S0-BPR-456

THE TRAITOR

Lavr Divomlikoff

THE TRAITOR

Translated from the French by
J. F. Bernard

DOUBLEDAY & COMPANY, INC.
GARDEN CITY, NEW YORK 1973

All of the characters in this book
are fictitious, and any resemblance to actual
persons, living or dead, is purely coincidental.

LE TRÊTRE was published in France by Editions Robert Morel

ISBN: 0-385-01472-4
Library of Congress Catalog Card Number 72–96234

Printed in the United States of America
First Edition

CONTENTS

PROLOGUE

For twenty years, Father Grigori had waited for this day. That it had finally arrived was a surprise. Ordinarily, the stages in a man's life are not laid out like a piece of music. Life does not progress from a first measure to a last. It unravels. The best that a man can hope for is to know where life begins. As to its end, he knows nothing. And he simply moves forward.

But Grigori's life was different. "That's how it is," the priest mumbled, and smiled slyly into his grizzled beard. "A perfect ending to a perfect plan." Then he added piously, "Thanks be to God."

He walked to the window. The chickens were pecking in the yard. He turned. The candle glowed before the ikon. Grigori stretched out his hand, as though reaching toward the finishing line. "No more chickens," he said softly. "I will never again see Petia the rooster." Then, without bitterness: "No more bows before the ikon."

His hand moved to his aching back. Grigori was forty-five years old, and he had the back of an old man. He also had the soul of an old man.

The soul?

He remembered his courses in atheism. Man weighs so much; his bones, so much; the blood, so much; the flesh, so much. And the whole man, so much. But how much does the soul weigh? A rather primitive argument, Grigori reflected, smiling. His beard was already half gray. Why? He moaned, his hand pressing the small of his back.

In a little while, he would see Nadson. It was an unpleasant prospect. Nadson, because it was his job to understand, was incapable of understanding anything. Just as prostitutes forget to love, as priests forget to work miracles.

Grouztchik had been better. If life were a movie, Grigori would be about to play his final scene with Grouztchik. But sometimes—rarely—life goes by the chain of command rather than a movie script. Grouztchik had been promoted, and then —who knew?—perhaps made a deputy, or liquidated. Verniak had replaced him. Verniak had been followed by others, until Nadson had finally been enthroned behind the desk.

It was no longer even the same desk. The old one, with pieces of cardboard under the left leg, shook under the fists of Grouztchik, who had been a smelter by trade. Grouztchik was enthroned, when he was not stamping about. Nadson's desk was of metal, and his soft, damp hand left an imprint on its surface.

Nadson "enthroned?" It would be more accurate to say "ensconced."

Grigori made a face. In a while, he would have to call Nadson "comrade" and slap him on the belly. He would slap him maliciously, as hard as possible.

Grigori plunged his face into the basin which Alona had brought. The cold water washed the last traces of sleep from his eyes, smoothed the lines from his cheeks. It also soaked his long hair and rough beard which were a bother to dry. The water on his skin, still warm from sleep, the chill: war.

War, and beardless cheeks. War, and young muscles. War, and brothers to be killed in uncounted numbers. "What a pity I was not old enough during the civil war," the priest thought. "I would have showed them."

Even so, Father Grigori's record was respectable enough.

Especially during the re-conquest, when the traitors had been tracked down. There had been in particular the incident involving a priest, also called Father Grigori, which always had a great effect in confession. "My son!" a horrified bishop had cried, "is it possible that you have never before confessed such a terrible crime?"

"Often," Grigori would have liked to answer, like an old lecher, "but I still find the memory of it pleasant." Instead, he had spoken of his lingering sense of guilt, and was complimented on his overly delicate conscience.

Grigori dried himself roughly with the embroidered towel, the gift of a lady parishioner, which Alona had laid out on the back of a chair. Then he gave his hair and beard a few strokes of the comb. A priest must never be too well groomed. It puts people off.

Well, perhaps today . . . No. A good actor never drops his role until he is offstage. And Grigori was a professional. Everyone said so. Either that, or he was a scrupulous and disciplined gambler. This was what Grigori himself believed.

He fell to his knees with a priestly grunt. It was time for prayers. Grigori thought of Christian morality. "To kneel oneself instead of forcing others to their knees. The slaves!" he grumbled.

A thought came into his mind: "Sunday, I said my last Mass." There was a moment of regret. "I am like a worn-out actress giving her farewell performance," Grigori chided himself. "Except that they wouldn't let me say good-by. I didn't realize it was my last Mass. I will be able to eat next Saturday night."

He made the sign of the cross several times, with the anxious piety of a persecuted priest. Many years before, in order to perfect the gesture, he had tried to imagine that somebody was spying upon him through the window. But now, he was thoroughly programmed. It was almost to be regretted.

Alona entered the room. Grigori recited the Lord's Prayer once more, for good measure. Alona liked him to pray at length. She frequently boasted to her cronies of the hours he spent on his knees.

Finally, the priest rose, placing his hands on his knees and pushing himself upright. Alona said, "Come, your Reverence. The clabber is ready."

Grigori, suddenly irritated, translated the two sentences into all the languages he knew. "Silly woman!" he concluded. Then he was annoyed with himself for playing this pedant's game. After all, he told himself, I am not an intellectual.

The association had been made. Suddenly, he understood why he despised Nadson, while for Grouztchik he had felt a warm, brutish sympathy. Nadson was an intellectual.

Alona was waiting, standing next to the table.

He would have to leave Alona. He would never again see that dark, round face, with its infinitely solicitous look; never again hear that voice tinged with adoration. What a blessing!

"She is nothing to me, and I am nothing to her," he reminded himself. "The proof is that she worships me. And one does not worship what one loves."

To Alona, he said, "You know perfectly well that the liquid and the curds should form one single mass. Why does this not—?"

"Here, take mine," Alona answered. And, before he could protest, she had exchanged bowls with him.

He was irritated. He was irritated at being irritated. "At least," he said, "I now have clabber that is really clabber."

Alona, her eyes on her bowl, ate the liquid with a spoon, without answering.

Grigori remarked that he must go to the next village that morning to visit someone who was sick.

Alona nodded in silence.

He knew what she was thinking. That he had no right to

visit anyone unless he had been officially invited. That the preceding year he had been suspended for just such a minor infraction of the rules. That, as a result they had scarcely eaten for a month. And, that she was ready to share with him any new act of martyrdom.

It annoyed him to know what she was thinking. He rose from the table, put on his cassock, hung the copper crucifix around his neck, and walked toward the door with only a slightly hurried step.

Alona timidly blocked his way. "Bless me, Father, before you leave."

He blessed her, and she kissed the hand which had just called down a bit of heaven's grace upon her. "As though she needs it!" he caught himself thinking.

He left the house. Or rather, he intruded into the street, into an alien milieu. He was like a spot in that bright, gray, modern communist street—he, a priest, wearing the vestments of another age, with the copper cross upon his breast. He walked on the wooden sidewalk, then on the ground, then in the badly paved street. His footsteps echoed, then were muffled, then were loud. He heard them above the noise of the street. He did not quite know how to walk. If he met a passerby, should he push past him or step aside?

As a Christian, Grigori reflected, I should be humble. As a dignitary of the Church, I have a right to the respect of laymen. As a priest in a communist society, I deserve only contempt. As far as my real function is concerned—but I won't think about my real function.

The men Grigori encountered lowered their eyes. The priest was a black, moving spot in the colorless communist street. He was out of the game. He was cheating, which is to say that he was bearing witness. Whoever cheats bears witness to the rules of the game. And men turn away their heads.

Why do they turn away, Grigori wondered. They should

look me in the face. Theirs are the eyes of knowledge; mine are those of superstition. Can it be that their consciences bother them?

It happened that some of the women he met stood flat against the wall and greeted him. One old woman embarrassed him by asking for his blessing in the middle of the street. He answered: "I cannot, my daughter. I would be accused of religious propaganda, and I would be expelled from the Church."

But the woman's eyes laughed with frightening gaiety. "Unless God wills it, not a hair of your head . . ."

Occasionally, young men wearing armbands called out to him: "Black crow! Filthy priest! Big belly! Go get yourself crucified! Go get drunk on mass wine!" Ah, how Grigori would have loved to take two of them by the hair and smash their heads together. Instead, in his reports, he commented favorably on the anti-religious zeal of the youth organizations. "Young so-and-so insulted me publicly and demanded detailed information on Jonas' sojourn in the whale . . ." But Grigori's reports did not tell all. He had his clerical weaknesses. Once, a fat businessman spat on him. The saliva, a large glob of it, lay white and frothy on the black cassock. It was the spit of a man whose salivary glands were in good working order and who thinks as a man should think in a communist society. And Grigori, standing humbly on the sidewalk, said: "My son, God will reward you in kind."

Grigori continued walking. He kept his eyes directly ahead. He had never been able to accustom himself to being a parish priest. He would have liked hats to be snatched off and heads to bow as he approached. He would have liked to be greeted with respect, and to have children clutching at the hands from which blessings fell. He caught himself thinking: "The sin of pride." And then: "I have been contaminated by their rhetoric."

He walked. The men he met hurried past him. Some crossed

the street as soon as they caught a glimpse of him, so as not to have to give way to him on the narrow sidewalk. If only they were openly hostile, the cowards! Grigori reflected.

He thought of Christ's entry into Jerusalem. How would it be to enter this village, riding on Bourdiouk's donkey, with the people singing and waving palm leaves? There are no palms. They would wave the branches of trees. And brutal Commissar Bursche would spread his leather shirt over a mud-hole for the donkey to cross.

One by one, Grigori recognized along the street the houses he had entered to administer secretly the last rites to men dying on beds without sheets, to baptize infants in a small zinc pail—and sometimes in a cast-iron pot from which the grease had not been entirely removed. He recognized houses which, their owners had confided, contained certain articles: a Bible, an ikon, a relic. All these things were mentioned in the report which he carried under his arm.

The file was written in Greek, and coded. Alona had sometimes asked softly, "Are you still working, Father?"

"My theology thesis," he had answered sanctimoniously. "It is going very well."

The priest was now outside the village. The flat fields stretched out along the road. The people whom he met were peasants, and they greeted him respectfully.

These people are still sunk in superstition, Grigori said to himself. If a few of them were hanged for it— A sophism. Many of them have already been hanged.

He walked on, and the mud splashed to his knees. The countryside was deserted. He drew near a clump of birches, stopped, and looked at his watch. In the distance, there was a rumbling. The truck was coming. Grigori, having made certain that there would be no witnesses to the meeting, began walking again. Behind him, the truck slowed, passed him, shifted into first gear. He caught up with it—what a relief to be able to run a few yards!—opened the gate, climbed up, and closed it. The truck picked up speed.

Within the truck, it was pitch black. There was no window. Grigori was not allowed to see the driver. He was not even supposed to know his destination. But he had guessed. Not long before, he had heard the deathbed confession of the former Chief Commissar of the Political Police. A spicy confession.

Grigori was in the truck for one hour. He kept close track of time. He did not entirely trust his superiors. It was best to avoid the surprises which the experts euphemistically designated as "conditioning."

He heard the sounds of a large city. There were frequent stops, then a sharp turn to the left. The truck stopped. The driver struck the metal wall of the truck a sharp blow with his fist. Father Grigori opened the gate and climbed down. He was in a dark, concrete garage. He knew the way. He opened a door, walked down a corridor, climbed a stairway. He thought again of the two limits: the beginning, and the end.

Twenty years ago, he recalled, I climbed these same stairs. But this dirty green linoleum was not here then. I didn't know what they wanted of me; but they had already taken my measure. They knew what I was capable of. The only real virtue of our regime is its insolence with respect to time. It counts in centuries. It assigns a man to a twenty-year mission. How far removed we are from the poverty of the democratic countries. And the individual? Bah! A fragment of collective life—and barely that. We are a regime of eagles!

A bitter smile was on Grigori's lips.

Or perhaps we are a regime of vultures.

Grigori knocked at a door. Would it be Nadson?

Yes. The nasal voice answered:

"Come in."

The priest entered.

Usually, Grigori entered this office with an energetic step, his cassock flapping around his legs. He would immediately remove the cassock and toss it over a chair, leaving the copper crucifix dangling from the armrest.

But today it was different. He shuffled into the room sideways, one shoulder forward, with a half-smile hidden in his beard. It was the entrance he used when he, poor priest that he was, called upon local administrators or party leaders to request permission for something. Grigori's mood had now changed. There would be no "Comrade Commissar" for Nadson, and no slap on the belly.

Nadson was a young man. His face was long, and yet plump. A man of contrasts. There were bags under his eyes. His lips were thick, dark; almost purple. He wore rimless spectacles. One manicured hand lay motionless on the desk. The other was on Nadson's knees, or in a drawer—doing something, Grigori did not know what. Grigori was suspicious of that unseen hand. Was there an alarm button, or a weapon?

The hand which Nadson kept free for use was now extended. There was a spot of dampness where it had rested on the metal desk—a desk on which Grigori had never seen a single object, not a pencil or a sheet of paper, except for a narrow desk pad with a blotter, yellow and immaculate.

Nadson's moist hand and Grigori's massive hand touched briefly, like two dogs sniffing each other, indifferently.

Nadson began with a joke, but without smiling: "Bless me, Father."

Grigori, forgetting that he was supposed to be jovial, replied: "Have they stopped making bonfires out of heretics like you?"

Nadson sensed the real antipathy that lay beneath the feigned threat. He gave a small, satisfied laugh. "Well, as you see," he replied, "we are no longer being burned."

The priest was angry. In his most humble and clerical tone,

he said: "Not on earth, my friend. But who knows what the hereafter may hold? There may be a special pot reserved for you to lick. A white-hot pot . . ."

The thought of Nadson licking a white-hot pot was quite pleasant. But not in hell. Here, and now. A real pot, heated on a gas stove.

Grigori sat.

Nadson said nothing. His heavy, dark lips made a silent, sucking motion.

Grigori grew impatient. "I received your message to come. What do you want? I gather that my mission is over."

"Precisely."

"Schluss?"

"Yes."

"Ah," Grigori said.

Deep within himself, he felt relief. But on the surface, at that instant, he felt no relief. He was still on stage.

Nadson immediately sensed his reaction. "Will you miss your cassock?" he asked.

Grigori would have liked to reply, "What an idiot you are!" But that would have been out of character. He said nothing.

"In any case," Nadson said, "you have no choice, since you were apparently unable to get yourself promoted to bishop."

"You were no help in that respect."

"What could we have done?"

"You could have put pressure on the Patriarchate."

"That would have ruined your chances for certain."

Grigori chewed on his beard. It was the mannerism of a country priest, one which had become habitual to him.

Nadson sucked an invisible cigar.

"As I was saying," he continued, "since you were unable to become a bishop, the authorities consider that you have reached the end of your usefulness in a subordinate position. Nothing can be gained by leaving you there any longer. I would be lying by omission, however, if I did not say that you have not entirely fulfilled some of our hopes. It takes more than good will, you know."

Grigori grunted. "You people! What more could I have done?"

"Well," Nadson replied in a pleasant tone, "let's say that if you had ended up as Patriarch, you would get better marks. But, it's not as bad as all that. Some of the higher-ups have been curious about you. One of them was afraid that you might want to remain a priest. Are you sure you don't? Haven't you enjoyed your pork chops bled white, and your little girls in confession?"

"Since you have no idea of what is involved in a mission, Comrade Bureaucrat, I'll thank you to keep your comments to yourself."

Nadson took the insult without a change of expression. He did not blink. Comrade Bureaucrat, indeed. And in a proletarian regime! He continued sucking.

"Here's my report," Grigori said, and carefully placed the heavy binder sideways on the desk, so as to introduce a discordant element. Nadson took it with both hands, thought for a moment, and then, with an air of finality, placed it in a drawer.

"Perhaps you have no intention of using it," Grigori said with heavy irony.

Nadson looked at him severely, sharply, through his prim spectacles. "Precisely, Comrade-with-a-mission. We have no intention of using it. Not now."

"You must be out of your mind. I've spent twenty years—"

Nadson shrugged helplessly.

Grigori's eyes blazed with a priestly rage. "Why?" he demanded.

"Because," Nadson explained patiently, "if we use your report now, it would be obvious, even to the idiots in your parish and especially to those foxes at the Patriarchate, that you have not suddenly seen the light, but that you were an agent of truth from the very beginning. That is not the effect that we are trying to achieve."

"What does it matter?"

"What do you know about it? Maybe you are not the only man on a mission of this kind. The greater the confidence of the people in their priests today, the easier it will be for us to destroy that confidence tomorrow. On the other hand, if the Church has the slightest opportunity to inoculate its followers against the truth, it will be able to generate as many antibodies as it needs. There are many examples of this. So, if we make use of your report right away, it would have an effect contrary to that which we—"

"I understand," Grigori said.

He looked at the bare desk, at the yellow blotter on which, a few minutes before, had rested the thick report covered with Greek symbols. How many hidden Bibles, how many clandestine books of psalms, how many hurried confessions, how many individuals had been compromised in those six hundred nauseatingly pink pages! There was enough to send ten or twenty men before a firing squad, and several hundred more to the salt mines. Most of the victims would be priests, of course; priests who went beyond the limits set down by law; priests who proselytized, who were dictators of the subconscious, who became dealers in the opium of the people. Old priests, whose heads were still filled with the temporal splendors of the Church in another age; and fiery young priests with the vocation of martyrs. Gleb, that hotheaded adolescent, who proclaimed: "I am the salt of the earth!" Grigori had said to himself, You'll have salt aplenty when they send you to the mines.

And there was the Archimandrite Seraphin, who raved: "Tongues of fire will come down and consume the Reds. They will dance naked in the squares, and they will hang themselves from the pylons of their own electrical systems. In their terror, they will scale the chimneys of their factories; they will go down into the darkness of their mines; and they will take to the air in their cosmic contraptions. The chimneys will be filled with brimstone, and, in the mines, oil will blaze. The Reds will fry upon the face of the earth like bacon upon a grill; and there will be weeping and gnashing of teeth."

Priests were not the only ones accused in Grigori's report. There was the director of a factory, a fat man, his face covered with sweat, his blue eyes hidden behind an opaque veil. "Father, what must I do to be saved? I have a family, and I am afraid. I cannot leave my job; and God will not leave me in peace. I know what I should do; but—well, that means Siberia. Yet, there was Nicodemus. And there was Joseph of Arimathaea, wasn't there? No? It's not the same thing? What about the rich young man who kept the Commandments? How should I interpret that? If only I could receive Communion. But that's out of the question. It would be known immediately."

"How would it be known?"

"I think it would show in my face."

Grigori had replied: "You believe; and therefore you will be saved."

There was also a regional official of the Party, who had said to Grigori: "Tell me, priest, do you have a list of prices? Do you have a church, like a movie theater? How much do candles cost? I want you to burn candles for me, at night, in secret, when no one is there, in front of my patron saint. My name is Aristarcus."

"I am sorry, comrade," Grigori had answered. "I have no ikon of Aristarcus."

My report contains instances of high treason, Grigori told himself, and they're going to let it gather dust somewhere.

He had expected the opposite—that there would be trucks with sirens gathering up the guilty at dawn. Men taken from their beds, quaking with fear, would be jammed into interrogation rooms. And Grigori would be there, without his cassock, his chest bare, but with his still eloquent beard, to remind them of their crimes. "The day that I was sent to jail for religious propaganda," he would say. "Do you remember how you came to my cell to encourage me? You said, 'One day, we will win.' Win against whom? And you, you copier of Bibles. You transcribed the whole of the Book of Isaiah for me, from one end to the other, for a dozen eggs. Don't deny it! And you, Comrade President, are you here too? You are a member of the Party, and you did not dare greet me in the streets. But at night you came to me with a bundle in your arms, and you said: 'This is my son. Baptize him. I will give you some concrete for the porch of the church.' You are all still glued to your old perversions as to a damp wall! You hang ikons on the inside of your cupboard doors, and you think that your duplicity— Well, you will discover that we have more than one trick up our sleeves, my children. Well, Theodosius! I hadn't seen you. Are you still having an affair with Matrona? Come here, my son, so that I may absolve you, as I did every Saturday. The only difference is that you may find it more difficult to sin again tomorrow. You will be placed out of temptation's way. You see, as an officer of the regime, I am better equipped to work for your salvation than I was as a filthy little priest."

In a single night, Grigori reflected, he could have wiped out twenty years of humiliation, of lies, of degradation.

And yet, he concluded, I must somehow rid myself of all the sacred oil that has dripped down my forehead, of all the altar wine I have guzzled, of all the kisses that have seared my hands, of all the signs of the cross—of those thousands of signs of the cross that have cramped my good communist fingers. Nadson, how can I wash away all those things? Grouztchik would have understood. He would have ordered me to go on an epic drunk. Or he would have sent me to a Turkish bath and told me to stay until I had sweated everything out of my system. Or he would have turned me over to a harem of little beauties and told them to make a new man of me. But Nadson understands nothing. There is no use trying to talk to him. Perhaps if I tried Latin?

To Nadson, he said: "As you wish, comrade. *Ad majorem factionis gloriam.*"

Nadson sucked his nonexistent cigar with a knowing air.

"You do not understand," the priest said. "It means, 'Blessed are the poor in spirit.' "

"That is not the customary language of the Church," Nadson objected.

"Purist!"

Suddenly, the tension was gone.

"Well then," Grigori said, "if I understand you correctly, there will be no arrests, no interrogations, no investigations? In other words, there will be no way for me to get back into shape?"

Nadson was shocked. "Certainly not," he sniffed. "In any case, procedures have changed since your time. Here are your orders. Tonight, you will write to Dobermann, professor of atheism at the university. You will tell him that his arguments have convinced you, and that you can no longer go on deceiving the people. That you now realize God does not exist, and cannot exist."

"Dobermann's arguments give me a pain," Grigori answered. "I haven't believed in God since my mother—you wouldn't understand. Let's say that I haven't believed in God for a long time."

"I understand very well; but that is beside the point. Dobermann needs a push this year to get himself elected to the Academy. Your conversion will bring him to public notice. In any event, those are your orders."

"But Dobermann is practically an imbecile!"

"He must become a member of the Academy. The reasons are none of your business."

Grigori smiled, and there was tension once more. "It may well be," he said, "that you don't know the reasons any more than I do."

Nadson clicked his tongue audibly. "Tsk, tsk. That's neither here nor there. You will write to Dobermann that you have been reading his articles for a long time, that they have gradually led you—"

"Onto the road to Damascus," Grigori murmured.

"—and that you would like to speak to him."

"As to a spiritual father, so that he may teach me to burn what I have worshiped, and vice versa. What will happen then?"

"Dobermann will ask you to visit him. You will have a moving encounter."

"A meeting of charlatans. We'll probably die laughing."

"Not at all. Dobermann will believe that he has really—"

"Really what? Won me over?"

"Well—"

"Converted me?"

"Precisely."

"What a scene that will be."

"You will take a metaphysical approach. Tell him that it is now your dearest wish to open the eyes of other men just as he has opened yours. He will offer you an instructorship at the university. It's all taken care of. There is an opening."

A hint of embarrassment clouded Nadson's impassive countenance. He pressed his lips together, then continued: "You will accept."

"I will accept?"

"You will shave your beard and begin a seminar for atheistic students at the university. In order to avoid any scandal, you will not return to your town."

"You people seem determined to make me spend my life in school. It's become a mania! How long will I have to stay in this one?"

Nadson made a gesture of ignorance.

Grigori, now growing truly angry, placed one hand on Nadson's desk. Nadson's own hand drew back instinctively.

"I know," Grigori said, "that the ways of the Party are unfathomable. Nonetheless, if it is the Party's intention to make a fool of me, they should tell me so. Don't raise your eyebrows at me. I've always spoken my mind to my bishops; and—no offense—they are as good as you. I hoped that I would at least be defrocked at Mass, in front of two thousand people, between the Elevation and the Communion. Then we would be doing something that would appeal to people's imagination."

Nadson's eyes were fixed on Grigori's hand. "Your nails are broken and dirty," he said. "You've become a real priest. At the university, you'll be able to clean your nails."

Grigori, with a brusque gesture, tore the copper chain from his neck and looked around for a chair on which to throw it. In Grouztchik's office there had always been chairs piled with papers. Nadson had no extra chairs. Grigori wrapped the chain around his fist, which he opened and closed nervously. The links cut into his flesh.

"So, there will be no big scene in the last act? I will not have the opportunity to flay the Pharisees of my parish. The opportunity to say, 'Hear me, good people! We're all been trying to pull the wool over each other's eyes. Karp, your churchwarden, is a pimp. Boria, the blind beggar, sees as well as you and I. The chief pillar of our church, Domna Evdokimovna, got the apartment she has by denouncing the family of Jews who were occupying it.' And you, Comrade Nadson, have decided to deprive me of this moment of jubilation."

Comrade Nadson, in a dark blue suit obviously imported from a less communist nation, looked at Grigori with distaste. "Isn't it curious," he seemed to be thinking, "how religion, whether real or pretended, generates bourgeois lyricism."

"Very well," Grigori went on. "I'll resign myself to it, even though it hurts. The expression on the pious face of old Firs if he learned that I, his hero, was a devil in disguise— Well, forget it. Who made all these changes in our original plan?"

"I have no idea."

Grigori stood up. He felt that he was smothering. He began unbuttoning his cassock. He wanted to remove it. The cross, hanging from his hand, made his movements awkward.

Nadson raised his hand in a pacifying gesture. "No, don't take off your cassock. I have another appointment in ten minutes. We'll have to finish quickly."

"You don't want my cassock as a memento?"

"Hardly. You have to go back to your parish to write to Dobermann."

"You mean I'm going to have to continue wearing this circus costume?"

Nadson pursed his lips. "Listen, Grigori. Don't be disagreeable. You've been living among village idiots so long that you've become childish. The university will do you good."

"What will be my assignment at the university?"

Nadson hesitated before the enormity of what he was about to say "Well—to teach atheism to the students."

"I said, my assignment."

"So far as I know, Grigori, you will have no particular assignment. At least not for the moment."

"Is this supposed to be a vacation?"

"I really don't know."

"Comrade Nadson, the service does not stop making use of an agent without a reason."

So strong was Nadson's antipathy for Grigori that he exceeded his instructions. "It happens," he said, "when there has been an error concerning an agent's abilities."

They looked at each other, the slight, young superior and the towering subordinate in his cassock, standing in the middle of the room.

Grigori shook his beard in a grotesque gesture of menace. Nadson's face wore a weak, but nonetheless victorious, smile. "Come, come, Comrade Grigori," he said. "I know very well that where there is a beard, there is religion. Perhaps you intend to excommunicate me?"

Physically, Nadson was afraid; yet, he risked irony.

Grigori took a deep breath to calm himself. "What am I accused of?"

"Inefficiency."

"If you look at my report—"

"That's unimportant."

"Grouztchik promised me—"

"Grouztchik," Nadson interrupted gently, "was wrong about you, Grigori. He thought you would become Patriarch. And you are not even a bishop, only a priest of the rank."

"I have confessed bishops."

"Most of them have already been shot."

"Comrade Nadson, I have accomplished my mission."

"No mission is ever accomplished one hundred per cent."

"I know of one which was."

"Tell me."

"That of Jesus, Jehovah's special agent."

"Grigori, Grigori. Hurry, write out a formal request. Maybe we'll let you keep your skirts."

"Do you think you could have done better?"

"Not among those fools of the Orthodox Church. With the Jesuits, I probably could have."

Slowly, Grigori unwound the chain from his numb fist and let the swinging crucifix strike his calf, his thigh, his knee. He spread his legs, threw back his shoulders, and opened his mouth to breathe yet more deeply. He had always considered himself an extraordinarily effective agent. He had just discovered that he was wrong. He was mediocre. He, Grigori! He wondered whether it could be true.

"Let's go over it once more," he said wearily. "I am supposed to return to my village and write to Dobermann."

"Explain your—your what?—your 'spiritual evolution'—to him. Mail the letter. Then wait. Dobermann will send for you. Leave, and don't go back. Say good-by to no one. Become Dobermann's altar boy. Accept the position that he will offer you. Do not try to contact us. Forget that you ever knew we existed. Is that clear?"

"Clear, Comrade Nadson."

Nadson's lips formed a malicious smile. "You have certainly lost your good habits, Grigori. You have my permission to ask me when you will receive your blue envelope."

Grigori asked nothing.

Nadson's smile grew broader. "Don't worry. You'll get it; and if you are a true priest you can always distribute it among the poor of your parish."

"Will there still be a parish?"

"You are joking, surely. Your church is being closed because of its sagging porch, which is dangerous to passersby. A public bath will be built on the site."

A foolish question came to Grigori's lips: "And the poor? Will they be done away with too?" But he suppressed it, turned on his heel, and walked to the door. Then he turned again, thrust out his chin, executed—poorly, because of his cassock—a regulation about-face, and left the office.

"Ritual!" he said to himself. "I've turned into a priest. I can't do without ritual."

He went down the steps onto the green linoleum.

"Have I always been a mediocre agent, or did I become one? Certainly, I became one, with all that mummery and foolishness that goes with being a priest. But they—they knew it beforehand. They sacrificed me. Professor of atheism. It's always religion. Enough! I've had enough! Is that all I am, an atheist? God, I'd give anything to have three or four fat German spies to interrogate. Or a commando raid at one of the frontiers—"

Then Grigori stopped. "Why, you silly old priest, you don't even remember how to hold a gun."

ACT I

Dear Comrade!

I almost wrote "Dear brother."

I have never had the honor of being presented to you. And yet, I know that you are, so to speak, the light of the people; but, as the saying is among the English, who are also called the British, a cat can look upon a king. And, in fact, for years I have nourished myself on the banquet of your mind.

I've never read a line of anything he wrote. But I wonder whether I'm not being too humble. "An excess of humility is worse than pride," says a Christian proverb. And pride—nothing is more dangerous, we are told in the service, than to overestimate our abilities. Well, so much the worse.

You are, dear comrade, the torch of learning in this nation. Or rather, you are not the torch, but the flame itself, since you shed the bright light of atheism everywhere.

That's much better. I think I've found the right tone.

You can imagine my embarrassment in confessing to you that I have been, until today, a messenger of the most retrogressive obscurantism; a stifler, an extinguisher. In other words, a priest.

I implore you, comrade, do not let this shameful title make you throw this letter into your wastebasket. Is it not said that "For every sin, there is forgiveness"? My purpose in writing to you today is to say, mea culpa.

I am going a bit too far. The first rule of the service is: Never do too much. Dobermann may well turn out to be the imbecile that I think he is. But he may also be playing the fool because it pays. And he may also be merely a fellow agent who has been given the job of keeping an eye on me. In any case, my letter will be published in the newspapers.

I ask your help today in purifying myself of the sin that I have committed.

Another piece of religious rhetoric. So much the worse. They will swallow it. But it is an intelligent analogy, so maybe they won't. We'll see.

Allow me, dear comrade, to begin at the beginning and to describe my Calvary to you at length; to explain

Well, no. That really won't do.

how I was able to sink so low; and how, thanks to you, I have been able to climb up to a level at which the air is at least breathable, in that it is no longer polluted by the suffocating fumes of incense.

Very good. I am going in the
right direction.

It all began on the day . . .

Which day was it? What was
really the beginning? Was it the
interview with Grouztchik,
which I usually think of as the
beginning, just as the Romans
used to date events *ab urbe
condita?* Or am I limiting
myself by believing in limits?
Perhaps there are merely roots,
roots of roots, and offshoots
of roots, going down an
indeterminate depth to childhood, to heredity? No. Every
chessboard must have a border;
and every billiard table must
have an edge.

Nadson's office; but the room bore no resemblance to what it would be twenty years later. Then, it was still Grouztchik's lair. Filled with smoke, foul-smelling, dirty. Like life itself.

There was a scratched and spotted table of wood, covered with piles of paper among which one could glimpse a glass, the neck of a bottle, an ashtray filled to overflowing, and—used as a highly suggestive paperweight—a bullwhip.

There were a half-dozen chairs, but none of them were vacant. They all held stacks of folders with dangling ribbons. In one corner, a typewriter sat on the floor, covered with dust. And a bottle, not covered with dust.

Behind the table, which reached to mid-thigh, stood Major

Grouztchik, a former smelter. His sleeves were rolled up, and his shirt was partially unbuttoned, revealing an allegorical tattoo which ran from one nipple to the other. Grouztchik raised his elbows. He smiled an ogre's smile, showing black and yellowed teeth. "Ah, there you are, boy. What do you want? Oh, yes. I asked you to come. Find a quarter of a chair somewhere and flop on it."

Grigori did not move. He was young, inexperienced, awkward. His complexion was pink, and easily turned to red. He stood midway between attention and rest, his hands balled into fists, simultaneously embarrassed and determined to stand his ground. He had just returned from the recently liberated areas, where he had been engaged in tracking down collaborators. Before that, he had been at the front, where he had risked his life every day. He had killed men in abundance. And, when there had been no ammunition, he had used his bare hands. From this, he had gained a deep confidence in his physical superiority.

Two of Grouztchik's subordinates were standing in the office. He treated them with the studied contempt of the self-made man. "You two," he said, "get out of here. Go see if I'm outside. I want to talk to this gentleman." They saluted and left. Grouztchik called one of them back. "Artemus, have you anything to do?"

"Nothing, major."

"Then go beat up the man we questioned yesterday. That will put him in the proper frame of mind for tonight. But be gentle. We want him to be able to talk."

Artemus left. Grouztchik smiled amiably at Grigori and rubbed his knuckles. "I have fists that can fell a bull," he said, "but I hurt one of them on that bastard yesterday. They have thick hides, my boy. But we'll get to them yet. Now, what did I want to talk to you about?"

Slowly, with his elbows spread apart, he lit a cigarette.

He did not offer one to Grigori. He kept his eyes down, staring at the small yellow flame. Grigori knew that, in a moment, he would look up and fire off a question. It was a well-known technique. What question?

Grigori set his face in a mask of impudence. He concentrated especially on keeping his eyelid muscles motionless. The eyelids could give one away.

Grouztchik shook the match, threw it to the floor, and inhaled, his eyes still lowered. Suddenly, he raised his head and his sparkling blue eyes were fixed on Grigori's carefully immobile face. "All right. Don't pretend to be an idiot. You're a nobleman's son, aren't you?"

This wasn't what Grigori had expected. The sons of noblemen were not allowed to study at the universities, or to become officers, or to occupy any command post. Until then, he had circumvented the regulations by lying about his origins. But Grouztchik had caught him off guard. Grigori hesitated. He looked Grouztchik in the eyes. Grouztchik was smoking, exhaling clouds of smoke through his crescent-shaped nostrils.

Grigori had often risked his life; but he was not so careless with his career. He was tempted to evade the question. To say, "I don't know anything about it. First of all, when I was born there were no more nobles. And my parents were not nobles. They were just gentlefolk." He knew that Grouztchik would despise him for it.

He answered softly: "Yes."

Grouztchik did not smile, although it would have made things easier for Grigori. Instead, he gave a short sigh.

"Good," he said. "If you want my condolences, you have them. Ancestors are a hell of a ball and chain for a man to have to drag around. We don't care about such things here. I might even say that— Well, that's enough. You've passed the test. There's nothing else we need to know."

"I hate the nobles," Grigori volunteered impulsively. He was no longer on guard.

Grouztchik seemed interested. "Why?" he asked.

"Because when a man has power, he should hold on to it."

Now Grouztchik smiled, paternally. "Very good, my boy. This makes things easier, in a way. At least you're not going to get bogged down in bourgeois idealism. Now, look here. You acquitted yourself honorably during the war. Were you hoping I'd say 'brilliantly'? No. Others did even better than you. I say 'honorably.' You volunteered for training, for assignments, for missions, for everything. To make a long story short, the higher-ups wanted to make further use of you, but they didn't know quite where you would fit in. Then someone noticed an incident in your file—a suggestive incident reported by one of your friends. Tell me, does the name Father Grigori mean anything to you?"

"There were so many—"

"Don't play the hardened killer with me. Father Grigori was a little old priest who had done no special harm to anyone, and whose beard caught fire one fine April night, near—"

Grigori remembered his namesake perfectly well: a plump little man, naked, with a long, greasy beard, which burned well. He was seated very low on the legs of an overturned chair. He remembered the smell of burnt flesh, the folds of yellow flesh on his belly. It was the first time in his life that Grigori saw a priest naked.

To himself he said: "I wanted to make sure that priests are men like other men, that there is no special sacerdotal organ. And that they have real beards, beards that burn." But aloud, he explained: "I hate priests."

"That's what everyone assumed," Grouztchik replied humorously. "You had nothing personal against the man, did you? He had already told everything without too much trouble. Did you know that?"

"I knew it."

Grigori was disoriented for an instant. He thought of what he was. It occurred to him that he knew very little about himself.

Grouztchik interrupted his thoughts. "Don't look so unhappy! Or do you have a stomachache? Chin up, boy, and eyes front. No one is going to blame you for roasting a priest. After all, this is not an ordinary profession. Everyone relaxes in whatever way suits him best. One man drinks hundred and forty proof vodka. Another amuses himself with little girls. You happen to like well-done priests. All that we require are results. For everything else . . ."

Now, twenty years later, Grigori had questions to ask himself, and questions to ask the swollen, seamed, formidable face of Grouztchik which remained in his memory: "Grouztchik, did you lie to me? Maybe you had already decided that my hatred of that priest was abnormal? That I would never be a really good agent? That I would have to be used within the limits of my ability? Maybe you had already sentenced me to conduct seminars in atheism?"

Grouztchik: "Look here, boy. Since you are obviously inspired by the best sentiments concerning our Apostolic Church, you seem to be the natural choice for the leading role in a little drama that I intend to produce. Sit down, will you? Throw all those papers on the floor, and leave the scribblers to sort themselves out as best they can. Don't pay attention to me. I'm going to walk around."

Grigori moved a file from a chair to the floor and sat down. As Grouztchik paced, Grigori's eyes followed his imposing silhouette.

"I can see that you are not exactly wild with enthusiasm. But you must understand . . ." Grouztchik explained. Why were the communists fighting? It was not to make common property out of the means of production, or to reduce the number of working hours per week, or for the pleasure of eviscerating a few particularly disgusting bourgeois capitalists. "None of this is really worth twenty million dead, is it, my boy?"

The real goal, he continued, was not social, or economic, or political. A man does not die for a planned economy, or for a classless society, or for a management committee. Or if he does, it is because he is a bourgeois idealist. A sensible man does not. "The priests have always understood that," he observed, "with their upside-down logic. The priests know what it is all about."

On the other hand, a man is willing to kill, or to die, to carry a bit of water to a thirsty friend, to carry it in his cupped hands, with the water running out between his fingers. But what is thirst? One does not thirst for the sea, or for train tickets at reduced fares. One is never thirsty for old-age insurance, or for vacations at the beach. One thirsts for only one thing: to be oneself. To be warm when one wants to be warm. To be cool when one wants to be cool. To drink when one is dried up. To develop to the full extent of one's potential, and to do so in every respect.

"People talk about alienation. There is only one real alienation, that which man finds within himself: alienation to God. The Christians understand this perfectly. They know that a man can be exploited, starved, killed, or nailed to a cross, and still be free. Because none of these exterior alienations count. Only one means anything: the slavery of love, the 'yes' of the slave to the master. If a man says, 'Thy will be done,' that man is truly alienated.

"We communists are fighting so that man may be totally free —which is to say that man must develop to his fullest and become fully himself. There is no real freedom without fullness. We have only one real objective, and that is to kill God. That Dostoevsky fellow foresaw this. You've never thought of that, have you?"

Grigori could have answered, "Yes, I sensed it. And that is why I am on your side." He left to Grouztchik the rather naïve satisfaction of unveiling the mystery. The self-taught master paced the floor, from one wall to the other and back again, filling the room with his arms and legs, his smoke, his musky, slightly alcoholic smell.

"Our entire history has already been written—and by a Greek, of all people. I don't remember his name; but he was a traitor. Everything was ending badly in the Caucasus, with a vulture nibbling away at the liver of the communist. But we, my boy, are going to change the final scene into a happy ending. All right? Nero was a child. He thought that he could destroy God from without. We'll give him zero for that. Oh, we've done our share of shooting priests. Many hundreds of them. And what happened? A bishop can make a thousand new priests in one fell swoop. We tried to do away with the bishops by a single stroke to break the chain, and we failed. It's a real hydra, I tell you. There's always one left to make two more grow, and each of those make two more, by scissiparition. We're fighting against infusoria.

"What we have to do is to reach the heart of this evil and cut its aorta. Do you understand? And you, my boy, have been chosen to be our spearhead in this struggle."

Grouztchik spoke of all those men in black, traitors to their species, who pile up gold and prayers and incense into a mountain higher than the world, reaching up into nothingness. "We say they are greedy, lascivious, and stupid, but that is all propaganda. If they were, they would no longer exist. In fact, they are ground down by chastity and distraught with renunciation, and filled with a sort of spirit—the evil spirit. God. Or Satan. It doesn't matter. And so, they are the enemies of mankind. Do you see? So, all that matters to them is faith. They live by faith. And we must destroy that faith. But we are not destroying it. We are making it rot away. And you, my young friend, will be the putrefying agent.

"An exciting prospect, isn't it? If I could pass myself off as a priest, I would do it myself. But who would ordain me? I look like Stenka Razine. But you'll see. It won't be an easy job. There will be fasts, and vigils, and prosternations. You'll have callouses an inch thick on your knees, and you'll get bumps on your head from knocking it on the ground. They'll spy on you, and interrogate you. They're not exactly altar boys, those priests. You've heard of the Inquisition? Well, they'll brainwash you. And you'll have to put up with it.

"Another thing. You'll be an anachronism in our pure communist society—a pariah and a scandal. You'll be insulted. You'll have to accept it, turn the other cheek."

Grigori was possessed by a bitter sense of exaltation. It was not the kind of mission that he had expected. Blood, violence—these were the things that he wanted. Yet he was flattered by the confidence shown in him. He felt himself slowly, gradually, flushing with pride. "I will bring you the Church Apostolic on a platter, steaming."

Grouztchik slapped him on the shoulder. "That's the spirit! But remember, we expect you to rise in the Church. You're not supposed to remain a country pastor. When you become a bishop, I'll even go to Mass, once, to kiss your hand. But you must promise not to laugh when you see me. And I'll tell you if your sermons are moving."

"A bishop?" Grigori asked. "But that takes years—"

"I'll give you twenty years, my boy. A man can do a lot in twenty years."

Grigori half rose from his chair. "Twenty years! But I'll be old! In twenty years I'll—" He was on the point of saying, "I'll have wasted my life." But Grouztchik smiled understandingly and placed his hand gently on his young subordinate's shoulder.

"By the time you are my age, Grigori, you will have learned

a great secret. I'll tell you what it is right now, but you won't understand it. A life is never wasted."

"Twenty years," Grigori repeated in agitation. "And for twenty years my life won't be worth living. It will be all praying and fasting and preaching. I won't even—" He stopped, overcome by a violent man's kind of shame, which prevented him from finishing. But he thought to himself, "Good God! No women! How will I stand it?"

Grouztchik, suddenly severe, said: "There is one thing which makes the whole thing worthwhile. And it is something that you, *sir,* should know: Service as such."

Grigori knew that it was not his rank as an officer to which Grouztchik was referring, but his family, who, for centuries, had served untiringly. Except that they had had as many women as they wanted. Grigori would have liked to refuse, but he knew that no one turned down an assignment. At least, not with impunity.

For two hours, Grouztchik gave instructions, predicted developments, described contacts and message drops, and warned against weariness and vanity, "the two great enemies of the service." And, all the while, he fanned the flames of excitement that accompanied the start of any mission.

"You will keep a record," he said. "You must try to have yourself transferred from parish to parish as often as you can. Keep close count of all the pious nonsense that you run across. Win the confidence of the faithful. And then, one day, twenty years from now, there will be a great reckoning. We'll hang them all, heads down, from their steeples. But we'll have to make people laugh. No martyrs. Only unmasked clowns. Understood?"

. . . It all began when I
returned from the war, in which
I had witnessed indescribable

atrocities by the fascists. I fell into the hands of a fanatic old man who conjured up before my eyes a burning vision of a world of goodness, justice, and human understanding—a world which he claimed we could build by following in the footsteps of Jesus.

Perhaps I can explain my feelings accurately by saying that the man took advantage of my innocence.

I was a child, not in years but in intellectual maturity. If that man were alive today, I would have him prosecuted for corrupting the morals of a minor.

That may be a little too pointed. I wonder if Dobermann will understand it. But the fact is that Grouztchik did speak to me of Jesus. On the very first day, he told me:

"If Jesus had not got himself crucified, he would have been the victim of his own practical joke." And he said:

"It's up to you to correct the mistake of that guy Pilate."

Also: "This Jesus, after

all, was responsible for a
certain amount of progress.
Without him, there would be
no communism. We'd still be
worshiping pieces of wood.
I've told you already, that
Jesus is the only real enemy
we have. You'll have to
make him look ridiculous.
But I warn you: he's a
worthy opponent. He doesn't
fight back. Therein lies his
cunning."

Dear comrade, I can tell you that this man hacked away at my soul with an axe. Within me, he dug a canal to change and pervert the course of my nature. I entered the seminary in a state of mind which, by reason of my inner exaltation, was not unlike that of a pure young man entering the Party.

The seminary . . .

The road was in disrepair, invaded by the shrubs which lined it. There were a few scrubby trees shivering in the wind. At the end of the road, beyond a path of loose pebbles, was a complex of buildings, the lower half sunk into the ground, grouped around once-gilded bulbous cupolas with crosses askew, supported by slack wires. There was silence. Each of Grigori's footsteps made a pebble roll, and every pebble struck other pebbles, dully. In the distance, a dog was barking.

The door. Low, vaulted, humble, guarded by an enigmatic ikon before which a red vigil light glowed timidly in the twilight.

Timidly also, Grigori knocked. His reticence was not feigned. Never had he been so ill at ease. He half believed that the first priest he met would guess his secret and order him away.

"Begone, Satan!"

He waited. The wooden door, with its spots of varnish, its asymmetrical bolts, its rusted lock, had the appearance of a spotted and forbidding face. Grigori, as a child, had often been taken to church by his mother to see the imprint of the Holy Face left on Veronica's pieced-together veil. It was that same face.

The door opened. Below, on the threshold, there stood a young man in a cassock. He seemed to be debating whether or not to slam the door in the visitor's face.

What should Grigori say? "I have been touched by grace"? "Is there room for a lost sheep in this house"? Or even: "I'm looking for a job"?

Grigori had no idea.

The other man looked at him. Their lips moved, silently. Above them, the red vigil light flickered imperceptibly. Grigori was the prodigal son. And the young man, with his slightly puzzled air, resembled the Virgin of the Annunciation.

His heavy, well-formed hand rested upon the door, tentatively.

Grigori would gladly have said, "I'm sorry; I have the wrong house," and then left. But he knew that Grouztchik would find him, even if he fled to the ends of the earth.

Suddenly, perhaps because of the young man's attentive air, which seemed to convey that he was more occupied with listening to an interior voice than with the presence of an intruder, Grigori heard the sound of music emanating from within the monastery. He recognized it. It had been painfully inscribed upon his memory during his childhood. A choir of male voices, deep and noble in timbre. Music from a thousand years in the past, and familiar for a thousand years. Their music.

"My mother used to sing that to me when I was still in diapers."

Almost at once, he felt an impulse to wound the porter, to hurt him, to smash his fist into that impassive face.

The young man replied, "That is the fifth mode. What is it you want, my friend?"

"To see the chief."

"The—?"

"The one in charge here."

The porter's eyes searched Grigori's person, his clothes, his eyes, for a sign of power. And, finding none, he questioned:

"Have you also come to make trouble for us?"

Grigori paled. "Why do you ask me that?"

"So that I may know." The young man explained: "If you are bringing us new trials, we will not sleep tonight. We will pray."

Grigori suppressed the words of sarcasm which rose to his lips, and substituted a smooth phrase: "I come not to bring you new troubles but to share those which you have, if you will permit me to do so. May I see your superior?"

They walked through abandoned interior courtyards. There was an occasional tree. Shutters were closed. Doors were boarded up. Walls had collapsed. Frescoes had faded. Desolation. And there was the sound of chanting, at times distant, and, at others, quite close, according to the direction which they took through the maze of courtyards. Grave chants, deliberate, naïve in expression, sublime in movement. Music from the depths of the twelfth century, Grigori reflected. In an instant, he saw the entire history of his country from one end to the other, and always, there was the same psalmodic chant intoned by male voices, addressed with stubborn serenity to the hypothetical ear of the Lord. The archaic words caused his throat to tighten. He opened his mind simultaneously to the beauty and to memory. He hastened to search for an explanation of his nameless emotion.

Their music, he told himself, is beautiful. I don't know why, but modern science can certainly explain it without difficulty. Wave lengths, and that sort of thing. Still, when I hear that music, my mother and her circle of humbug priests, in whom I once believed with all my might, seem to come alive again. But that's nothing to be surprised at. It's called association of ideas. I'll have to be careful. I'll probably have the same reaction to the smell of incense, and to the taste of warm sacramental wine. I wonder what the superior of this monastery looks like. It doesn't matter. All these priests look alike. They are a separate sex—not entirely men, since they wear skirts, and not wholly women, since they wear beards.

It was difficult to remember precisely what had happened next. He recalled only that he had waited for a long time in a small room with a well-scrubbed floor. To occupy his mind, he tried to distinguish the sober odors of soap, incense, leaves. The window was open, and a tree, growing against the window, was moving in the wind. Above the rustling of the leaves, the chanting of the monks still rose, with a false note from time to time, at once familiar and noble.

Then the priests arrived. Obviously, they suspected nothing, and were content to ask vague questions. No one said, "Begone, Satan!" But neither did anyone welcome Grigori's candidacy for the priesthood with the enthusiasm which he had expected. One of the priests said, "A vocation is always deserving of the greatest respect. Surely no one would argue otherwise. Even so, there is nothing so much to be regretted as a misunderstood vocation. At this moment, we are in the midst of a national crisis the like of which we have not known in the past twenty-six years. It is not impossible, citizen, that you have been the victim—how shall I describe it?—of a collective emotion, and that you have interpreted that emotion in a religious sense. In itself, that is praiseworthy, but not significant. It is by no means certain that you personally have received a call. Naturally, these are all things that we must try to discover, with God's help."

These priests, Grigori reflected, talked like university professors. He had hoped for more local color.

So much darkness, so much emotion, and so much duplicity should have opened my eyes. But I was the victim of what I accepted as knowledge, fervor, and charity. You yourself have often said it: these men

And if you have not said it, let's say that I read it between the lines.

bear no resemblance to the foolish caricatures described in our official anti-religious propaganda. They are perfectly capable of insinuating themselves into a defenseless mind and injecting their soporific poison into it. And I placed myself in their hands.

Obviously, nothing could be less true. Never did I surrender myself to them. The holier I thought they were, the more I hated them. Also, there is nothing soporific about their poison. On the contrary, it is a marvelous stimulant.

There were three priests at the seminary. In Grigori's memory, they were the three ikons of a triptych—impassive, aloof, representing the visitation of the three old men on the Feast of Pentecost. A malevolent trinity in black and gold. Contemplating life from the height of the ikonostasis, controlling it with their stiff hands in a silent incantation. Unfeeling as mummies. Whether they were dead or alive mattered little. The folds of their cassocks, like those of their chasubles, were arranged in unconsciously hieratic order. Faith works such wonders. The color of death; and eyes open, but turned inward.

Three priests.

The first of them was the oldest, Father Mitrophanus, hardly more than a shadow, a wraithlike body, a ghostlike voice. Disincarnated by age, by sanctity, and by a dream cherished for eighty years. Professor of theology, and an experienced demonologist. He had a devotion to Mary so intense that he was unable to speak of her without a shiver of delight. "Think of her," he preached, "as a Jewish girl; a good little Yiddish woman standing at the very summit of the human pyramid and exposed to every breeze. What is more defenseless than a girl

—and a Jewish girl at that? And yet Mary is the most perfect thing that man has ever produced. You must be very careful not to fall into the error of Rome known as the Immaculate Conception. God gave us Jesus, but he did not give us Mary. Mary was created by man, as the oyster creates its pearl, so that he could offer her to God."

The second priest was Father Nicephorus, rector of the seminary and professor of Greek. He was dark, slippery, unctuous; a true olive-oil priest. And he was on excellent terms with the civil authorities: "Well, well, Comrade Commissar, what are you going to accuse me of this time? One of our seminarians gave a fruit tart to a little boy again? Why don't we just forget about it? He didn't know a fruit tart was religious propaganda, or that he was running the risk of converting the poor little communist soul. The poor little communist soul didn't know it either. So far as you are concerned, I can't offer you a fruit tart; but how about a glass of currant vodka? And don't say that I'm trying to convert you. You know how I feel. Each of us has our work. Yours is to make communists, and mine is to make Christians. Believe me, some day we'll be working together, trying to make Christian communists. No one is more attached to your social order than we who wear cassocks. A clean slate. You know that Jesus was the first socialist in history. He specialized in overturning the stalls of the capitalists in the Temple. The only thing is that there are certain practices— Well, I need you in this world, but only for a matter of twenty years or so. On the other hand, if I am right and you and I both end up there in front of the same judge . . . Remember, Comrade Commissar, in heaven as on earth, one hand washes the other; except that it is for eternity. Won't you have another glass of vodka?" As he spoke, Father Nicephorus' eyes were like black olives behind his steel-rimmed glasses. His beard, his hair, like black enamel laid on silver. His smile was that of a Greek, charming and perfidious. And, after the commissar had gone, he fasted for three days to expiate his glass of vodka. Had he enjoyed it, then? Pharisee!

The third priest was Father Michael, the youngest, professor of liturgy. His face was flat, pale, bony, diamond-shaped. His eyes protruded so that they were merely colorless orbs level with his forehead. His rubbery mouth was barely able to restrain the flow of invective which rose to his lips. If truth be told, it restrained it rarely. "The communist yoke has redeemed the excesses of the Inquisition," he taught. "All the churches are united. Yes, I admit it, I am united with the papists. In our time, we are expiating the bonfires that they ignited in past centuries. And the more we expiate, the more quickly will we see the rainbow in the sky once more. Let us speak frankly. For the Christian, there is nothing better than to die a martyr. It's all very well for us to open up the untarnishable faucet of Christ's blood every Sunday. But how do we feel about letting some of ours flow?"

Father Michael had a tenor voice, grating and violent. His liturgical invocations were like shrieks of pain. When he celebrated Mass, he sounded like a woman giving birth. At the same time, he swung the censer as though it were a battle-axe.

And yet, it was not these men
of blackened gold who were
most important. You know,
Comrade Dobermann, the in-
sidious and sensual effect of
a high, narrow room, its walls
hung with tapestries and
bristling with banners,
somber, empty, silent, its darkness re-
lieved only by a candle here and
there. It affects you, so to
speak, through every pore and

through every sense. Your
eyes are filled by shadows
and candles in regular
sequence, and by dim re-
flections of the gold.
Your ears are held by the
even chants, the ritual
words, or by the silence
punctuated with a murmur
of prayers which are of
yesterday, of half a
millennium ago, and perhaps
even of tomorrow. Your nostrils
are assailed by the scent, faint,
humble, and austere, of
stale incense. Into your
hands, custom places a smooth,
soft candle. On your tongue,
there lingers the taste of
the bread and the wine. You
are surrounded. You are invaded.

Grigori wrote no more. His chin rested on his hand, his fingers moved in his beard. Yes, the chapel was impressive.

It had been designed for a thousand of the faithful within its erratic form. Everywhere there were nooks and alcoves, pillars where the ceiling sloped. The whole was painted in the inexpressive, sacral style of the classic age. It was loaded to the gills with small ikons of gold or silver, enhanced by the presence of several pedestaled ikons, also of gold. Before them, huge votive lights of red and blue hung from the ceiling on draw-chains. The irregular floor randomly sloped and rose and changed from wood to brick and back again. The dimness was lighted by spots of color from the few panes of stained glass that were still intact, and by this alone, for the chapel was almost without windows, almost a vacuum, a closed world, and enchanted, where relationships were alien, where the laws of society, physics, and mathematics no longer applied; an ethereal space where phantoms reigned at will, over subjects cast in their image.

In their image . . .

Grigori could see in his mind the seven faces of the seven seminarians, the only subjects of that forsaken kingdom, raised toward the crucified and glorified Christs, toward the saints both immobile and kinetic. Shining eyes, sunken cheeks, pale mouths at the service of the eyes, brows, and mouths of their sovereigns. Hands folded in imitation of the praying hands of images. And we speak of stigmatists! At any moment, the seven seminarians could have been suddenly transferred to the walls and covered with gold leaf, and they would have been indistinguishable from the other sacred gentlemen of the ikonostasis.

And I? Grigori thought. Did my face stand out? Why is it that no one ever said, "That face is not like ours"? But it would be useless to explain this to Dobermann, since he must believe that I had the faith, that I was one among others. But what was I in fact? An actor in make-up?

Perhaps, he thought, without conviction. An actor, made up from within by fasting, exhaustion and prostrations, by texts repeated and chants chanted. It is as easy for a man to simulate prayer as it is for a woman to simulate pleasure. Probably because neither is ever wholly unreal. The rhythm, the invocations, the hypnotic repetition of ejaculations. It happened that I, like the others, sometimes cried, spontaneously, "Lord, have mercy!" And yet I did not believe. Lenin wrote that quantitative values proceed by degrees, and that, at a certain level, they become qualitative. Lenin was referring to economics; but the same thing holds true of religious incantation. The spiraling invocations of the litanies induces hypnosis. No, I was not different. I experienced exactly the same thing as the others. The only difference was that my sacred ecstasy was a trick.

There were seven cassocked seminarians on their knees. Seven seminarians standing, then seven prostrate on the floor. Seven foreheads struck the floor and seven posteriors were raised toward heaven in a derisory posture of worship. There were seven voices, dissonant at first, their consonants interwoven, then later finding a harmonious cadence and the contrapuntal timbre to hymn their own abasement. The music of slaves. Pray to Jesus. Beseech him. Throw yourself on the floor, press yourself against it, become one with it, enter into it, treat it as one loved, for it conquers pride, the very sense of individuality, and therefore brings one closer to God.

"Grace," Father Michael shouted, stamping his foot, "is in these planks, these pieces of tile, this grouting. There is more grace in the floor under your feet than in all the splendors of our ikonostasis. Love this hard, cold floor. Let your bodies bear the marks of it. Let your hands be covered with splinters. Let your brows be covered with lumps, and your knees with callouses. The gymnast needs a stationary bar to practice his specialty, and you, when you practice yours, need the floor."

I was really one of them, Grigori thought. But who can say? Perhaps Pacomius or Vsevolod were like me, certain in their hearts that there was no God. Really, we were working not for God, but for ourselves. They mollified us. They used to tell us: "Some day, after you have graduated and been ordained, you will be ready to work for God. But, at present, there is no room for pride. Make yourselves over by imitating Christ, but do not expect positive results. The seed germinates beneath the soil. Do not try to make it grow before its time. Your present task is to try to enter into the ground so that you may some day germinate and grow."

From that standpoint, what was the difference between them and me? Like them, I was on an assignment, and I was leading the life of a larva, in the hope that one day I would be free of my cocoon. Was I one of them? Let's see. It is not the opinions of chiefs that count, but those of peers. The superiors and the saints on the walls saw around them, at their feet, seven thin faces, all alike. But my comrades, those who studied from the same worn Bible, ate at the same table, jostled me over the same zinc tub that we used as a sink; did they detect on me the scent of a lost sheep?

Grigori smiled, happy and malicious, proud of his virtuosity even at the distance of twenty years. Those lambs had sensed in him not a lost sheep, but a converted wolf; a superior animal who had had his claws blunted, a dilettant ready for martyrdom. They used to say to him: "After all, you were an officer"; and, "You had a career in the world, whereas we have only Our Lord." They feared his outbursts, his strength, and even his friendly teasing, they were wary of his borrowed, painstaking humility. They nicknamed him "the hard-boiled monk," and "the boyar in a cassock." They remarked on his lack of flexibility. But never did any of them suspect that he was a hypocrite.

It gave Grigori a rare equivocal pleasure to remember his first introduction to his fellow seminarians. It was in the refectory, where once more than a hundred monks had taken their daily meals. There was a long, scrubbed table of wood, one end of which was occupied by the six seminarians who sat there in a corner of the room, in the growing darkness of evening. High windows showed the sky still bright; and against it one could see the branches of birches, and birds circling in the heavens. Before the six seminarians were six wooden bowls filled with broth.

The door opened and Grigori entered, enveloped in a floor-length black cassock, holding a bowl of wood, the seventh, in his hand. It was empty. He paused at the threshold. He dared not cross the room, walk to the far end, sit at that table where he had no assigned place and where the broth had already been served. Two priests pushed him ahead of them. He went forward between them as between two angels or two policemen. He had a strong impulse to turn and run. But Father Nicephorus and Father Michael would never have allowed him to leave like that. In their way, they were like Grouztchik.

The three men crossed the room halfway and stopped in the middle. The six seminarians did not rise, but neither did they touch their broth. They watched, and they waited, in a spirit of resigned expectancy.

Father Nicephorus said: "I bring you a new brother. Make him welcome."

No one moved, neither Grigori nor the seminarians.

"He has not enjoyed the same advantages as you," Nicephorous continued. "He has not had the benefit of years of ecclesiastical instruction. He will do his best to catch up with you in your studies, as well as on the path of charity. Help him. His name is Grigori. Go, Grigori."

Grigori crossed halfway the space which still separated him from the table and then stopped again. He was, he knew, the last arrival, and also a Christian. Therefore he must take the lowest place. At the same time, he felt nothing but contempt for these apprentice priests. He was, after all, an officer in a victorious army. He knew that he deserved the place of honor. He deserved it also because he was insincere and therefore more intelligent. He would willingly have taken the lowest place, but only if it was obvious to everyone that he had chosen it willingly. He knew that he was wrong. The place you must take, he told himself, is that which will best enable you to do your job. A proud man is a poor intelligence officer. Therefore, take the lowest place. But which is it?

He had no idea. Rudely, he glanced over his shoulder. Father Michael was watching him with impatience, and Father Nicephorus was smiling his oily, subtle smile. Grigori, now angry, strode to the table, threw one leg over a bench, and dropped into a seat next to one of the seminarians. He did not know which place he had taken, but at least he was seated. The seminarians had taken no notice of him. Their eyes remained fixed on the priests standing in the middle of the room.

Grigori still held the wooden bowl, the wooden spoon, in his hand. He dared not place the bowl on the table, for that would have been to ask for food. The broth had already been served. Grigori clutched the bowl to his chest. He did not care if he went hungry, but he was determined not to expose himself to ridicule. He would have given anything to be back in his battalion mess hall, where he knew what was expected of him.

The two priests did not speak. They waited. In the semi-darkness, their parallel silhouettes, separated by the space which Grigori had occupied, were motionless.

Grigori felt someone touch the bowl. It was the seminarian next to him, who took the bowl and smiled, a smile tinged with a certain shyness and yet a certain self-assurance. After a moment's hesitation, Grigori released the bowl. His neighbor placed it on the table noiselessly, carefully, in front of Grigori. Then he dipped his spoon into his own bowl, filled it with broth, and with great care, spilling not a drop, emptied it into Grigori's bowl.

Then Grigori's other neighbor pulled the bowl toward his. They struck with a small sound, flat and intimate, and another spoonful was emptied into Grigori's bowl with all the majesty of a crane moving its hamper.

One by one each of the other seminarians took a spoonful of his own broth and emptied it into Grigori's bowl. It was done in silence. One of the men pulled Grigori's bowl toward him. The others rose and carried their full spoons to his place. One red-faced peasant allowed a few drops to fall to the table. Immediately a ripple of gaiety spread. Smiles appeared on gentle, closed faces. Someone laughed aloud. There were taunts, but their irony was so gentle as to have lost its edge:

"Pacomius! You've done it again!"

"Pacomius, you'll never change."

"Pacomius, you never miss a chance."

Pacomius, even redder than usual, bent his large, ungainly body over the table, carefully scooped up the spilled broth with the tip of his spoon, and then sat down again. His neighbors gave him quick jabs with their elbows.

In the middle of the room, the two priests turned slowly toward each other and, in the gloom, exchanged silences.

ACT II

If you consult the records of the local militia during my last year in the seminary, you will find proof of how blind I was. I was one of those men who, wearing a blindfold, are certain that they are racing headlong toward truth, but in fact

Always let your lies be as close as possible to the truth. That is one of the axioms of the service.

are going in the opposite direction. If ever I have the happiness to see you in person, you will not have to refer to the militia's records. You would see proof of my folly in the scars of my body.

Scars. Grigori's fingers sought them out with morose satisfaction. One, hidden by his mustache, was the result of a blow which had opened his upper lip from end to end. There was another on his side, where he had been struck by a rifle butt and his ribs broken.

Grigori was in his third year at the time. For two and a half years, he had worked with the diligence of a dedicated agent. The course of studies did not follow a logical chronological cycle. Some of the seminarians had been there for six years, for it had been necessary for them to begin by learning to read. Others had just arrived. Ordination was conferred upon the initiative of the rector, who decided that one or another of his students was ready for the priesthood, and who was not required to explain his decision to the Patriarchate. A certain amount of friction resulted from this situation. The Patriarchate was in need of priests and attempted to accelerate the process of preparation. Nicephorus never gave in. Wearing his most unctuous smile, he would answer: "Your Holiness needs a hundred priests, and I have only seven seminarians. Let these seven places, which will be filled, be filled by men who are ready. In other circumstances, we might rely upon the laws of quantity to provide us with quality; but today that is not possible. Grace, if it is to be allowed to come to rest, requires a landing field which has been properly marked."

At that time, Pacomius was reciting the psalms in his cell. Abraham was occupied with refuting the Roman schism. Vsevolod, prostrate on the floor, at the end of his strength, was gasping: "Humility! I demand humility, Lord!" Grigori was conjugating Greek *-mi* verbs until his head swam. Macarius and Thomas were quizzing each other on the Old Testament. And Alexander, having tied a string to a doorknob, was teaching himself how to swing a censer in cadence.

While the seminarians were thus waiting for God's grace to ripen, in time, of course, but out of season, as in a hothouse, life went on in the modern communist society around them. Some men passed the closed churches and said: "No one can find a house or an apartment, and yet these old barns remain empty." Others saw the same locked doors and thought: "Death is upon my soul, and the church I used to visit with my grandmother is not open."

Meanwhile, Party directives and denunciations by local activists were piling up on the desks of those responsible for public education, were filling their files and swelling their brief cases. And, simultaneously, certain decisions were beginning to take shape in their minds. These decisions concerned, among a thousand other things, a certain seminary located in a former monastery; in a complex of buildings admirably suited to become the headquarters of a youth organization which would be created specially to occupy those premises.

Plans were commissioned, and spread out on desks to be studied. High officials made tentative claims of jurisdiction over the monastery in order to gain leverage, then gave up their claims, or exchanged them for others, and thereby gained prestige and a small profit. Architects razed walls which they had never seen and, with the bulldozers of their imaginations, leveled the mounds of earth in the monastery graveyard and made a handball court of it. Hundreds of gallons of fictive paint were spread over frescoes four centuries old, by virtue of the miracle of budgetary anticipation. Red pencils struck out "cells" and "oratory" and "chapel" and wrote in "showers" and "offices" and "auditorium."

Files were compiled, tied by secretaries with black ribbon, and dispatched. Much gooseberry vodka was drunk by the authorities. Father Nicephorus undertook draconian fasts. Increasingly urgent memoranda were dispatched to officials of the Party. The most scrupulous of these functionaries soon severed relations with the priest, so as not to be obliged to drink his vodka under false pretenses.

One night, three truckloads of soldiers drew up a short distance from the seminary. The buildings were surrounded, and Captain Lodzianko, at the head of ten men, presented himself at the main door. With Lodzianko and his soldiers, but to the rear, well hidden behind their broad backs, walked a political commissar, a small mule-faced man, camouflaged from head to toe by an overcoat with a fur collar.

It was five o'clock in the morning. Fog swirled around the twisted cross which crowned the cupola. There was an odor of freshness and of earth. "Ready whenever you are, Comrade Commissar," the Captain said in his most official tone. The dark little man made a gesture of acquiescence. Even his nose was hidden in the fur collar. Lodzianko, who, being an educated man had of course no religion, gave a ringing order: "Vaska! Let's see if we can awaken these joyful cenobites!"

The joyful cenobites, if Lodzianko had known, had already been awake for an hour. They had begun with individual prayers in their cells, and then assembled in the chapel for the first community prayer of the day. Afterward, they had gone to the refectory for a slice of black bread and a glass of water; for it was Lent, and the milk which was their ordinary fare was forbidden them. After a prayer of thanksgiving, they had shared the daily chores. Some swept the courtyard, others hoed the garden. Alexander brushed off the refectory table, and wondered whether it would be sinful to eat the two crumbs which he had found among the straws of his brush. Pacomius was polishing the bell of the main door with a mixture of vinegar and salt. Thus, the joyful cenobites were busy; and everyone sang the liturgical canticles proper to the feast of the day, so that a faint humming rumbled through the monastery.

Father Mitrophanus, in his cell, had already succumbed to the temptation which assailed him daily. He was composing a new litany to the Virgin, endlessly polishing each invocation:

"Holy Virgin, wild rose of the Arabian desert, living rose of the sands;

"Pray for us.

"Holy Virgin, daughter of Sem, sweet succor of the Gentiles;

"Pray for us.

"Holy Virgin, rustling olive branch on the tree of Abraham;

"Pray for us."

Father Michael prayed. Eloquently. Passionately. He prostrated himself. He rose. His eyes popped. His movements were so energetic that the flame of the votive candle flickered in the breeze of his prostrations. He was praying to his patron saint, the Archangel Michael, patron of knights. He had chosen him when he became a monk, and he had a particular devotion to him. In counterpoint to his ritual prayers, he repeated unconsciously the flamboyant words which constituted his true orison: "Archangel, archangel with the fiery sword! You and I know that Satan exists . . . Archangel! We do the work which no one else will do . . . Fiery sword! It was you, and not Gabriel . . ."

Father Nicephorus was writing an adulatory letter to the political commissar of the district. He did not know that the commissar at that very moment was not five hundred yards away, standing behind Captain Lodzianko. "Comrade Commissar," he wrote, "I have heard rumors to the effect that certain highly placed persons, poorly informed rather than badly motivated, plan, at some time in the still distant future, to undertake certain projects which will cause grave harm to our institution, an institution which owes so much to your kindness. Is it possible that you may be able to obtain more precise information on this matter? I am told that a youth center is planned . . . Be that as it may, you may be sure that, victorious or defeated, we will be ready always to welcome you with open arms into our sacred precincts, and I anticipate the pleasure of sharing with you a glass . . ."

Nicephorus, as he wrote, allowed his imagination to wander. He ruminated on the various improvements which he wished to effect in the seminary plant. The cross over the bell tower should be straightened; the crumbling cupola should be repaired; the exterior walls should be whitewashed, at least in front; and the faded image of the Virgin over the entry portal should be repainted. "If God will grant me the strength and a little whitewash . . ."

He was interrupted by Pacomius, pale and free of his customary awkwardness. "Father," he said, "I heard noises around the buildings. I looked out of the peephole and saw armed men on the road and others in the bushes."

Nicephorus put down his pen, carefully replaced and tightened the lid on his inkwell so that the ink would not be wasted. "Go," he commanded. "Tell everyone to assemble in the chapel."

Grigori, as it happened, was already in the chapel, scrubbing the floor with a great splashing of water. His cassock had been gathered to his waist and secured there by the narrow leather belt that he wore. His feet were bare. He splashed about, and in the hollows of the wooden floor, the water formed small pools around his toes. He had already scrubbed the choir and the forward part of the nave. There, the floor shone as though it had been waxed, and the golden reflection of the ikonostasis was dimly visible. The chapel was shorn of the solemn air which it assumed during the divine office. It had become a familiar place of work. There was nothing intimidating about the ikons. Grigori did not even see them. It was as though the saints had withdrawn in order to avoid getting their feet wet. But they would return later, in time for services.

Grigori watched, however, as the mortals entered. There were the seminarians, some with their cassock skirts tied around their waists, and others, with no cassock at all and with their brooms still in their hands. Father Mitrophanus came, like a captive bird; Father Michael, profoundly troubled; and Father Nicephorus, serene. In order not to spoil Grigori's handiwork, they gathered at the far end of the chapel, where the floor was still dry and dusty. They made careful signs of the cross, and looked at one another anxiously.

Father Nicephorus stepped forward briskly and walked to the edge of the clean section, where the water mixed with dust had established a boundary of foam and gray bubbles. He made a solemn sign of the cross, his eyes fixed on the Royal door, then, turning his back to the altar, he faced his assistants and his students, who stood waiting silently. They hardly recognized their rector. His face was no longer that of a Greek, and his features reflected a new harmony, a detachment. The nose seemed more aquiline; the eyebrows, more finely drawn. The eyes and mouth had lost their air of obsequious coquetry. His black hair and beard, touched with silver, formed a somber frame for his countenance.

Behind him, the saints, like a flight of pigeons, had hurriedly resumed their accustomed places within their haloes of gold. They were present; and they somehow resembled Nicephorus. As the mortals had entered through the nave, they had entered through the choir. The chapel was once more a chapel.

The rector spoke: "Brothers, it may be that the hour of our great trial is upon us. Let us endeavor to pray for our enemies, not with our mouths but in our hearts.

"I am confident that, even if we should be dispersed, most of you will find the means to pursue your vocation. Those of you who may not choose to continue—remember, priests are not the only ones who are saved.

"Brothers, there is much that I could say; but it would be much better for us to pray."

A wild hope sprang up in Grigori's mind. If the seminary was to be closed, if all the seminaries were to be closed, he would be free. He would be given another assignment.

Everyone followed Father Nicephorus' example and knelt. "Our Father, Thou Who art in heaven . . ."

No more glances were exchanged. Each man was occupied wholly with himself. Each conferred hastily with his favorite saint, with the Virgin or with the Saviour who were enthroned to the right and to the left of the altar. Father Mitrophanus edged into a corner, before an ancient Marian ikon painted on wood, a tiny shrine which he loved above all others. Pacomius was striking the floor with his forehead with such force that it was plain he would have bumps later. Alexander had crouched down rather than knelt. A piece of string was hanging from his pocket. At the end of it, no doubt, was the doorknob which he used as his censer.

There was a loud knocking at the gate. The seminarians started. The priests continued to pray, ignoring the knocking. ". . . the power, and the glory. Amen," Nicephorus concluded. "Grigori, my son, answer the door."

Grigori rose. Nicephorus half turned toward him, revealing a profile at once human and humble. "Remember," the rector warned, "these men are the representatives of our legal government, since we have no legitimate government."

Grigori left the chapel at a run. The men who were pounding on the door in the distance, who were beating at the gates of his prison, were his comrades in uniform, his liberators. At last he would see a face that was not blurred by preoccupation with the hereafter. He knew that, to those men, he would be the enemy; but he would be comforted by the very sight of them.

As he approached the gate, Grigori heard the familiar curses, the coarse voices of enlisted men. He remembered the war, the damp grass, the large, heavy, supple bodies of his men leaping through the underbrush. Life!

In his officer's voice, brutal, raucous, he roared above the noise: "Don't break down the door, for Christ's sake!"

There was an immediate silence. Grigori could sense the amazement of the soldiers; and he was aware, too, of the impropriety of what he had done. Remember your mission, he chided himself.

The door opened. It revealed to the soldiers a seminarian with downcast eyes, the humility of his posture emphasized by his bare shanks and feet. Thus Grigori confronted the armed might of Caesar.

Captain Lodzianko stood on the threshold, a Hercules with the curly locks of a cherubim. An upper tooth was missing on the right side. The gap was useful for spitting.

From head to toe the officer inspected the seminarian with the bowed head. Grigori was solidly built, a strapping young man; but his cassock concealed his frame and his muscles. The captain saw only the bent body, the sunken cheeks, the thick beard of a young man. "Get out of my way, little priest," Lodzianko said good-naturedly. "I want to speak to a grown-up. Aren't you ashamed of yourself? At your age you should be carrying a rifle. If we had depended on you to save the country, my men here would all be good little krauts by now."

He turned toward his soldiers. "Can you see this one using a slit trench in those skirts?" Then, to Grigori: "Don't worry. If you were in my outfit I'd soon have you in shape. You may have the makings of a good communist."

The soldiers snickered.

The political commissar, his nose still buried in his fur collar, hid behind the captain's back.

"Go on, talk," Grigori said to himself. "Talk, little rear-echelon captain. You are doing your job, and I'm doing mine. And mine is more important. You can humiliate me, but it is I, and not you, who know the great mystery. I belong to the service. I am an agent." And he lowered his head even more, so as to hide the smile playing on his lips.

Grigori was happy. The truculence of the captain, the loud, coarse voices and awkward gestures of the enlisted men both shocked and delighted him. Three years in the seminary had heightened his sensitivity, but he had retained a nostalgia for his former life of violence.

"Among these men," he told himself, "is my truth."

He moved aside to allow the men to pass. The captain, the commissar and the soldiers passed him in single file. A giant trooper put his hand on Grigori's bowed head and gave it a jocular shake.

"Look. The walls all have drawings on them," said one of the soldiers when he saw the exterior frescoes.

"They're beautiful," observed a naïve young corporal with a pug nose.

Someone more educated, wearing glasses, corrected him: "These are non-cultural depictions."

Grigori fell in at the end of the line.

"Where are they?" the captain roared. "Where are these holy priests?"

"In the chapel, Lieutenant. If you will follow me—"

There was general indignation. "He doesn't even recognize a captain's insignia!"

Grigori enjoyed his small revenge. It was amusing to tease village idiots.

The captain marched through the monastery with swinging arms, his narrow hips and wrestler's shoulders moving in silent cadence. He halted before the chapel, looked up at the saint depicted over the portal, spat eloquently on the floor, then opened the door with a mighty kick.

He and his men stomped into the chapel, where the seminarians and priests were chanting a psalm in the seventh mode. Grigori could distinguish the thin, quavering voice of Father Mitrophanus, the ecstatic articulation of Father Michael, and Pacomius' rounded bass.

The soldiers halted, confused. To some of them, the chant recalled images of their childhood: their mothers, and priests with long beards, and the lugubrious services of Holy Week which ended with the bittersweet taste of the Easter cake.

Lodzianko's voice thundered; but a single voice cannot drown out a well-trained chorus. When the verse had been duly completed, Father Nicephorus gave the signal to interrupt the chanting. He walked toward the intruders and bowed to them in silence.

"Are you the boss?" Lodzianko asked.

"I am the rector," the priest responded in a low, firm voice.

"Read this."

A typewritten sheet passed from the red hand of the soldier into the gray hand of the priest.

Father Nicephorus was an administrator, and he grasped immediately the substance of the document. "This says the twenty-third," he remarked. "But the twenty-third was yesterday."

The political commissar moved backward, backward, and hid among the soldiers. The captain was left to offer an explanation. "Precisely," he said. "There have been delays. For that reason, we must proceed immediately to the expropriation of this—this—"

He hesitated. He wished, without knowing why, to appear polished, educated, even distinguished. He wished to wound the priest, and deeply. He had intended to say, "to the expropriation of this hideout," but he caught himself in time and said instead: "of this haven."

Silently, Nicephorus bowed his head.

The seminarians and the soldiers were face to face. Grigori, who had been the last to enter, stood behind the soldiers, his arms folded. He was overcome by a strange feeling: that for the moment, his friends were the men he saw opposite him, the seminarians. He saw their apprehensive faces, their apparent dignity, and he sensed their fear—that incontrollable contraction in the pit of the stomach. He had eaten their black bread and their broth, drunk their water. With them, he had prayed to the point of physical exhaustion during the long Lenten nights. He knew the weakness and the smell of each of them. He had sewn buttons for Vsevolod, who could not handle a needle and thread. He had chopped wood for Alexander, who was sickly. He had tutored Macarius in theology. His enemies had become his friends, and his friends had become his enemies. As by a sign, he now found himself apart from one group, and behind the other. Because Father Nicephorus had sent him to the gate—had he been chosen?—Grigori was in a position to observe the reactions of the seminarians from without; and, for that reason, he was conscious of belonging, albeit temporarily and precariously, to their group. There was nothing mysterious about it. He had seen close friendships develop between members of a military unit, only to disappear without a trace when one of the men had been transferred. Yesterday, only those who wore certain insignia had been one's brothers; today, a different insignia had the power to confer brotherhood. It was in this sense, and in this sense only, that Grigori felt he also was a seminarian.

"How much time will you allow us, to leave?" Nicephorus asked, in a voice so dry that it seemed alien to him.

"You do not seem fully aware of what is involved, ah, comrade priest," Lodzianko said, becoming more and more courteous. "So far as your personnel are concerned, you must all accompany us to headquarters so that we may verify your identity. We hope to detain you no longer than is absolutely necessary. Regarding the buildings and their contents, I must refer you to the final paragraph of the directive."

The final paragraph read as follows: "The premises will be vacated, cleaned, and disinfected by the date given above. The contents of the premises will be turned over to the district commissar."

"Captain," Nicephorus asked, "are you the district commissar?"

"No," Lodzianko answered, "certainly not." He spoke with a mixture of deference for the person of the commissar and distaste for his function. "But he is here. Commissar, where are you?"

"Here," the commissar answered, from behind the soldiers. Grigori saw his low, timid silhouette. The commissar was eager to remain out of sight, but the soldiers moved apart, and the little man found himself standing face to face with Nicephorus.

"Commissar," the rector asked sternly, "what do you intend to do with our holy images and sacred vessels? I submit that these objects are the property of the Patriarchate, and that they are of considerable value. You understand that if something should happen to disappear, I would be obliged to report it to my superiors."

The commissar coughed, and finally answered: "You are mistaken, citizen. You will recall that the buildings of this monastery and everything contained in them were confiscated at the beginning of the Revolution. Later, a cultural association was given permission to make use of them; but that association has now been dissolved. You will also recall that this property was consigned to the Church only by the occupation army of the Nazis. Surely you know that a recent law has abrogated all administrative decisions implemented by that authority. Thus, from a legal standpoint, we have returned to the point where your ecclesiastical wealth—"

The commissar scratched his nose, which remained hidden somewhere in his collar.

"Everything is perfectly legal," the captain added firmly.

"Everything is legal," the commissar corroborated in a thin voice, as though excusing himself.

Nicephorus did not answer. But, behind him, Father Michael said in a flat voice: "Everything is le-gal."

There was silence, and deep embarrassment. There had been none of the expected violence. The clerics had offered no resistance. Weapons had swung uselessly from their straps. The soldiers had struck no one with their rifle butts. Not a drop of blood had been shed. The prayers chanted so recently and with such sincerity now seemed exaggerated, almost pompous. So much excitement on both sides—and all over a strictly legal formality.

Nicephorus did not budge. He had no intention of facilitating the intruders' work. The commissar hated direct confrontations. Captain Lodzianko awaited orders. The soldiers looked at the seminarians with natural wariness, as though afraid of the evil eye. Grigori was fidgeting in his corner. He was eager to see all these things, the "contents" mentioned in the directive—the banners, ikons, lecterns, candelabra and censers—carried away in a great and grotesque procession. He wished the chapel to be bare, naked; the murals on the walls to be covered with paint; and its space to be handed over to pagan children for them to play their games and sing their marching songs.

"Comrade Commissar," the captain said at last, "I think that we are already behind schedule."

"Yes, certainly."

"Should we get to work?"

"Yes, I think so."

Lodzianko turned to his small troop. He spoke in his hearty command voice: "Men, you have one hour to clean out this place. At the end of that time, I want the corporal here to be able to show me a place that is fit for self-respecting communists. Corporal!"

"Comrade Captain?"

"I'll skin you alive if I find a single holy picture around here."

"Yes, Comrade Captain. Not a single one. What should we do about the paintings on the walls?"

"Do whatever you want. Camouflage them with cow dung if you want to. But get started!"

Loud voices. Heels clicking. Salutes pointing up the caps still on the soldiers' heads.

The corporal winked at one soldier, shouted an order to another. The men stacked their weapons in a corner with much clanking of metal against metal. One of them stood guard as though it were second nature to him. It was all routine. And so it began. A soldier's large, coarse hand seized upon the mahogany frame of a Virgin. Others grasped at frames of chiseled, dentelated gold. The large ikons moved, swaying, borne between pairs of enlisted men. The austere faces of the saints, emaciated by fasting, blackened by age, nodded, then righted themselves. There were muffled curses; and then, open blasphemy, uttered good-naturedly. A candelabra rolled to the floor with a crash. The corporal uttered a great oath.

Father Mitrophanus, with his white hair and transparent skin, still prayed before his favorite Virgin. The corporal with the turned-up nose spoke to him: "I'm sorry, grandfather, but we'll have to take that one too."

Mitrophanus looked at him without understanding. "This one too?"

"Yes, grandfather, that one too. It's the law."

Mitrophanus smiled gaily. "Well, my boy, since it's the law, take it! Take it!"

The corporal shrugged one shoulder apologetically and lifted down the panel of painted wood. Mitrophanus raised his white, shriveled hand and blessed the corporal.

Slaves! Slaves! Grigori thought. He doesn't even defend his Virgin.

The corporal, however, paused in surprise. One of the soldiers had witnessed the scene and called out, "Comrade Corporal! Now that you've been blessed, are you going to say Mass?"

The corporal ignored him. He held out the ikon to the priest. "Grandfather, maybe you would like to kiss it for the last time?"

"I'd like to very much," Mitrophanus answered gently. "I have grown fond of that piece of wood. Look how beautiful the colors are. And the Virgin—isn't she pretty, with her dark eyes and her long fingers?"

"Yes, she's very beautiful," the corporal agreed.

"Here, take it," Mitrophanus said. "Good-by, my dove. Farewell, holy little Jew. You're only an image, you know, no matter how lovely you may be. The real one is more beautiful than you; and no one can take her away from me. Take her, my boy, take her. God be with you."

The group of seminarians and priests had not budged. They seemed to believe they were forbidden to leave the chapel. Step by step, they retreated toward the choir as the soldiers gathered the ikons and piled them in the courtyard. It was all done without mockery, without rancor, and without remorse, and only muttered curses were heard when a large ikon proved difficult to move through the chapel door.

Gradually, the walls were laid bare. Grigori, from where he was standing, could see the naked wall, the high white surfaces, and spots of blue and green mold. And these little priests do nothing to defend themselves, he said to himself. Vsevolod, the proud one; and even Pacomius, like a force of nature. They submit. If it were I—

Suddenly, Grigori's voice rang out. "You bastard! Stop where you are!"

The soldier turned. He was tall, ugly, with an air of stupidity as his mouth hung open. He had walked in his dirty boots into the forward part of the nave—the part where the floor of brick and wood had been scrubbed so thoroughly that it mirrored the length of the ungainly ikonostasis.

Grigori stepped forward, shouting like a child: "I'm the one who scrubbed that floor! I did it, you understand? And now look what you've done, you clumsy fool!"

The soldier looked down. Pieces of mud had fallen from his boots and soiled the floor. He said nothing. He seemed more and more uncomprehending.

Grigori lost all control of himself. He forgot where he was. He forgot the danger. He forgot his mission. He spoke to Captain Lodzianko's man as he had spoken to his own men when he had discovered a dirty firing pin or an unpolished belt buckle. He was caught up in his own rage, and his epithets mirrored his state of mind. "Filthy pig" alternated with "infidel"; and the name of God punctuated an accusation of sacrilege. After two sentences, there were no more words. The gross, brutish face of the soldier drew Grigori's hard, well-trained fist like a magnet.

Behind the man, the golden ikonostasis rose. Above it, painted on the ceiling, was Christ the King, enthroned and judging. To the left, a crucifix of wood; to the right, Veronica's Veil. Everywhere, the same Face, mysteriously knowing. Everywhere, the same eyes, opened, onto another world, observing simultaneously the Grigori who was there and the Grigori who was elsewhere. Those inexpressive and all-seeing eyes spurred Grigori on to greater violence, to an ecstasy of liberation. Now, at last, he was cleansed of three years of humiliations, of prayers, of devotions. Freed of pieces of painted wood, of confessions of imaginary sins and mandatory exercises in asceticism. Finished with the abnegation of self for the sake of another being, whether God or man. Grigori drew back his fist and struck. The soldier reeled, raised his hand to his chin.

Lodzianko, who had been speaking to the commissar in a corner of the chapel, turned, saw what was happening, and rushed forward. The seminarian, his cassock still caught up around his waist, his legs apart, his calves bare, faced him.

Nicephorus stepped forward and placed a restraining hand on Grigori's forearm. The young man's muscles were so tense that the forearm trembled. "My son," the priest said, "remember Malchus—"

Lodzianko's voice thundered: "I'll take care of you, priest!" Grigori's fist smashed into his face, and the officer spat a tooth to the floor.

"Now," Grigori said, intoxicated, "maybe both sides of your ugly face will match."

He regained consciousness in a dark, silent cell. His ribs were broken. His face was contorted in pain. His bruised arms and legs seemed unable to function. Well, he reflected, I'm lucky. They could have killed me.

He clenched his teeth to keep from moaning.

I wonder what came over me, he asked himself. But that's not important right now. I should be worrying about how I'm going to get out of this. I could ask to see Grouztchik. But how will I explain it to him? I'll tell him the truth. Then he'll ask how I could have been so stupid.

Immediately, the justification of a subordinate came into his mind. I was not stupid at all. I took advantage of an opportunity to prove to the priests once and for all that I was on their side. I punched Captain Lodzianko in the mouth in the line of duty. I was able, and rather cleverly too, to provide the priests with what are called "guarantees."

Several hours were sufficient for Grigori to come to believe this explanation. He forgot the floor scrubbed by his own hands, the irritation provoked by the searing dispassionate scene in the chapel, the frustration engendered by three years of prostrations. He was convinced now that he had acted coolly and with all deliberation. He refused to answer any of the questions put to him by his interrogators. Instead, he demanded to be taken to Major Grouztchik.

Days passed. Grigori became impatient. He received little food. His guards answered his requests and his complaints alike with blows of their nightsticks. "We can't let him lose all those beautiful purple and yellow spots," they joked.

Grigori held his temper. His battered body caused him pain, but he was sustained by an inner exaltation. He was conscious that he was on a mission. If he was being allowed to rot in prison, it was only better to confound the enemy. Never for a moment did he doubt the efficacy of the secret services of his country.

Finally, he was blindfolded, led out of his cell. There was a truck, and, with many curses and kicks, he was loaded into the vehicle. A short ride. He was removed from the truck. A stairway. A corridor. A right turn. The odor of tobacco and vomit. Then, close, the odor of alcohol, very strong. A familiar voice: "Take off the blindfold and get out."

The harsh glare of an electric light. A few inches from Grigori's swollen face, Grouztchik's ogre face, fierce, intelligent. It had been two and a half years since they had seen each other.

"Well, my boy, I understand that you've been getting special treatment. I see that you can still stand up—and at attention, no less. It probably did you some good. You have to have gone through it yourself to keep from making mistakes. I know, from my own experience, twenty years ago, with the Whites—"

Grouztchik's index finger was on Grigori's chest, pushing, gently; and with irritation, Grigori felt himself falling backward. Grouztchik laughed, caught him, cleared a chair with his knee, and pushed Grigori onto it. He sat behind his desk and, his elbows spread, began to light a cigarette.

He's not looking at me, Grigori told himself. He's going to ask me an unexpected question. But what question?

In order to compose himself, Grigori looked around the room. In one corner was a small puddle of indeterminate but nauseating composition. Grouztchik had just conducted an in-depth interrogation. The smell of sweat was about him, and his gestures were those of a slightly excited animal.

Who was his victim? Grigori wondered vaguely. An enemy of the people? An American spy? A German collaborator? Poor man, he must have suffered. But it served him right. I haven't complained; why should he?

Grouztchik had lighted his cigarette. Suddenly, his blue eyes looked up at Grigori. "Have you changed your sex?"

"What?"

"Don't say 'What?' I'm asking you if you've changed your sex. That would explain it."

"Explain what?"

Grouztchik brought his fist down hard on the desk. "Our little friends in the anti-religious brigade are all faggots. Have they converted you? You can't even answer a simple question any more. Answer yes or no! Well?"

Grigori mumbled that he had not changed his sex, Comrade Major.

It was a curious thing. Nothing that he had undergone in prison or in the seminary had humiliated him so much as his answer to Grouztchik. He blushed to the roots of his hair. He felt as though, for the very first time, he had been injured in what, if he had not been a communist, he would have called his dignity.

"Ah, good," Grouztchik said. "Then perhaps you can give me a quick explanation of what happened."

Grigori had imagined a different scene. Now he understood

that he too was undergoing an interrogation, and that it was to his own best interests to give satisfactory answers. Groutzchik was no longer his superior, but his judge.

"My assignment," he began, in the hostile silence, and went on to give the arguments which now, despite their logic and simplicity, no longer seemed so convincing. He finished by repeating several times, "You see, they could have been suspicious of me. But now they know, and my mission—"

Grouztchik, leaning forward, spoke rapidly, tersely. "Did the priests have any reason to be suspicious of you?"

"No."

"And you, did you have any reason to think that they were suspicious?"

"No."

"Were you aware of the consequences of your action?"

"Yes."

"You told me that you were hoping all the seminaries would be closed."

"That's right."

"And that would have meant that your mission would be canceled?"

"Yes."

"Therefore, you were expecting, and in any event hoping, for your mission to be canceled. And yet you let yourself be beaten up under the feeble pretext of defending your floor? Answer me!"

Grigori had no choice but to answer. Grouztchik's voice was commanding, and his enormous fists were clenched on the desk.

"Yes."

"Those idiots were taking down the ikons, upsetting the candelabra?"

"Yes."

"Wouldn't it have been more convincing for you to lose your temper over an ikon?"

"Yes."

"Couldn't you see that yourself?"

"Yes."

"Well, *what?* Do you believe in God? Is that it?" Grouztchik asked the question in a different tone; in a final, almost affirmative way. Grigori experienced an unexpected feeling of relief. He was certain that, for once, Grouztchik was making a mistake; and he knew that the service never remained in error for very long.

"No," Grigori answered. "I do not believe in God. I believe in God less than I ever did. I hate priests more than ever. They haven't perverted me, if that's what you're thinking. The people at the seminary were country bumpkins, or else men with repressed ambitions. Nicephorus is a Machiavelli. Michael is a Savonarola. Mitrophanus is a maniac who thinks that he can cast out devils. I was at the point of being able to understand one of their mysteries, of being able to see how they are able to lead astray even some good men. We've always thought that it was by their morals; but it isn't, for there is no such thing as morality. Policemen can take the place of morality. It is by their liturgy, Comrade Major. The incense, the candles burning in the darkness, the music. Believe me, the Church does not capture a man by its virtue; it casts a spell on him by its liturgy."

Grouztchik smoked and listened. "My boy, you've reassured me. I thought you had become a turncoat. Or should I say a turncassock? I mean, that you had gone over to the other camp." He said it frankly, almost ironically; for he had never really believed it. But Grigori was not concerned, and the sense of relief persisted. For now Grouztchik was speaking in a fatherly tone, in that of a superior who corrects in order to encourage.

"Listen to me," Grouztchik went on. "I don't believe for a minute your story about having gone to jail to convince the priests that you were on their side. It occurred to me that you might have been touched by God's grace and that you had become an apostle. All the same, I would have been surprised. I'll tell you what I think now. If I'm wrong, tell me, and we'll try to understand each other.

"Here it is. As unhappy as you were in your seminary, you've lived there. And, after all, habit is a form of attachment. Perhaps unconsciously, it was painful for you to see the soldiers taking apart the world in which you lived. But that resentment didn't rise to the conscious level until they touched something that concerned you personally—the floor that you had just finished scrubbing with your own hands. And that was the moment of crisis for you. Still, you needed a pretext to justify your feelings to yourself; and so you invented one. You pretended that you wanted to win the confidence of the priests.

"That's something that you're going to have to be very careful of, my boy. This whole idea of becoming a martyr in order to prove something is an attitude that you got from the priests. Even if it's something that occurred to you afterward, it was because, without knowing it, you've been influenced by their way of thinking. You were walking in their footsteps. Be careful! Those footsteps lead to Jerusalem.

"Remember this: suffering proves nothing. Nothing, ever, to anyone. Moreover, there's never any need to prove anything. When you're fighting for a cause, the only important thing is to win. And in order to win, as the peasants say, do what you must do. But, above all, don't do more than you must. All things in moderation, my boy. That's the wisdom of the ancients. If I believed for a minute that you really ended up in prison 'in the line of duty' I'd have you thrown out of the service in a minute. I prefer to believe that you acted in a moment of weakness, or out of high spirits, or for any other reason that I can think of. Let's say simply that you got drunk while on duty. It's a serious offense—but one that can be pardoned. Now, are you sure you understand what I'm saying?"

"Yes, Comrade Major."

"Remember, no zeal. Never. Remember the peasants. Do only what you must do. Or remember the philosophers: all things in moderation. Your mission should be like an egg: full, but not overflowing. Otherwise, I'll have to send you to raise geese for the rest of your life."

"Geese, Comrade Major."

"Now, I'm going to have you released from prison right away, so that you'll lose as little time as possible. You'll have to get in touch with Father Michael somehow, and have yourself ordained as soon as possible. Then—"

"Michael, Comrade Major?"

"Yes, Michael. The old one is in a looney bin."

"And Nicephorus?"

"The rector?" Grouztchik's brow wrinkled. "Well, we had a little accident with the rector. We turned him over to a young idiot for interrogation—a young and *zealous* idiot, as it happened. And, as we might have known, he messed up the job. It was your fault. Indirectly. While you were busy beating up Captain Lodzianko, your rector made a pedantic and unfortunate allusion to a certain Malchus, who occupies an honorable place in the Scriptures. Well, our idiot got it into his head that Malchus was the pseudonym of the rector's correspondent in the Vatican."

"And then?" Grigori asked awkwardly.

Grouztchik shrugged. "Those greenhorns! When I get through with them— And then? Well, let's say that the Father Rector has received the crown of martyrdom and gone to his happy hunting ground, while the greenhorn in question has been transferred to the customs service, where he will spend the rest of his life—after spending sixty days in the stockade."

Grigori lowered his head and was silent. He thought of Nicephorus. Nicephorus the Greek, with his silver-streaked beard, his astute smile. He thought of Nicephorus, transfigured before the armed intruders: his aquiline nose, his impenetrable expression, as though he were looking inward, and his trenchant voice. Nicephorus had never touched Grigori's heart.

Grouztchik, now truly upset, rose from his desk. "I hate accidents of this kind. They're stupid, you know. Especially since we didn't get anything out of Nicephorus. Not a word about Malchus, obviously; or about what's cooking at the Patriarchate. Not even about clandestine hermits. Absolutely nothing, my boy. You know how they do it, don't you? At a certain level in their training, they repeat over and over again a special formula that they call the Prayer of Jesus—you should know about this—and they reach the point where they don't feel anything. At least, they pretend that they don't. You can beat them as much as you want, and they smile like angels. Well, they don't actually smile. They—how can I describe it?—they *dematerialize*. They disincarnate themselves. You have to be an idiot to give the third degree to a priest who is able to do that. There are other ways . . . Incidentally, if you happen to learn that trick, you'll have to let us know about it. It could be very useful on some of our assignments."

Grigori bowed his head, stunned. He thought of the other Father Grigori, the one with the greasy beard, on that April night. Why had he not been able to "dematerialize" himself? Had he not been a true priest? Perhaps Grouztchik was barking up the wrong tree.

"And now," Grouztchik said, "you'll have to go back to

your cell. But"—his voice was low—"we have to make sure that no one will suspect you and I are in cahoots; not even your guards, or anyone on my staff." His voice was softer yet. "And since you are so concerned about persuading the good fathers of your sincerity—"

Grouztchik's enormous smelter's fist crashed into Grigori's upper lip. Grigori's blood, with the taste of iron, covered his mouth and dripped onto the papers on Grouztchik's desk. Grouztchik bellowed: "Artemus! Get this idiot out of here! He's messing up my files!"

Artemus ran in, cursing. "Aren't you ashamed? Bleeding on the major's papers?" Grigori was led out, pressing his palm against his mouth to staunch the flow of blood.

When I was released from prison —a confinement which I surely deserved, and during which I was treated harshly, no doubt, but not unfairly—I immediately began trying to locate my former teachers. You will gather, from that fact, how totally my mind was given over to error.

In a way, I had hoped that I wouldn't be able to find them; but, in a society like ours, anyone can find anyone. The state is omnipresent, and the people live as they did in the Middle Ages. I suppose this is also the case in the colonized

countries. No one is neutral.
Everyone is either an informer for the government,
or a conspirator against it.

The nurse, a Neanderthal type wearing a filthy white smock, said: "The priest? You can probably find him in the garden. He's harmless. I haven't had to punish him a single time. Guess what he said to the chief medic. He said, 'I am in the kingdom of the possessed; and you are the king of them all.' The chief, you know, is—well, he put 'incurable' on the priest's file."

Grigori walked from the reception desk and ventured into the kingdom of the possessed. It was a world which seemed to him characterized by a disgusting violence. Combat, interrogations—these were things which he understood. He knew that, between the sessions of interrogation, agents were in the habit of refreshing themselves with glasses of vodka drunk in all good humor. But these patients and their nurses, who created a daily hell for one another, were beyond his experience. He had never seen a world of padded cells in which, to the technological horror of electrotherapy were joined the indecencies of childhood. It seemed a caricature of government police methods. Grigori was afraid. He walked hesitantly, not knowing whether he feared the patients or their keepers more.

He passed people wearing white smocks, and some wearing pajamas of coarse blue fabric. He looked away from them. He thought of the gentle Mitrophanus. "I haven't had to punish him a single time," the nurse had said.

If hell existed, Grigori reflected, it would be an insane asylum, where everyone would be whipped into acting out their dreams.

He passed the dining hall and looked in. There were wooden tables, heavily stained by patches of an indeterminate liquid. There were bits of lettuce leaves and scraps of bread on the tables and on the floor. A sickening odor of sauce turned Grigori's stomach, and he hastened his step. In his mind, he saw Mitrophanus, old, very white, ethereal, eating at these tables, his elbows against his body, assaulted by the shrieks of the hysterics and the silences of the melancholics.

Grigori followed the corridor. There was a door which opened into a dormitory. He saw fifty iron cots jammed together, covered with identical striped spreads. The odor of disinfectant—and occasionally that of eau de cologne—contested with that of filth for supremacy. There was none of the masculine odor of the barracks. No manly sweat, no rifle oil. Here, at night, Mitrophanus stripped his emaciated body under the insulting eye of the nurse on duty, and slid between his sheets. On top of his quilt, one would see his sparse white beard, his thin hair—unless he had been forced to shave—and his bright, knowing eyes.

At a bend in the corridor Grigori encountered a patient. Their eyes met. Those of the patient were not knowing or bright, but clouded, alien; the eyes of a dog on a biologist's torture rack. Would they also be the eyes of Mitrophanus?

The garden was nothing more than a courtyard containing four scraggly trees and bordered by a covered walk. In the far corner, Grigori saw him, perched on a low post, like a small bird, looking up at the sky; and, despite his patient's uniform, he was instantly recognizable, because he was different: Mitrophanus.

Grigori walked toward him, stopped, hesitated. The body of the angelic old man, no longer hidden by a cassock, its thinness emphasized by the grotesquely voluminous pajamas, was that of a wraith. His white hair, so sparse, so fine, had been shaved, like that of someone infested with lice, or that of a recruit; and the skull, fragile and pink, was naked to everyone's eyes. His beard had also been shaved. It was beginning to grow out again, a white and irregular down, like that of a pigeon barely out of the egg. The priest's head had taken on the shape of a formless rock. But it had suffered no dishonor. Grigori had thought to find a violated angel wallowing in shame. Instead, he saw that Father Mitrophanus, although deprived of his cassock and his beard, had remained as untouched by insult as by persecution. He could see it in the old man's eyes. They had remained the same: almost colorless, lightly tinged with blue, gentle, rich in their damp spark of tenderness.

"It is I, Father. Grigori."

"Ah, good morning, Grichenka, good morning."

Mitrophanus showed not the slightest surprise. He had recognized his visitor immediately. He inquired after his affairs with a sort of distracted solicitude. He had not gone mad, as Grigori, without knowing quite why, had expected.

Grigori explained why he had come: he wished to be ordained as quickly as possible. It was a case of a most urgent vocation.

"Well," Mitrophanus said, "I think it's a very good idea." Then, as indifferent to the nurses watching him as to the patients, and with the same gesture, at once affectionate and detached, as in the seminary, he blessed Grigori. "But," he continued, "you have come to the wrong person, my poor boy. I can't help you. You must go to—I don't really know—to Nicephorus, or to Michael. As you see, I am residing with the poor in spirit." And he smiled, angelically.

Grigori was disappointed. He had imagined the priest as a victim of persecution, as having been thrown to the medics and the maniacs as to the lions. And he had felt a mixture of pleasure and of inexpressible compassion for the unfortunate old man.

"Father," he said, "your sufferings are mine."

Mitrophanus, in all innocence, was astounded. "Are you

suffering, Grigori? But I am not suffering. I ask you, suffer no more. As for me, I can assure you that I have never been happier."

Grigori thought of the filthy pillows in the dormitory, of the crusts of bread under the narrow table in the dining hall, of the simian nurses. "Happy?" he asked.

"But of course, my dear boy. There are only two kinds of people in this place: those who are possessed, and those who are poor in spirit. The latter are empty, naked, stripped of everything. They are cold, trembling, and they await the coming of the Lord. I ask them to teach me my trade—which is the imitation of Christ; and they do it better than anyone else, for they are the poorest of the poor. They truly have nothing; not even reason. They are totally deprived; really open and ready to receive their God. Do you understand? They are as deprived and as open as a furrow in autumn. And that is why they are the poor in spirit. They tell me stories, *their* stories. And I tell them a story also: that of Mary. We understand one another very well. But occasionally I experience a sinful thought: they will be saved before me, and I envy them their good fortune. They are pure. They are like the sea with which the moon does whatever it will.

"And then, my son, there are the others, the possessed. With all my heart, Grichenka, I pity them. But what a blessing they are for me! Never have I had so many excellent subjects!" His eyes shone with eagerness. "Our government could not have found a better place for me!"

"What do you mean by 'blessings' and 'subjects'?"

"Come, come. A demonologist locked up in an institution for the insane! If only you knew how many old acquaintances I have met here. There are some who speak to me in tongues that I do not understand. But many speak Hebrew, or Greek. And, of course, Latin."

"They must be intellectuals who have gone mad."

"I am not speaking of those who are mad. Such men can hardly speak even our own language. No, those who speak to me are demons. We have theological debates, you see. It is delightful, when their tongues are untied. They are very clever sometimes, for they are creatures of God. I met one who compelled his victim to believe that he was a skillet. It was pitiful. The poor man walked around all day throwing his arms up into the air, hissing and crackling, without stopping. We asked him, 'Vania, what are you making?' And he answered. 'Pancakes.'

"I watched him closely for several days. Once, when he collapsed, exhausted, to the ground, I bent down next to him, put my hand on his elbow and my mouth close to his ear, and summoned his demon. 'Urobach! Urobach!' "

"You had recognized him?" Grigori asked.

"With a little practice, one can recognize them easily enough. In my time, I was a fairly good exorcist. I called him, first in Greek and then in Latin. But Vania only looked at me with glassy eyes. Then I played my trump card. I began speaking Hebrew. Vania had not even finished grammar school; yet, from his mouth, in answer, there flowed the purest Hebrew of the classical period!"

"What did he say?"

"Oh, we spoke of one thing and another. Urobach pleaded with me not to exorcise him. 'If you chase me away,' he said, 'I'll have to go back to hell, which is no more pleasant for devils than for men. Let me stay in Vania.' But I answered: 'Unclean spirit, limb of Satan' "—and here Mitrophanus' hands trembled with rage—" 'you ask me to allow you to continue to torture Vania, who has never harmed anyone?' The demon answered, 'I'll never torture Vania again! Or, at least, only a little. If I stopped altogether, I would be recalled immediately. Let's compromise. From now on, Vania will make only a hundred pancakes a day.' But I answered: 'A hundred pancakes? Never! Not more than three, do you understand me, demon?' Finally, we compromised at twelve pancakes a day.

"To be certain that Urobach does not try to trick me, every morning, as soon as I wake up, I sit on Vania's bed and say: 'Make your twelve pancakes!' Vania makes them. And then, for the rest of the day, he stays quietly in the cupboard."

Grigori could think of nothing to answer. He had been away from the seminary for two months, and the supernatural had become alien once more. The asylum had affected Mitrophanus after all, he told himself. The old priest had not been so demented before.

But, in fact, it was Grigori himself who had changed. In the seminary, he had listened to stories of demons in a different spirit. Within the monastery walls, everyone lived a faith which was fantastic without being absurd; a philosophy which, while no doubt false, was rigorously logical. Here, that faith and that philosophy were mere superstition. No, Mitrophanus had not changed, unless he had been rejuvenated by the abundance of devils which had suddenly fallen into his hands.

Of my teachers, one was in
an insane asylum; and he ad-
mitted to me that it was an
ideal home for him. He had
sunk into a swamp of diabolical
superstition and beliefs based
upon the Scriptures of my sect,
which frequently allude to the
existence of immaterial and
malevolent spirits over which
the priests are able to exercise a
mysterious control. Comrade, I,
a priest, can swear to you that,

even in the improbable event that such spirits exist, we have no power over them, and have never had any such power.

Obviously, this is all nonsense. Any priest would answer that I am a bad priest, and that such powers are not conferred by ordination but by God's grace.

I began searching for another of my teachers, one whose madness was less gentle. He had been deprived of authorization to exercise his ministry, and he was working as an unskilled laborer in a factory. A group of Christians told me where to find him, after I explained who I was.

I had assumed the furtive ways by which we recognized one another, and I had no trouble in convincing the faithful of my sincerity. It is enough to persecute any community, to any extent, for all its members to become instantly recognizable by the fear which haunts them, as

though a distinctive sign
were visible on their foreheads.

It was a building which, before the Revolution, had been middle-class. There was a dirty staircase, soiled and torn wallpaper. Broken windowpanes had been replaced by old newspaper, or had been mended with tape. There was, inevitably, the smell of cabbage. And also that of children. From the kitchen came the rattling of pots and pans; and like anything pertaining to household chores, and therefore to an organized manner of existence, it was a reassuring sound.

There was a double door, painted black. Grigori pressed the button. There was no sound of a bell. He knocked, and waited.

He had already gone to the Patriarchate where fat deacons had informed him that he could not be ordained until the seminary authorities had certified that he had completed his studies. However, not only did Grigori have to obey his orders; he also was determined to prove his loyalty to Grouztchik. In order to do so, he must become a priest, a wearer of the miter, and, as soon as possible, a bishop. Then intelligence and sabotage would be within his purview and within his grasp. With Nicephorus dead and Mitrophanus insane, Michael was his last chance.

Grigori knocked. A feminine voice, deep, careful, tinged by anxiety, asked: "Whom do you want?"

Grigori gave the name of the persons with whom the priest was living. He heard the woman's voice: "Euphrosyne Fominichna, it's for you."

The apartment, naturally, was occupied by several families. Grigori wondered whether he would be able to talk privately. Would the other people know who Michael was?

There was another voice: "What do you want, friend?"

Grigori repeated the name, and added, in a lower voice: "I want to see Michael." He dared not say, "Father," a word banned among enlightened men.

Women's voices whispered on the other side of the door. There were now three voices. One was calm, rich. Another, unsteady. The third, deliberate and low, said: "Open the door, Mother."

The door opened. There was a vestibule, long, dark. Before Grigori stood a small, aged woman, her half-smile unable to mask her trepidation. It was she who had opened the door. Behind her, leaning against a closed door, was a young woman, with large, high breasts; her face was unsmiling, flat under her dark hair. Like that of a Laplander. At the opposite end of the vestibule, in the light of an open door, Grigori could see another woman, rather large, holding a pan in her hands and cleaning it. It was she who had first answered Grigori's knock; but he could sense that his presence did not concern her, that she had emerged from her kitchen out of curiosity, to see what would happen.

Grigori drew back a step. He was afraid to enter this house of women. It had been three years since he had spoken to a woman. Even before that, he did not speak to women. He simply took them. In the seminary, he insulated himself against temptation. Chastity, he discovered, was easier than commonly believed, so long as a man was on his guard, not against sin but against temptation. For he learned that it was not sin, but temptation, which men found delectable. Not once had Grigori cheated on his mission. With a conviction which was sometimes lacking among his believing fellow seminarians, he repeated, a thousand times a day, impatiently, pretending to pray to himself rather than to God: "Lead us not into temptation."

Here, however, there were no safeguards, no real faith, no religious exercises, no little seminarian's formulas. He felt himself to be vulnerable in the presence of these women. He was dressed like any layman; but in order to protect himself he would willingly have donned the cassock, which he had shed with such relief.

He explained once more that he wished to see "Michael."

"Come in," said the old woman, with evident reluctance.

The young woman moved aside to let him pass.

It was a large room, with two windows on the street. Clean. Furnished with comfortable, shabby old pieces. There were two folding screens. One, of silk, had been meticulously mended.

"He sleeps over there. That's his corner," the old woman said, pointing to one of the screens. "You can wait for him there."

"You may wait here," the young woman said.

Grigori could hear the clattering of pots and pans from another room, and the third woman singing in a pleasant, throaty voice. He did not know what to do. He would have liked to hide behind the screen, to escape from these women. But to walk across the room, to let them inspect the way he walked—perhaps to make a laughingstock of himself? It would have been much easier for him to attack an enemy machine-gun nest.

"Well, then, take a seat," the mother said.

He dropped onto the flat cushions of an ancient armchair. An armchair too low for his long legs. He had hoped to regain his composure when he was seated. He had been wrong. He was still at the mercy of the two women, who had remained standing and were looking at him wordlessly: the mother in the middle of the room, her hands on her hips; the daughter, leaning against the buffet, withdrawn. Grigori did not know what to do with his hands or his eyes. In order to avoid looking at the girl, he inspected the buffet—an enormous mahogany piece, the kind of furniture which was no longer manufactured.

"Well," the old woman said, "I'll have to look after my dinner. *He* will be home soon."

She hesitated. Grigori could think of nothing to say. He inspected the buffet.

The old woman came to examine the visitor. She bent down. It was as though she were sniffing him. She glanced at her daughter. The two women whispered together. Grigori had the impression that the mother said, "Keep an eye on him," or, "Watch out for the silverware," and that the daughter had answered: "He'd better not try anything." In any event, she was leaning against the buffet with all her weight, her hands and her back pressed tightly against it. The mother left the room.

Grigori, with an effort, turned his head. He looked out of the window. His neck was stiff, and his feet were in an uncomfortable position. But he was determined not to move. He waited for Michael as for a liberator.

Suddenly, behind him, he heard a loud creaking. Someone had opened the buffet. Grigori did not turn. Instead, he huddled in his armchair, without knowing why, as though he were about to be attacked from the rear. Silence. Then he heard the voice of the girl, very serious and, at the same time, very virginal:

"I know who you are. You're one of them."

Grigori did not move. His muscles relaxed, his spirits soared. He was himself again, the Grigori he had been three years earlier. This young woman had found him out. He would probably have to kill her. This was something that Grouztchik had not foreseen; what would he say? Along with the exaltation of imminent action, Grigori experienced the apprehension of the agent about to be unmasked. What would his superiors say? Agents were forgiven everything; everything, except failure.

He waited.

Nothing happened.

Grigori thought of the secret organizations of which he had heard without ever really believing they existed: the Trotskyites, the monarchists. It happened sometimes that an agent disappeared. And he had been lured into a trap.

The window opened on the street, he reflected. If he made a break for it, he would not be killed by a drop of two stories. No, not killed; only exposed. And an agent is like a sophisticated woman. Scandal was the only thing Grigori feared.

Grigori waited. Next to his ear—he had not heard the young woman move—he heard her voice: "Look."

He sprang up, ready to strangle her. Then he stopped. The two doors of the buffet stood open, and on the interior side of this he saw row upon row of them: small, large, painted, copper, wooden, silver, and gold, chiseled, polished, glistening. Ikons. Perhaps twenty of them.

Grigori fell upon his knees, made a large sign of the cross, and struck his forehead on the floor. When he raised his head and glanced at the girl, she was looking at him with approval in her eyes.

Grigori grinned openly, showing his teeth—the smile of a pious, trusting, simple boy. He had resumed his role. "How did you find me out?" he asked.

She did not answer his smile, except within herself. "We have ways of knowing our own."

She hesitated for a moment, then clasped her hands together, one over the other, in the ritual gesture. "Bless me," she said.

Grigori shook his head. "I am not a priest. Only a seminarian."

She looked at him with a new expression, one which conveyed passionate admiration and, at the same time, pity. The man who is about to sacrifice himself is even more touching than the man who has already done so.

Still, she did not smile; but now she and Grigori spoke openly as they waited for Michael's arrival. She told him of the exile and death of her father, who had been a priest; of her quiet life with her mother and her work in a fabric mill; of her belief in God.

"We prefer to remain hidden," she explained. "That way, we can sometimes be of help to others."

Michael arrived. He was dressed as a layman, with thick gloves, motorcycle goggles in his hand, and clips on the legs of his pants. He was clean-shaven. His eyes blazed.

Grigori went forward to ask his blessing. Michael removed his gloves with short, brusque motions. When he spoke, it was as though he spat. "So, it's you, Malchus! You're the last one I expected to see. Pacomius, perhaps, or Vsevolod. The others. Where are they? The only one I've seen is Alexander. In the name of the Father, the Son, and the Holy Ghost." He made the sign of the cross, a very small cross, as though regretfully, on Grigori's forehead. "So, you're not tired of your cassock? You were eager for a taste of persecution? It's a little premature, my boy. I see that you have scars. Have they calmed you down?"

"Where is Alexander?" Grigori asked.

"He's all right. They let him go. He's been ordained. He has a church; he says Mass. I spend *my* time tightening bolts. In this country, you have to have a yellow permit to be able to practice. Just like the prostitutes in the old days. They took mine away from me. 'You are no longer allowed to say Mass, priest,' they told me. Alona, leave us alone."

The young woman bowed and left the room without a sound.

Michael turned away, sighed heavily, and threw his gloves

and goggles behind the screen. He returned, bent over, and laboriously removed the clips from his pants. "Well, are you pleased with yourself?"

"Father," Grigori murmured, "I don't understand what you mean."

Michael drew nearer, thrust his pale face close to Grigori's pink, heavily scarred countenance. "You don't understand? Saint Peter! It's Saint Peter, I swear! You simpleton! Don't you know that you don't believe in God with your fists? Do you know that Nicephorus was tortured to death because of you?"

"Because of me?"

"Yes, because of you. He was arrested because he tried to speak to you when you hit the captain. Three days later, some women went to the prison to bring him some food, and the guards told them that Nicephorus no longer had need of food. That he would not need anything, ever. In other words, that he was dead. And how did he die? What does one die of in prison under this devil's regime? Of what?"

Michael's lips trembled. He bit them to keep himself from sobbing, or perhaps from cursing. In a small, broken voice, he went on: "Father Nicephorus was an angel on earth." Then, angry once more, he roared, "Do you think that *you* can take his place?"

Grigori, his arms folded, answered: "That question is the reason I've come to see you. I think that I've learned enough to be ordained. But I need a certificate showing that I've completed my studies. You're the only one—"

"I'll give you the certificate," Michael interrupted.

"You know my vocation," Grigori continued. "I'd like to take my vows as soon as possible."

Michael looked at him obliquely. If he could see into my heart, Grigori thought, he would know. And he bore Michael's piercing scrutiny, a look which seemed capable of tearing the truth from him.

"You will never take vows," Michael said finally.

"But Father! You know that I've always intended to be a monk! You know it!"

"Yes," Michael answered drily. "But you; do you know the last words of Nicephorus, the martyr? In the truck, while they were taking us to their headquarters, he whispered to me: 'They should all be priests, except Grigori.' Then, after having prayed and meditated, he turned to me again and said: 'A priest, yes; but a monk, never.' His last thoughts were of you. Be satisfied with that."

Grigori could hardly control the tears of rage and frustration which rose to his eyes. "Father," he said, "I don't understand why you are so bitter. It's not my place to judge you, of course; but I wonder whether you did not misunderstand Father Nicephorus' words. You know that if I don't become a monk, I can never become a bishop."

Michael looked at him once more, staring into his eyes. This time, it was of himself that he asked the searching question which sprang into his mind. But he found no answer. He sighed. With a malicious smile, he said to Grigori: "What if that was precisely what Father Nicephorus had in mind?"

ACT III

It was then that I learned the ecclesiastical authorities were opposed to my taking of vows, although it was my dearest wish to do so. I puzzled at length over the reasons for this extraordinary decision on their part—a decision that no argument I put forward could reverse. At the time, I could discover no basis for it, although the matter seemed to me to be the most important thing in my life. Today, however, I have come to think that the priests—who strive to understand men in order to be able to master them—had sensed in me that unyielding love of truth and that devotion to dialectical reality which now cause me to reject the Church and turn to you.

This is the only possible explanation, and it did not

take me long to think of it. Even so, it came as a great shock. I was so certain that my confessions had deceived him! How on earth could he have guessed . . . ?

Father Grigori, bending over his letter, smiled bitterly, in self-mockery. He recalled that he had been on the verge of tears—no, worse, tears had actually come to his eyes—when Michael had told him: "You will never be a bishop." Why? Because of his mission? Because of Grouztchik? Because of the great harm that he would have been able to do to the Church which he hated? No. There had been another reason; a secret, childish, absurd reason. For three years, he had dreamed of the solemn moment when he, as a bishop, in the middle of the liturgy, would proceed to the ritual washing of the hands. Acolytes, vested in gold brocade, would offer to him a silver basin—or one of tin, it mattered little—and an embroidered towel. He, Grigori, would dip both hands—his strong, competent hands—into water which, according to the season, would be cold or warm; and he would rub them together and then dry them on the crisp, immaculate towel decorated with red and blue (or yellow and black) embroidery. And this would be on the very threshold of the Royal door, while the people stood rapt in prayer and austere and glorious chants thundered beneath the cupola. Grigori, without knowing why, had been haunted by this vision of himself ever since he had assisted a bishop in a similar ceremony of great pomp. It had seemed to him that these moments of dreaming compensated for all the unhappiness, the privations and the pious exercises which he was compelled to endure.

And now, there was nothing. He would be only a country priest, dirty, and married.

Married? Yes, of course! If he could not take his vows, he must, in order to be ordained, either wait until he had reached the canonical age, which he had no intention of doing, or—marry. The thought of it, as of old, made the blood rush to his face, and he blushed deeply. The scars in his face were scarlet. Marriage! A woman! The prohibition against thinking of women, enforced for three years, suddenly existed no longer. It required an act of self-mastery for Grigori to restrain himself from rushing into the street and falling upon the first woman he saw. His knees felt weak, and he was obliged to sit. His past experiences crowded before his eyes, and blood pounded in his temples. He saw a mass of images pitifully alike and yet disturbing individually. He felt drained, powerless. He felt the urge to ask pardon of the hundreds of women who came before his mind's eye, demanding that he take them all, simultaneously.

After several seconds, Grigori regained his sense of reality. He might be allowed to take a wife; but a wife was only one woman. Even so, it would be several months before he would be allowed to have this one woman; and then only if Grouztchik did not find another solution.

He put on his cassock and went to see Grouztchik, who seemed puzzled. "Well," he said, "this puts us in a difficult position." Then, in a tone somewhere between amiability and the irritation of a superior, he added: "For that matter, you should be the one who is angry. The priests have made a fool of you. These are not very auspicious circumstances in which to begin your mission."

Grigori, stiffly at attention, thought, Then why not cancel the mission? But he said nothing.

"How long did you rot in that seminary?"

"Three years, Comrade Major."

Grouztchik paced the room, emanating a strong odor of sweat and tobacco. "You understand, my boy, that this is not going to make us change our plans. But I'd like you to tell me what happened."

Grigori himself did not know. He thought that he had the complete confidence of his superiors. Nicephorus had always treated him in exactly the same way as the other students.

"Do you think it might be your family?" Grouztchik asked. Grigori's family seemed to preoccupy the former smelter. "You understand, they were nobles, and I like that. They were leaders. They were people one could work with. I mean, of course, in olden times. Not the court parasites, but the tough ones—the men who worked the land and fought the wars. Maybe the priests prefer pious little mama's boys who are more pliable. What do you think?"

"The liturgical calendar is full of princes," Grigori answered. "Nicephorus told me several times, 'You will be an administrator.' I thought he meant that he had singled me out as a future bishop."

"Well, then," Grouztchik reflected, "it must have been something that happened at the very last minute. Can you guess what happened?"

"I hit the captain—"

"What are you trying to say? That the priests concluded that, since you couldn't control yourself, you would never be able to control others?"

"That's very possible."

"No, it's not. It's not something that logical. They must have sensed that you were not really one of them. Priests have a feeling for that sort of thing, believe me. But then, why would they let you become a priest at all? They could simply have thrown you out. Well, what's your explanation?"

"I have no explanation, Comrade Major."

"You should have one. You're the one who spent three

years with them. If you haven't learned to understand them, what good are you?"

Grouztchik was carried away by his irritation. In a moment, he would explode. Grigori waited, at attention, like a soldier in the ranks who submissively puffs out his cheek so that his superior's slap will sound louder. But Grouztchik's temper subsided as quickly as it rose. He fell to his chair and said: "Sit down somewhere, my boy. We're going to have to decide where to go from here."

A pause. Grouztchik lit a cigarette. "I know absolutely nothing about this hocus-pocus business of yours. Suppose you tell me what's going to happen next."

Grigori explained that he could be ordained a priest, but that first he would have to be . . . married. Later, if he was a successful priest, he would be allowed to wear the miter; but he would never become a bishop.

Grigori had blushed when he said "married," but Grouztchik appeared not to have noticed. Or so it seemed. He puffed wearily on his cigarette. "Would you be able to hear the confessions of bishops?" he asked.

"Yes, though usually they prefer monks."

Grouztchik smoked.

"Comrade Major, there is a solution."

Grouztchik raised his eyes slowly, indifferently, like a beast who is awake but pretends still to sleep. "Well?"

"Widowers may become bishops."

When Grigori left Grouztchik's office, his heart was light. He would have a wife for several months. He would have his fill of her, exhaust himself on her. She would have an accident, a runaway truck, probably. Then Grigori would take his vows. Nicephorus would be overcome; and a victory over a dead man, Grigori reflected, is the sweetest victory of all. His real mission would then begin. He, Grigori, through his own efforts, would destroy the Church. He would dethrone her, crucify her, annihilate her. He would bury her, and crush underfoot any traces of her that might remain. There would not be a single black priest left, not one lazy pastor to awaken in the people the hope of an escape from the authority of the government into the realm of the supernatural. During that period of intensive activity, of informing and accusing, he would be too busy gathering intelligence, organizing networks of agents and outwitting the patriarch himself, even to think of women. One day, perhaps, when the victory was won, it would be the time for orgies. But Grigori did not dwell on that possibility. Perhaps his honeymoon would be enough to last him for the rest of his life. He would take as his model the saints who, after a period of frenetic debauchery, had channeled their energies into an equally unbridled asceticism in order to fulfill the duties of their mission. A shimmering lake, and then a torrent in a narrow, black ravine. It was thus that Grigori saw his life. The color black obsessed him, surrounded him, as it surrounded the faces of the saints in the ancient ikons.

In the street, for the first time in three years, Grigori allowed himself to look upon women. He stopped when he saw them coming, his mouth hanging open. He turned when they had passed and watched them with an air of astonishment. He devoured them with his eyes, so hungrily that a grandmother, accompanied by a young girl, shook her finger at him and shouted, "At least take off your cassock, you shameless gawker!"

Grigori was immediately overcome with shame; the shame of a seminarian and that of an agent on assignment combined. He wished for the earth to open up and swallow him. He wanted to kill the old woman. He wanted to shoot down the passersby. He had sinned against the Sixth Commandment; and thus he had abandoned his cover. He was ashamed of his black cassock, of his desires, of his behavior, of his shame itself. The young girl shrieked with laughter at his discomfiture; and he could have killed her.

With an effort, he regained control of himself. He walked slowly, breathing deeply, his eyes downcast. He saw only the feet of the passersby; and, occasionally, to reward himself for his self-control, he raised his eyes to mid-calf. What if Grouztchik had seen him acting like a lecher in the street? He would have been dismissed from the service, disgraced. Or Nicephorus? An offense against purity is always the gravest sin, because it is one over which the will has no control. Nicephorus the saint, Grouztchik the wild beast; the two became as one in Grigori's guilt-stricken conscience.

Then the problems began to occur to Grigori. Grouztchik had said, "Do whatever you want, but do it quickly." At first, he had thought of giving Grigori a female agent as his wife. "I have some, you know. And," he added with a leer, "some of them are not bad at all."

Grigori had agreed; but Grouztchik quickly abandoned the idea. "First of all," he said, "I would be using two agents for one job. Second, it would take a really extraordinary woman to carry it off without arousing suspicion. She wouldn't have had three years in the seminary to prepare for her assignment, you know. And, finally, if we use one of our own people, we won't be able to kill her. In our business, my boy, it's dangerous to play-act. We must avoid fiction, phony scenes, and novelist's solutions. No. I'm afraid you'll have to go out to find a woman on your own, like a grown man."

It would not be easy. Why should a woman become the wife of a priest, perhaps face deportation or death, and certainly subject herself to humiliation and harassment? Why should any woman be willing to cut herself off from ordinary people who lived according to the norms of society? Not to preach the Gospel to the world, saving souls, like her priest-husband. Her only glory would be to fix his cabbage soup—

and without meat, at that. Who could possibly be willing? Most priests were monks nowadays, vowed to celibacy.

Grigori was seized with a childish fear. What if he could not find a woman? To begin with, he knew no woman. He could not call out to one of the street-sweepers, "Hey! Citizeness! How would you like to marry a priest?"

He returned to Michael's house to tell him of his decision: he would marry and become a secular priest. He knocked, and Alona opened the door.

Alona held herself erect, respectfully. Grigori saw her slightly oriental features, her dark hair drawn back tightly on her head. Behind her, the wallpaper of the vestibule depicted stylized vases, brown on yellow, faded almost into invisibility. Alona, the dark vestibule, the wallpaper in the style of 1910—Grigori saw them all, and understood that he would marry this girl. It could not be otherwise. It had been so written somewhere, in a great marriage register, since the beginning of time.

Alona led him into the room and said—and this, too, had been written from all eternity: "My mother is not here."

They were alone, facing each other. Slanted rays of light from the windows, with their high, oblong panes, fell upon them and upon the shabby furniture. Grigori thrust the fingers of one hand into his short, unkempt beard, and moved them slowly. He did not know what to do with the other hand, but his embarrassment was only superficial. His awkwardness, sincere as it was, was in keeping with the personality he had assumed. He was not troubled by it. On the contrary, he almost enjoyed it. He did not speak. And Alona did not invite him to be seated, for she was waiting. She, too, knew.

After the embarrassment and silence had built up, Grigori turned to Alona. "I have something to say to you. It is not possible for me to become a monk, as I had hoped. Still, I wish to become a priest, and, in order to do so, I must marry. I would like you to be my wife."

He looked directly into her face as he spoke, but she kept her eyes cast down. He was pleased with his little speech. It had been very simple, very honest. If this young woman answered "yes," she would be condemning herself to an early death: the runaway truck. But that was unimportant. Only Grigori's mission was important.

Alona raised her dark eyes and spoke without smiling: "I do not know you, but I have always prayed to become the wife of a priest. And today, when you came in, I knew that I loved you. I shall love you always."

She has the slave's vocation, Grigori thought, like all true Christians. I've made a good choice.

If the old woman had not shamed him in the street, he might now commit an irreparable blunder, and everything would be different. But the woman had made him ashamed. Her words, addressed to the seminarian, had reached the agent. To Alona, he said: "Let us pray together."

She opened the buffet in which the ikons were enthroned. The images of gold were reflected, in shades of red, from those of silver. The saints' faces, black, impassive, frowning, looking on the man and the woman.

"Wait a moment," Alona said. She found matches and lighted a candle before the holy images. The tiny flame flickered in its blue glass, and then was still. It burned steadily and silently before the rows of ikons.

"Now," Alona said.

They knelt together, side by side, their hands joined. Grigori had thought that they would pray in silence, individually, but Alona looked at him in surprise, and he knew immediately what she expected. In a voice little more than a whisper, an inexpressive, almost instrumental voice, the voice of Orthodox priests since they first existed, he began to pray. The prayers he chose were moving; prayers unfamiliar to Alona. He chose the most lyric ones in his repertoire, those in which the ancient language of religion had become as honey in the throats of the most gentle and impassioned of the saints. Father Mitrophanus had known many such prayers, and had offered them, like caresses, to his Virgin. Now, Grigori recited them, and into the inexpressive inflections he introduced as much sweet warmth as he was able. He felt Alona's hand in his, warm and firm. After a few minutes, he fell silent. She looked at him, disappointed. Oh, all right, Grigori told himself. She likes it.

He began to pray again, in the same voice as before, not unctuously but, on the contrary, roughly, barely singing: the voice of magical incantation. The little flame within the blue glass now burned without flickering. The faces of the saints looked down without expression upon the young couple kneeling before them. There was the Saviour, the Virgin, Saint Nicholas, Saint Alexander, Saint Vladimir, Saint Sergius of Radoneje, Saint Seraphin, and others; a true assembly of saints, gathered to bless the wedding of an assassin and his victim. But they did not bless. Rather, they maintained a careful silence. A gust of wind through the window caused the flame of the vigil light to dance, and a shadow crossed their countenances. Other than this, there was no reaction. They were merely witnesses; and they would not bear witness until the end of the world.

Finally, Grigori stopped and said: "It is enough."

Alona heaved a sigh of satisfaction. Everything had happened as she wished. She looked with affection at the bearded and poorly groomed seminarian kneeling at her side. On his face, he bore the scars of a hero, a martyr. He was the one to whom, in God, she would sacrifice her life. He was her Christ. One finds the Christ that one deserves.

They were married three weeks later. Grigori had sufficient

time to overcome the madness which had taken possession of his senses. Alona made it easy for him to do so. There was no coquetry in her, other than that remote, almost oriental abandon promised by her ways, her looks, and by the submissiveness that characterized her.

She would not address him by his Christian name. He foresaw that, as soon as he was ordained, she would insist upon calling him "Father." It was a pleasure which he must not deny her.

Grigori quickly observed that Alona was without education, even religious education. She loved, she hoped and believed, all by instinct. Literally with her heart. For a moment, Grigori toyed with the idea of attempting to develop her mind. But then he remembered. What good would it do? Within a year, she would be dead.

Alona loved Grigori to read books which she did not understand. She hovered over him respectfully when he reviewed his courses in Greek. Her faith was pagan to the extent that she believed in several degrees of initiation. For herself, she was content to be in the outer circle of believers, so long as Grigori had access to the most secret circle.

She was a laborer, unskilled, and she was satisfied to be such. She mistrusted science: "These things are not for people like me." But she added, with a metaphor which came to her naturally: "You are able to walk safely in the dark night of knowledge, for you have the lamp of religion."

Grigori awaited their marriage patiently. Occasionally, at night, in his bed, he had abandoned himself to wild reveries. But, he reasoned, it was all part of his mission. Any seminarian, he told himself, would do the same—and would feel just as guilty about it as I do.

When he and Alona were together, he was attentive but proper. She took the opportunity to explain to him her concept of the role she was to play: to free him from all worldly cares so that he might devote himself entirely to God. For Alona, the flesh was part of what she regarded as "worldly cares." She wished to be "the servant of the Lord," through the intermediary of her husband. And Grigori treated her as such.

It was Michael, forbidden though he was, who married them. Reluctantly. He regarded Grigori as the assassin of Nicephorus. He told Grigori so in the clearest possible terms during Grigori's prenuptial confession, in the apartment where they were then all living together. "What about the death of Father Nicephorus, who was a saint?" Michael had asked. "Are you not going to accuse yourself of that sin?"

Grigori, bearded, kneeling in his cassock, had looked up at the priest, who was standing, clean-shaven and wearing a leather jacket and work pants, with the embroidered stole hanging incongruously from his shoulders. "I confess it, Father," Grigori answered, "among the sins which I have committed unknowingly."

Michael did not approve of Grigori's marriage to Alona, and he did not take the trouble to hide his opposition. To Alona, he said, in Grigori's presence: "What you need is a good and gentle man. Grigori is not good. If he is saved, it will be because of spite. But then, there have been men who became saints out of spite." And Grigori had smiled through his thickening beard.

The nuptials were long and solemn. Alona and her mother were astonished at the number of friends who attended. They came from all sides, bearing gifts. The chapel was full. Everyone who could sing at all joined in with the choir. The witnesses held the golden crowns suspended over the heads of the bride and groom. The incense billowed into the air; the candelabra, bristling with candles, illuminated from below the ikons painted on the walls. Dozens of saints, carrying lances, banners, crosses, books, ciboriums, and pennants, stood as silent witnesses to the sacramental union. The clouds of incense which swirled around them seemed at times to make them move their lips; and their unblinking eyes looked down solemnly upon the man in black and the woman in white. Alona wore a simple summer dress, with a small veil pinned to her hair. Grigori, in a moment of vanity, had thought of being married in his lieutenant's uniform; but that would have been impossible for both the seminarian and the agent. He had borrowed a black suit from a cousin of Alona's.

Grigori had been fully prepared to play a part, but it had not been necessary. The wedding had been like all other weddings. The music had been beautiful. And Grigori had been possessed by a very real emotion. Occasionally, he cast a concupiscent glance at the bride; and, on each occasion, experienced a stab of guilt. His throat was tight, like that of any man who binds himself to a woman for the rest of his days. He did not pretend not to know that, in a year, Alona would be dead. He had forgotten it, temporarily.

After the ceremony, Grigori felt a sense of relief, as though something had really taken place; as though there had been a transformation in his life. It was a feeling which had been absent the previous day, when he and Alona had undergone the civil ceremony, a simple registration with the authorities.

Outside the church, they were surrounded by their friends. Some presented them with the gifts which they had brought to the ceremony. But there was no explosion of mirth. The felicitations of the guests were dignified, respectful, out of consideration for Grigori, who, as everyone knew, was destined for the priesthood. Nonetheless, every face shone with heartfelt joy.

Alona was calm. She did not smile. Grigori, infected by the atmosphere of celebration—he would have preferred a bit more noise and gaiety—truly felt himself to be a newlywed. He asked Alona why she did not smile, and she replied: "I do not have to smile. I am happy." His reaction had been a moment of irritation. Christians, he said to himself, are full of paradoxes. But it was a transient irritation. At the apartment, where everyone gathered, Grigori joyously drank a toast with sparkling wine. It was the first alcohol he had tasted in three years, except for the sacramental wine. It went to his head. He drank no more, for fear of betraying himself.

One of their guests called out the traditional "How Bitter It Is," but timidly, because of Grigori. The seminarian, like a good fellow, was not offended. He turned toward his wife and, with a look, asked her whether she was willing to follow the custom of the people. Until that moment, they had kissed only once: the nuptial kiss, during the wedding ceremony. Alona, without the slightest embarrassment, kissed him full on the mouth, a long, loyal kiss, a symbolic kiss, to satisfy their friends; but a chaste and passionate kiss.

"I wish these people would go home," Grigori whispered.

"But they're our friends," Alona answered. And now she smiled.

Grigori had already noted that, in many respects, it was Alona who took the initiative. It was she who arranged the details of the wedding; she who established the affectionately respectful tone of their exchanges; she who decided on their first kiss. Grigori justified this arrangement on the basis of his mission. He told himself: I will let Alona decide the things that are unimportant. This will increase people's confidence in me.

The wedding guests left. Alona's mother had arranged to sleep at a friend's house in order to give the newlyweds the entire room—a kingdom—on their first night. Michael worked a night shift, and would not return until morning. They were alone.

First, they prepared dinner. Grigori wished to help, but Alona was firm: "Your place is not in the kitchen." He went into their room. He did not know what to do with himself. Memories of his past life sprang into his mind. There had been moments, if not of true sensuality, then at least of debauchery. Through the windows, he saw the streetlights go on. Occasionally, an automobile passed. From the other rooms in the apartment, he heard the sounds of their neighbors laughing, quarreling, rattling dishes. Alona would never be done in the kitchen. Then she was back.

After they had eaten, she went to the kitchen to wash the dishes, according to the schedule arranged with the neighbors. Grigori offered to wipe as she washed, but Alona, shocked, refused even to consider it. And Grigori was left alone in the bedroom.

I hope, he thought, that she's not going to be coy with me tonight. I'm not going to be able to force her, with this damned mission of mine.

He sat at a table, opened a book. It was a book of hours. He closed it in irritation. Alona returned, removed her apron, hung it carefully on a nail, and as though it were the most natural thing in the world, came to Grigori and sat on his lap. Nothing was foreign to Alona; she even knew how to become the wife of a priest.

Before going to bed, they prayed together, but briefly. Afterward, Alona showed herself to be not only docile, but also tender. Grigori understood with difficulty. He had never had a tender mistress. They had been passionate, venal, ravished. But never tender.

Grigori awoke after an hour's sleep. Alona's head was resting on his chest. Alona's breath was on his cheek. He lay with his eyes open in the darkness, and began a series of meditations which, in similar circumstances, he would pursue for the next seventeen years.

Grigori had no natural bent for philosophy, but the glorious satiety of his body inclined him to it. He felt himself to be content, with the kind of contentment that he had hitherto known after a long march in the mountains, or after a bloody and victorious battle.

His mind wandered lazily to the subject of sacerdotal marriage. He had learned in the seminary that Roman priests did not marry. Dostoevsky was right, Grigori reflected as he lay quietly on his back in the narrow bed, with Alona's hair spread out over his bare chest. The Romans have never understood the humbly human element of Christianity. Since I'm almost a priest, I'm in a position to know. I can understand that a man might want to give his all to God; all his attention and all his love. But how unrealistic that is. One would have to have no parents, no friends, no country; nothing but the cross. That may be enough for monks, but even the Roman Church doesn't pretend to require such an attitude of her priests. They argue that celibacy spares their priests the unpleasant side of conjugal life—the arguments and so forth. If they taught their seminarians how to wield authority (and, occasionally, the whip), there would be no problem in that respect. But such things are no more than a pretext for something else. The fact is that the good Fathers of the Council of Trent were shocked at the idea that hands which had touched a woman's body the night before would handle the Eucharist in the morning. What a thoroughly Roman concept! And yet wasn't it a Roman who said, "If anyone tries to become an angel, he becomes a beast"? The Fathers were sophomoric about this. Even if we abstract from the fact that a priest must fast and abstain before saying Mass, we cannot deny that a woman's body is at least as pure to the touch as a piece of bread or a clod of earth. They say that our bodies are temples of the Holy Spirit, and then they make such lewd distinctions. They allow their priests to drink and smoke, but they don't allow them to obey God's commandment: increase and multiply. It's obvious that Rome has angelic ambitions. And it's obvious she is wrong since she requires that they be true men, capable of sexual relations, and then denies them the right to exercise that capability.

Grigori stopped, struck by the incongruity of his loyalty to the Orthodox Church. Well, he corrected himself, why not? Lies should be as close as possible to the truth. A man must take to heart the interests of the community to which he is assigned. I hate our Church; but that doesn't keep me from hating that of the Romans even more. For that matter, I hate ours precisely because it is so reasonable, logical, clever—and therefore dangerous. If we have been preserved from such things as the Inquisition and the religious wars, it is because the natural instincts of our priests fulfilled their natural function and had no need of such monstrous perversions.

Shortly after my marriage
to a rather stupid woman—she
was not an evil person, but she
had been stultified by her father
and by other ecclesiastics—

"Stultified" is not quite the
proper word, but it will do in
this context.

I was ordained a deacon. At
that time, I entered into close
contact with the Patriarchate.
There I found—to my
disappointment, I confess—not
a trace of fanaticism. Instead,
there was a spirit of sordid
repletion, of self-satisfaction
which was in direct

contradiction to Christian morality, and of permanent compromise with the socialism which the Church affects to despise.

That is very well said. It's true that I did not find what I had expected at the Patriarchate. There was no trace of that vast anti-communist conspiracy of which I had been certain the Patriarch himself was the guiding spirit. There was nothing except fat deacons, worthless priests who had fallen into a soft job, and a pair of political commissars who wore their cassocks so badly that I recognized them as police agents even before I asked them for their blessing. I couldn't resist asking their advice on theological problems. In other words, I treated them as they deserved to be treated. I've never had any use for the police.

A permanent compromise with socialism? Yes, certainly. These priests and deacons were there for precisely that reason. The Patriarch, who is no fool, had deliberately chosen to surround himself with the worst, most deceitful ecclesiastics he could find. They served as buffers between himself and the government, and effectively absorbed all the blows aimed by the state at the Church, starting with its head.

I said they were "self-satisfied." That is an understatement. All these bureaucrats in cassocks thought they were deceiving both the state, under whose nose they continued to pray to God, and God himself, under whose nose they consorted with the worst enemies of religion—all in the name of "a good cause." They must have prayed to their Christ in the following terms: "Look, you know I'll never be a martyr, so why not accept me as I am? You'll have to admit that I'm more useful here than at the stake."

I wrote of "repletion." Naturally, in all churches, there is a secret and necessary connection between sinecures and gastronomy.

I remained a deacon for only a short while. It had been noted that I had both sufficient education and a certain degree of natural authority which qualified me immediately for higher functions. A few weeks later, I became a priest; which is to say that, in the eyes of the faithful, I was another Christ.

Neither more nor less than that.

The night after his ordination, Grigori awoke after one or two hours of sleep. The room was not in total darkness, for a candle was burning before the prudently closed doors of the buffet. The small blue glass of the vigil light had been placed at the corner of the shelf formed by the lower, wider section of the piece.

Alona was breathing deeply, alongside her husband—her Saviour, as she had called him, in ecstatic humility, earlier in the night. Grigori's eyes were open. A delicious fatigue coursed through his body, induced first by continence, and then by satiety.

For weeks, he had prepared carefully for the priesthood; as carefully as any other deacon. During religious services, or in the solitude of the monastic cell set aside for him, he prayed with the same care, the same professional conscience, to a God in which he did not believe. With one part of his mind, he wanted to play the game according to the rules, to omit nothing required by his mission. Another part of his mind, trained and exercised in piety, found it easy to slip into prayer. It had become easier for Grigori to pray than to think of other things, so long as he was in a suitable place, made the ritual gestures, and fixed his eyes on sacred objects. He had not the faith to pray, but he had acquired the techniques of prayer. And, as the experience of the mystics has proved, technique plays as important a part in the things of the spirit as in those of the body—in acrobatics, or virtuosity, or craftsmanship. Certain prayers—the Prayer of Jesus, for example—sometimes sprang into Grigori's mind without any conscious effort on his part. These were prayers which, so to speak, prayed themselves. Occasionally, he would catch himself at it. "Look at me! I'm praying. Isn't that ridiculous? How long have I been doing it?"

At such times, Grigori did not merely repeat words. The words themselves contained the germ of a thought, a fragment of attention which, like a piece of cloth attached to a turning wheel, recurred regularly. Thus a part of Grigori repeated unceasingly, "Jesus, have mercy"—as though he expected Jesus could hear him.

Sometimes Grigori worried. It seems, he told himself, that the priests, with their underhanded tricks, are trying to graft a piece of alien skin onto my body. A piece of Christian skin. If I'm not careful, I'm going to start believing without knowing it.

This was not something that Grigori would have thought of himself. Grouztchik had pointed it out to him. Now, in his bed, he smiled at his fears. He was a priest, and the transformation that he had vaguely foreseen, and even almost expected, had not taken place. His face, his hands, his secret parts, had not changed in the slightest. He looked at the steady flame burning before the closed doors of the mahogany buffet and thought of the other Grigori, the bearded priest, nude and yellow, half impaled on the leg of a chair, his bushy beard inviting a lighted match. He smiled at the recollection of it. The old priest had given them a great deal of fun that day. The cycle was complete. It was now Grigori himself who was a priest. He smiled again in the darkness, spitefully. Now, let the priests beware!

Nonetheless, Grigori had been disappointed. He had vaguely expected to undergo a private initiation. After the Mass, the bishop would lead him blindfolded to a secret place—a cave, or an underground chapel. In Grigori's daydreams, he would say: "Henceforth, you are one of us, and you are permitted to know the true mysteries of the faith." Then he would show Grigori holy books other than those of the Bible, other objects of worship. He would teach him another, more efficacious liturgy; perhaps a criminal liturgy, with its roots in Orphism, or in the secret cults of Attis or of Baal.

The Blood of Christ, Grigori said to himself. They're always speaking of blood. There must be blood somewhere. Perhaps the fresh blood of a newborn child, a circumcised child.

Or the bishop, with a clever Voltairian smile, would say: "My dear fellow, you must now learn to disbelieve what you have learned until now. God does not exist. Believe me, I am an expert. The liturgy is a farce. The sacraments, a trap for idiots. No priest believes in God; but we live very well, I must say, on the faith of those who do."

Or else, the bishop might whisper to him: "You are a priest; one of us. You are now part of a vast conspiracy to overthrow the communist regime and establish the supremacy of the Church. Your assignment . . . your contacts . . . your agents . . ."

Nothing like that had happened. Two deacons, one a tottering old man and the other a young giant, had put their hands on his shoulders and led Grigori around the altar under the tearing eye of the bishop on his faldstool. Three times, Grigori kissed the four corners of the altar and the vestments of the bishop. This rite was literally breathtaking and symbolized his openness to the service of God. Even Grigori had been moved. As he glided about the altar like an angel on an errand, under the damp and tender eyes of his superior—who bore no resemblance to Grouztchik—he was careful not to step on his overly long chasuble. He felt that he was being subjected to a rite at once honorific and humiliating, very old and very mysterious.

One thing had been lacking: the submissive love symbolized by the exchange of kisses. Within himself, Grigori had laughed at the old man presiding at the ceremony. The bishop, Grigori sensed, had no pride, no strength, no backbone. For that matter, it was rumored that he was collaborating with the government, and that he did not fast as often as he should. He looked upon Grigori with an expression of tenderness. Grigori despised tenderness.

As Grigori circled the altar, the choir sang, "Holy Martyrs, who have suffered and received your crowns, pray to the Lord that our souls may be saved." This antiphon was intended to signify that the holy martyrs would aid Grigori to make progress in self-renunciation and strength, and he echoed it with all the strength of his devotion to the service. Then the choir sang: "Glory to thee, Christ-God, praise of the Apostles and joy of the Martyrs who preached the single Trinity." Grigori knew that this chant was intended to assimilate him to the other elect; and he was glad, for he still believed that the latter formed an exclusive and secret society. Finally, the choir intoned, "Isaiah, rejoice! A virgin has conceived and borne a son, and his name shall be called Emmanuel." From this, Grigori was supposed to gather that his priesthood was founded upon the Incarnation of Christ; but, at this point, he lost his footing among such theological subtleties.

The crucial moment of the ceremony arrived, Grigori knelt on both knees (at his ordination as a deacon, he had knelt on only one), signifying that, once and for all, he accepted on his shoulders the heaviest of burdens. Then he placed his arms on the altar in the form of a cross, as a sign of total submission, and lay his head on the altar to await the coming of the Holy Spirit. A shiver ran through his body. What if the Spirit truly came down upon him? What if, when he raised his head, he found that he was a true believer?

No, he thought in amusement, Christ would not play such a dirty trick.

Slowly the old bishop, with one tearing eye, rose from his chair and placed the end of his episcopal stole on Grigori's head. He made the sign of the cross three times over him, and touched Grigori's forehead with his papery hand. (The cross, the cross, always the cross, Grigori said to himself. It is an instrument of torture. I know all about torture—but from the other end.) Finally, in a quivering voice, as though he were sobbing, the bishop intoned: "The grace of God, healing all wrongs and filling every void, ordains the pious deacon Grigori a priest. Let us therefore pray that the grace of the most Holy Spirit will descend upon him."

"Kyrie eleison!" the choir thundered.

Grigori thought of his wife who, in the first row of the congregation, wearing a badly cut purple dress made from the wardrobe of a deceased aunt, was repeating with the assurance of faith: "Lord, have mercy!"

When Grigori rose, he was a priest.

Then the episcopal hands, with their ruddy, twisted fingers, garbed Grigori in the vestments of his new rank and in the sacred stole which he would be required to wear when he exercised his office. The episcopal lips, sunken but animated by a constant interior motion, like those of a rodent, pressed against Grigori's cheek, as the other ecclesiastics—the priests, acolytes, and choir—sang: *"Axios, axios!"* He is worthy! He is worthy!

A wan smile appeared on Grigori's worn face. Yes, he thought, I am worthy. Worthy of the service, worthy of Grouztchik, worthy of my assignment. The smile lent a thoroughly mystical air to his countenance.

Grigori was summoned to receive the Eucharist. He went forward, triumphant. As he swallowed the bread and the wine, the bishop admonished him in a touching tone: "Receive this pledge, and keep it intact until your last breath, for an accounting will be required of you at the second and terrible coming of our Lord, Saviour, and God, Jesus Christ."

Grigori raised his eyes and, to his astonishment, thought he detected in the squinting eyes of the prelate a mysterious, threatening expression. An accounting, he knew, was the ecclesiastical equivalent of an interrogation. The word evoked a brief, unpleasant feeling. For a moment, he thought that he had been discovered, stripped naked; and that the flaming sword of the Archangel seared his eyes. Almost immediately, he regained his composure and reverently kissed the hand of the damp-eyed bishop.

Now, lying in the darkness, he recalled his exit from the church after the ceremony, wearing his cassock, and his new crucifix hanging from his neck. Alona had been alongside him, a half-step to the rear in irritating servility. He had stopped for a moment on the sidewalk and looked at the billowing white clouds in the sky, at the high, dilapidated buildings, at the busy street with its modern efficiency and its modern ugliness. Disappointment and relief. Nothing had changed since the imposition of the bishop's hands. The sky was the same. The ceremony just concluded had been but a comedy played out with a superabundance of props; and it had also been a stage in the accomplishment of his mission. In a few days, an unknown secretary in the service would add a line or two to his file: a decoration that he could not wear for the next seventeen years.

The vigil light burned. Alona was breathing deeply. On the other side of the screen, Grigori's mother-in-law was snoring.

He had blessed her earlier, with becoming solemnity. Her snores were soft, humble; not like the proud trumpeting of some. Her snoring, Grigori said to himself, was devout. Then, in the darkness, he smiled broadly.

I am a priest, he reflected, and this implies several disparate functions. From now on, I will have a special relationship with God, with my superiors, with my fellow priests, and with my flock. I will be obliged to obey, to administer the sacraments, to teach, and to help those who need me. I will also be expected to exhibit passive resistance to the regime. Now that I am sacrosanct, I can't go around hitting people in the face. I must learn to bear all things with a humility becoming to an agent on assignment. I will have my reward later, in seventeen years. The government has time. So far as my ecclesiastical superiors are concerned, I will behave with military propriety and discipline, and they will have nothing to complain about. After all, I've had enough experience at it.

At the same time, I will have to keep my files up to date. Somehow, I must arrange to embark on a career as a confessor of bishops. Respectful severity: "For your penance, Comrade Bishop, seven days of fasting." They will like that.

Good. For my fellow priests, the same system: friendliness, and files. Everyone knows that I was in the war. I'll play the hardened officer. That's always popular with our dear priests.

So far as my flock is concerned, all I have to do is fulfill all my responsibilities to them. That shouldn't be difficult. I'll find out what they expect of me, and do only that. I must always play the other man's game. Offer no resistance. Become like water in the hands of the enemy, fluid and elusive. That is the basic credo of any agent on assignment. Total submission is total escape. No problem.

In my contacts with God—or what they call God—I'll make use of our faked telephone-conversation technique. I dial a non-existent number, listen to the record repeating over and over,

"The number you have dialed is not a working number," and carry on a conversation while imagining the answers of the other party and keeping my own end of the conversation as vague as possible. I'll be on one end of the line, and there will be no one at the other. I'll talk into the receiver, and I'll hear my own breath in the earpiece. But I must be careful not to exaggerate, that's all.

Grigori's program was now laid out. The details would be filled in from day to day. The mother-in-law snored. Alona took deep, calm breaths. The vigil light, on the corner of the buffet, reflected, serene and secretive, on the mahogany doors. Grigori smiled and rubbed his beard. His relaxed body eased its vigilance.

Did he sleep? He was not sure. Perhaps the doors of the buffet had not been closed securely. Slowly, with an almost inaudible creaking, the doors swung open, separating one from the other like vertical lips, like the shell of an oyster, moving forward in the darkness of the room, pushing back the air, grating on their hinges, pausing in their movement for an instant, then beginning again. Finally, like joined hands that open outward gradually to show their palms, the doors' inner faces were exposed and the room's dim light was reflected by the ikons of gold and silver. The hands and faces of the saints were but spots of black; their vestments, only reflections. The buffet seemed a great mouth; a mouth about to speak.

ACT IV

It happened once that I held in my hands four slender books; four volumes of memoirs. I was moved by the thought that within these covers was contained the entire life of a man from his first whimper to the final rattle. For my own life, I do not need four volumes. A few pages will be enough; a few pages on which to spread myself in an attempt to enter into the paper itself, just as, in the seminary, I spread myself on the floor in order to become one with the earth. For, truth to tell, the life which seems the longest in the living is the shortest in the telling. The seventeen years which remain—the approximately nine hundred times I played at transforming bread into flesh and wine into blood, the 1,328 pink pages I filled with information—it bothers me to burlesque such things for the greater glory of Comrade Professor Dobermann. It was all so stupid. Saving souls is a daily routine, and no atheist would ever understand that. Pretending to save them is a still more meticulous and painstaking job. Nonetheless, I had my moments.

As soon as I had been ordained,
I was given a parish in the
provinces. I arrived there
fired with enthusiasm, and
began my ministry in the best
possible frame of mind.

Our anti-religious propaganda, although it accomplishes an extremely useful purpose, constantly makes errors so obvious that the overall effect is to harm the cause of atheistic humanism rather than to further it. For example, it has been customary to say that priests make a great deal of money. I can tell you, Comrade Professor, that, since taxes took 87 per cent of my salary, my life was characterized by the same amount of luxury as that of John, the one who is called the Baptist, when he lived in the desert.

In fact, to make ends meet, I was obliged, from time to time, to draw on my agent's salary, which was piling up from month to month.

Strange as it may seem, this situation, instead of weakening my vocation, had the opposite effect. I established order in my parish, a parish which had been on the verge of perdition. I celebrated not only the offices tolerated by the government, but also—I admit it—those which were forbidden.

I even ignored those very wise laws which prohibit visits to the sick and to the aged who had need of the consolations which I was in a position to give them.

Nonetheless, I was soon brought face to face with a problem of conscience despite my blindness at that time, despite the process of atrophy which my moral sense had undergone under the influence of Christianity. Should I abide by the law and refuse religious instruction to all minors? Or should I, in accordance with the custom of the Church, take advantage of the innocence of children and fill their minds with clerical teachings?

That is not far from the truth. I even asked my superiors for written instructions on this point. I was well aware of how the government operated. The religious indoctrination of minors was regarded as a very serious offense; and I knew that if I acted on my own initiative, I could be blamed no matter what I

chose to do if someone
decided to make me look bad.
At that time, the service was
already beginning to lose
some of its prestige. As I recall,
Grouztchik was under
direct attack and was losing
the great freedom of action
which he had previously exercised.
A new class of men had
come to power. And this was
why I received contradictory
instructions on this point. . .

Grigori had been deprived of his illusions regarding even the service which he loved with such passion. He remembered Grouztchik's lapidary message in answer to his request for instructions: "You can't make an omelette without breaking eggs, so do what a true priest would do—and to hell with the bureaucrats. Your mission takes precedence over everything else."

And he remembered, too, the pedantic instructions received from his "political adviser": "It is, of course, unacceptable for the young people of our country to be placed in danger of corruption by too much zeal on the part of a single agent in pursuit of an isolated mission. Certain evils are necessary, but they must be kept at a minimum. Thus you are allowed—but not encouraged—to give communion to young children. Under no circumstances, however, are you to give them any instruction whatever in Christian doctrine. It is necessary that they see the rites that you perform for what they are: absurdities. They will reach that stage as soon as their minds begin to develop; and, at that moment, our own propagandists will begin their work."

I was therefore obliged to make God
and the devil come to a compromise.
That is, to teach only the
children of those parents who
absolutely insisted that I do
so; those who had made up
their minds to sacrifice every-
thing—even the future of
their children—to the
errors in which they themselves
persisted.

And, on each occasion,
I wrote
up a report.

Children occupy a very special place in the Gospel. They are treated even better than harlots, centurions, and publicans. Grigori had no children. God did not so bless his household; as Grigori was the first to admit, he had done more than his share to ensure against children in the first two years of his marriage. Then, after Grouztchik's replacement, and Grigori's subsequent disenchantment, he lost interest in precautions. He could have had children. All secular priests seemed to have them by the dozen. But the stork refused to visit his house, and the children that could have been his were left to shiver in the no-man's-land of the unborn, awaiting another father. It was just as well. He regretted nothing. It would be difficult enough to get rid of Alona now. And, for that matter, what future could there be for children under a government so ungrateful that it would reward an agent who had just completed a twenty-year mission with a professorship in atheism? There was no regret, but there was bitterness. A man of forty-five who has no children, like a man of twenty who has no wife, is not wholly a man. "Human nature," Grigori remarked in a moment of sarcasm, "has been no more changed by the advent of socialism than by that of Jesus."

In the preceding ten years, Grigori had read many books; books by serious and cynical authors, and books by satirists. He had experienced those disappointments which bring a man to maturity—the disappointments both of a priest and of an agent, which seemed a great deal for one man. He had aged. He was afflicted by rheumatism as well as by misanthropy. He no longer smiled when he told himself that all he needed to become once more the promising young lieutenant of twenty years before was a proper shave. When he looked at himself in the mirror, he saw the face of a man with the furtive air which had become the hallmark of a priest in a socialist comedy, and, at the same time, a resemblance to the face of his grandfather, who had been a patrician. It was strange; for, in reality, Grigori's face took on a cunning look only when he saw himself in the mirror, when he became a priest face to face with an agent of the government. In the presence of others, he sometimes had the look of a snarling dog who has just been beaten; but, most often, he seemed a figure of benevolence and authority with just a touch of what fools call paternalism.

Children. He had none of his own; and he was unable to treat those of others as his own. Children, with their indiscriminate confidences, frightened him. He did not love children, and he disliked deceiving children. Whenever he distributed Communion and placed the golden spoon in the mouth of a wide-eyed child, he experienced intense irritation. He would have liked to shout at the parents: "Do you know what you're doing? Why are you condemning your child to a lifetime of lies?" And sometimes he told himself: "I am the lie," as solemnly as Christ had said, "I am the truth."

He would have liked to cry out, to shout above the choir's hieratic chants, "Do not suffer little children to come unto me!"

But he did not cry out. He gave Communion; and sometimes he whispered into the ear of a young mother who divided her loyalty between the Church and a communist youth organization: "Bring little Vassia to church more often. It is necessary that the smell of incense become familiar before he encounters that of good and evil."

Thus, Grigori played the game of both Christ and the state. Vassia would be a religious child; but, in the heart of Vassia's mother, doubts would begin to take form after hearing the priest use arguments taken from the textbooks of the atheistic propagandists of the state.

I am walking a tightrope, Grigori told himself, just as Christ walked on water.

I should explain to you that
in all my parishes—there were
four in all, corresponding to my
rapid advancement in the hier-
archy of the Church—the majority
of my parishioners were old people,
and especially women. No doubt, this
particular failing on the part of
our sisters is to be explained by
the backwardness of former ages,
when women were uneducated and were
treated as children. Today, of
course, they are our equals in all
things, and even travel
about in the cosmos.

Nonsense.
Women, obviously, are

slaves. But then,
Christianity, as Engels
says, is a religion of
slaves.

From the very beginning, Grigori delighted in bullying the old women who came to church long before a service was scheduled to begin and left long after it was over; those who tried to corner him in order to extract one more blessing, and who rattled on for hours over their smallest sins. "No!" he preached, "Christianity is not a religion for the frail, the weak, the old. Who are the aged but those who have already begun to die? It is written: 'Leave the dead to bury the dead.' What we need is a new, young strength, capable of sacrifices and deeds!"

He refused the old ones who came too often for his blessing, holding out their cupped, wrinkled hands to him. "Go home!" he said. "I've already blessed you this morning."

To some of the males of his parish, he entrusted the honorable task of extinguishing the candles. And only Alona was allowed to arrange the flowers brought to the church. The women who brought them would insist that they be allowed to place their offering before this or that ikon. And Grigori would reply: "Let's not play favorites. Alexander is a handsome saint, all right; but that's no reason to neglect Akaky."

No matter how offensive his words—he delighted especially in imposing severe or ridiculous penances upon the more bigoted of his parishioners—his popularity was not affected. If the faithful did not regard him with the same affection as they had his predecessors, they nonetheless feared him; and fear was an emotion which they found somehow agreeable. "This new one," the old women whispered among themselves, "is a real one!" And by that they meant that he was a true priest; a true servant of Christ. Some of them, aware of

Grigori's origins—although he was at pains never to discuss such things—would add: "He is a true master." Gradually, their faded eyes weeping with humiliation, they came to worship him.

So far as Grigori himself was concerned, his surliness disappeared. He began to bless his people mechanically as did most of his confreres, and he no longer gave way to anger. When he spoke of his parishioners as "my harem of scarecrows" or "my battalion of cripples," it was with barely disguised affection. It pleased him to find them there, willing to be insulted and to thank him for it. There were times when he, as a soldier, was touched by their inexplicable devotion. At such times, he would say, not without hypocrisy: "Charity is the strength of the weak, as it is the weakness of the strong." And when their follies and their sins, which would have scandalized a true priest, were brought to his attention, he would only smile with satisfaction and tell himself that such things confirmed the total failure of Christian morality.

In any event, old women crouched before pet ikons and Christian morality itself were of no importance. Jesus had been right to tell the moralists, with an air of boredom, to read the commandments. And the communists were right also: Christian morality does nothing for man that communism does not do equally well. St. Augustine had recognized it: "Love, and then do whatever you wish." It was understood, of course, that if a man truly loves, the trap of love will have closed upon him and he will no longer be capable of evil. How foolish the Voltairians were, Grigori reflected, with their plan of preserving Christianity for the people so as to keep them in bondage. What a farce! Religion, far from being an opiate, was a stimulant. And so much the worse for me, Grigori said to himself, if I am a Marxist according to the spirit and not according to the letter—to paraphrase the vibrant words of Comrade Saint Paul.

In the light of these things, Comrade Dobermann, it should be clear that, during the seventeen years of my ministry, I was what is known as a good priest.

Oh, yes indeed!

I tried simply to place my people in direct contact with the Divinity; and I attempted to do so with them just as they were, without subjecting them to any kind of degrading emotional preparation. I had always been struck by the propaganda methods of the Jesus of the Gospels. Unlike our activists, Jesus first recruited his followers; only later did he teach them, as though he was in a kingdom which had already been conquered. This was a performance which even our most accomplished experts in subversive warfare cannot equal. In selecting his followers, he did not attempt to arouse their indignation against an oppressor or an enemy, or offer them the hope of a reward. Instead, he asked for their complete loyalty. His method was the direct opposite of that which is sometimes used by the Church herself and which resembles the

methods of insurance companies.
Jesus demanded all, immediately.
It is thus that I acted with my
parishioners; and I must admit,
Comrade Professor, that, despite
everything that our professors of
atheism can do, in our country
one still need only ask and he shall receive.
I am astonished to see the diffi-
culties encountered by the Party
in this respect. The Party's
demands are quite reasonable; and
yet, when the people give, they
do so grudgingly. I can tell you
that I myself encountered no such
difficulties in this respect.

Grigori stopped writing and looked at the lined gray paper, half covered with his large, black, slanted script. He looked at it with a kind of amicable hostility. Was he about to sign a declaration of independence, or a commitment to final servitude? Would Comrade Dobermann understand anything of the erudite lies which he would read that very night or the next morning? The simple trick of using a past tense has transformed the present into the past.

Grigori raised his head, looked around the room. He almost expected new scenery set on the stage for a new comedy. But it was not so. The wallpaper was still patched and dirty. The ikon was still in its corner, dimly lighted by its candle. The photographs of Alona's relatives were still in their place. Alona herself was sitting on her bed, mending socks, silent and almost incorporeal despite the weight of her body with its bony frame, which the years had deprived of all gracefulness. Grigori's hands were poised over the paper; large hands, hairy; hands made for beating, twisting, and striking, protruding incongruously from the sleeves of a threadbare cassock which, from long use, had almost lost its black color. The past, Grigori reflected, although revoked, was still present. He experienced a feeling both of disgust, as though obliged to put on a shirt which he had already worn too long, and of relief, as though he had allowed himself to remain for five minutes longer in his lumpy, but nonetheless warm bed.

He thought of his parish. Tomorrow, it would be without its pastor. He thought of his parishioners as, twenty years before, he had thought of his platoon. "My men." No, he corrected himself maliciously, not my men. It would be more accurate to describe them as "my women." Unless, of course, I use the word "man" in its generic sense. "My souls." Women also are men. Even so, there are some males. Many of them, in fact. More than in the other parishes in this area. They've been won over by their reliance upon authority, and by the perpetual and silent devotion of their pastor.

It was true. Grigori was not an unctuous speaker, nor did he thunder from the pulpit. He was a man of action; a man who did his priestly work as a matter of course, as other men smelted bars of metal or put their shoulders to the wheels of their broken-down tractors. He was quick to blame, and quick to praise. His time was that of his parishioners. He was happy if he was paid for his services, but he asked for nothing. He did not apologize for existing or for doing his job. In a time of anguish, he represented a certitude. The soldiers in the more fortunate regiments used to say, "So long as So-and-so is our commanding officer, we'll be all right." Grigori's parishioners exhibited the same attitude. With such a priest, a man had to fear neither God nor Satan.

Grigori had never been a procrastinator. In every situation, he weighed both sides of the question carefully, and then announced his decision immediately, without fear of being thought hesitant or indecisive. It was a style which inspired confidence. He had been able to reconcile couples troubled by misunderstandings. And, occasionally, he had ordered others to separate, because he knew that they could not live together in peace. He had brought several young people back onto the right path by offering them the harsh exaltation which they had sought vainly from the bureaucrats. He had reconciled parents with their children. Above all, he had helped many to bear the injustices visited upon them. These victims had come to him in secret, and they felt for him a gratitude which would endure so long as they lived:

"Father, if it hadn't been for you, I would have cut my father-in-law's throat."

"Without you, I would have beat up that cop."

"Thank God you made me return the money."

"You were right in telling me to stay with him for the sake of the children."

Grigori smiled, proudly, ironically, spitefully, tenderly. My souls. The lives upon which I have left my mark.

This has nothing at all to do with the fact that I am a priest, he told himself. My ancestors all did the same thing as well, if not better, than I, simply because they had the muscle.

Would I be pleased, Grigori wondered, if those few dozen souls retained their respect for me—or if they came to despise me—when I become a professor of atheism?

He shrugged. Such things, he knew, were unimportant. The question of whether or not he had been a good priest was really this: had he fulfilled his mission? His mission had been to be a good priest. A good priest does not confine himself to performing little services for his parishioners. A good priest is not a boy scout. A good priest is a saint.

Am I a saint? Grigori wondered, almost without wincing. Those who do not know believe that a saint is one who resists temptation. Grigori, looking back over the seventeen years of life just completed, asked himself: have I had temptations? Yes, certainly; but not ordinary temptations. He had fasted when he was supposed to; and he had turned away, with sincere indignation, Domna, with her beautiful white arms. "Go," he had said. "I have no time for wanton sluts like you!"

No time? It had been the truth. His parish, and his files, had been more than sufficient to occupy his time.

The temptation to violence, common enough in itself, had assailed him with particular intensity. He would gladly have given some of his penitents a beating in place of absolution and penance. But the most characteristic temptation had come with a visit from the church warden; a man who was an agent of the same government which Grigori served. But what an agent he was! Sordid, base, greedy, and cowardly. With him, Grigori had succumbed to temptation, but only venially; and, in so doing, he had rendered a service to the Church. The satisfaction he had derived had been triple, and paradoxical. He still experienced a fierce joy from the memory of it.

The church warden, a little man in a tight, striped jacket, had come to him one night, complaining that Grigori had baptized an infant without informing the authorities of that fact. "You understand, my good little Father," he had said, "that we cannot allow such things. The law is the law, and we have to obey it. I am responsible for what is done in our church. God is God; but the rules are the same for everyone. So, you see, priest, if you cannot abide by the rules, we will not be able to keep you as the priest of this parish. Let us give things their proper names. When you baptize, bury, marry, and say Mass, you are serving us. We are the ones who pay you. In a manner of speaking, we are your employers; and, as such, we can require that you obey the rules. Now, if you do not agree with the rules, this means that you are an enemy of the regime; and, as you know, it is our patriotic duty to report it to the proper authorities.

"You baptized Vassilitch's baby, and I was not told about it because Vassilitch is an assistant director of a factory and pretends not to believe in God. But this did not stop him from paying you. The money, Vassilitch's money, is there, in your pocket, priest. I'm sure you have no intention of paying taxes on it. Isn't that so? In other words, Vassilitch is trying to deceive the Party—I happen to know that he has applied for membership—while good Father Grigori is trying to cheat the government."

He clicked his tongue disapprovingly, and his eyes rolled in his head so that Grigori could see only the whites of them.

In a corner of the room, Alona was seated on the bed, bent over her sewing. Her presence, ordinarily so immaterial, now weighed heavily in the room. Above her head, a candle glowed, the ikon glimmered.

Grigori felt a rage rising from deep within him; the kind of rage he had sometimes experienced as an officer; a rage which filled him to the tips of his fingers. He was seated with his elbows on his knees, leaning forward, facing the church warden. He said nothing for a moment. His hard eyes were fixed intently upon those of the little man. Suddenly, he rose, a huge figure in his black cassock, bearded, menacing. The warden flinched. Alona, in her corner, cringed; or rather, crouched, like a diver, and waited.

Grigori turned toward the ikon, trembling with pleasure at the anticipation of the demanding and difficult role he was about to play.

"God is my witness," he said in a solemn voice, speaking with slow deliberation. "He knows that the indignation stirred in my heart by your iniquity is the same as that which He himself experienced in the presence of the money changers in the Temple. Church warden, I owe it to your immortal soul to treat you in the only way that your hardened heart is capable of understanding."

Still facing the ikon, Grigori made a large and devout sign of the cross. He was conscious of playing a part; but he was also thinking fervently of the warrior saints of his Church: Alexander, Vladimir . . .

Alona seemed to become smaller, heavier, denser. The warden drew back further into his chair, blinking, sputtering, aghast, his eyes still rolling. Grigori, with his left hand, lay hold of the warden's shirt collar and necktie with such force that he had difficulty drawing a breath. With his right, Grigori, the former officer, struck methodically at that pale face as, in another life, he had struck the red faces of thieves and drunks in his platoon. But the satisfaction he derived was not the same. Grigori was not punishing. He was correcting.

When, with an effort, he dropped his hands, the inspector collapsed into his chair, his open mouth gasping for breath, holding his nose with a thumb and forefinger to stop the flow of blood.

"Now," Grigori said quietly, his voice barely tinged with pleasure, "if you report that I baptized Vassilitch's child, I'll have to report that you offered to keep quiet about it in return for a sum of money. And, as for my method of pointing out to you the error of your ways, you may boast of it. I won't be hurt by it."

The church warden rose to his feet, swaying, still holding his nose. He reached the door. He turned, and pointed to the uneven floor. "Father," he said, in a nasal, abject, penitent voice, "I'm sorry. I've spotted the floor there . . ."

It was blood.

Grigori folded his arms and said, almost jovially: "It will be taken care of. Now, my son, go in peace."

The door closed behind the warden. Alona breathed more freely. Grigori would never know what were her thoughts at that moment, for there were none. She judged no man, and least of all her husband, who was also her Saviour. She knew only that Grigori had run a great risk for the sake of the parish, and she loved him for it, if it was possible, more than she had before.

Grigori went to the painted wooden table where the basin and jug of water were kept. He washed his hands thoroughly, calmly. The soap, poor as it was, cleansed nonetheless. Never, Grigori thought, will I wash my hands before the Royal door, in the sight of the praying faithful, attended by priests in vestments of gold and surrounded by the chants of the choir.

When he had dried his hands, he sat behind another table. This one served as a desk. He made an entry, in coded Greek, in Vassilitch's dossier. He had already written: "Had his son baptized in secret." Now he added: "Has applied for membership in the Party." Grigori then recorded the source of this information.

Violence, Grigori reflected, is a temptation; but it is not one which can condemn a man to hell. Violence does not exclude purity. Often, the two are inextricably bound together.

Grigori knew that, before he had been transferred to the intelligence service, when he had leaped into a trench dug by the invader in the sacred soil of his country, with a submachine gun clutched under his arm—then, he knew, he had been pure. He would have been able to receive the Eucharist without committing the sin of blasphemy. He had killed; but he had done so in a rage of love and not of hate. But then his rage had gone off the track.

The truth was that Grigori, like all special agents, had experienced only two serious temptations. One was that of the lion; and the other, that of the serpent. Excess and deficiency. Zeal, and fatigue. Excess, paradoxically, could lead to a complete change of sides; and deficiency resulted in the itch which caused an agent to reveal himself.

The first temptation—the magnificent, princely temptation—made itself felt sporadically, like summer lightning. It was not unlike treason to the service; and it was an even more abominable treason to Christ.

Well, thought Grigori, hunched over his letter to Dobermann, I know enough about religion to understand that. I am closer to the one they call Christ, at least so far as understanding is concerned, than many cardinals, or popes, or Constantine the Great.

This temptation had afflicted Grigori only rarely; but when it came, it had done so with almost crushing force. It had occurred when a healthy, strong young man knelt before Grigori for confession. It had occurred when, in the course of a sermon, he felt that he was dispensing happiness and virtue to a congregation which included more males, or more truly devout members, than was usual. And when an official of the government or a member of the Party summoned him in secret and proposed Nicephorus' bargain: "I will give you my protection in this world, if you will give me yours in the next."

The temptation had made itself felt for the first time on an Easter night, in the capital, shortly after Grigori's ordination. He was officiating at a service, with several other priests from the Patriarchate, in one of the few cathedrals which remained open for use. It was a pontifical Mass. The celebrant was an enormously tall, thin old man, clothed in white and gold and ablaze with precious stones. It was known that he slept in a coffin; and he fasted so rigorously that he would soon be dead. The government, dissatisfied with the pace at which he was dying, and with his growing popularity, had arranged for him to be poisoned shortly. These circumstances had endowed the liturgical celebration with an extraordinary nobility. It had lasted the entire night. The cathedral itself had been filled—one could see only a sea of faces transfigured with joy, a wave of red and white candles, a fog of incense and smoke—and the crowd of the faithful had spilled beyond the cathedral doors into the courtyard and out into the square itself. The surrounding streets had become impassable. Horns of blocked automobiles blared incessantly. Policemen roared. But nothing had been able to override the fierce shouts of joy which resounded constantly around the cathedral. Each priest in turn, surrounded by clouds of incense, had stood before the ikonostasis and, in a great voice, had announced to the milling, ecstatic throng, the ancient message:

"Christ is risen!"

For weeks before the Mass, Grigori had fasted, prayed, and celebrated the liturgy. His head was spinning. The evangelical jubilation preserved by the Oriental Church was, in its essence, contagious. Grigori rejoiced with his fellow priests because a Christ in which he did not believe had risen from the dead—a feat which he knew to be impossible.

The golden censer—for the Patriarchate had kept its wealth—had smoked in Grigori's hand as he had advanced toward the congregation. At the two ends of the transept, the double choirs were chanting the insistent rhythms of the paschal antiphons. Grigori did not hear them directly, for their voices rose into the cupola, then descended upon the congregation like a sound from the heavens, the harshness gentled, the harmonies blended into a music which was at once unearthly, unchanging, absolute.

Grigori halted. Thousands of candles, thousands of eyes surrounded him. Behind him, above him, around him, red vigils burned in uncounted numbers before the black and gold faces of the saints encircling the faithful. Above, a fog of incense dimmed the cupola's golden sky.

Grigori hesitated. His tongue was glued to his palate. He knew that, at the first sound from his mouth, there would be a response in a voice of thunder from all sides. It would grow, roll to the doors of the cathedral, erupt into the square, where, for three hours, it had already resounded without interruption.

He opened his mouth; and, immediately, before Grigori was able to utter a word, a child's voice screamed the response:

"He is truly risen!"

Grigori smiled, pierced by an impure ecstasy. Temptation drew near and descended upon him from the misty cupola, rose to meet him from the crowd of the faithful wholly attentive to the sound of his voice; a sound which he was about to hurl into their uplifted faces like a torch into a haystack.

He spoke. He cried:

"Christ is risen!"

And, since he was an intellectual priest, he spoke it in all the languages at his command. In Greek, as a mark of homage to Byzantium. In English, in German and in French to announce the good news to the outside world. In Latin, to hurl puerile defiance to Rome. And in Hebrew, to mock the murderers of Christ.

The faithful, in a frenzy of love, gave a great cry; a sound like fire sweeping through a field of wheat, in which the flame is passed from row to row like an all-consuming wave:

"He is truly risen!"

Before the immensity of that response, face to face with that enormous crowd and with the power of the word, a thought flashed into Grigori's mind: With such power in my hands, how could I not become prince of this world? And the temptation remained with him from that moment. By means of the advantages provided by his status as an agent, he would become a bishop, and acquire an influence of such magnitude over the people that the regime's hold would weaken. And a regime which loosens its hold must, inevitably, fall. In its place, Grigori would establish the absolute dictatorship of the Church. Perhaps he would be Patriarch; perhaps the *éminence grise;* or perhaps by then he would be a corpse. It did not matter. What would matter was that a total regime—which is much more effective than a totalitarian regime—had been established in one country and would shortly cover the world. The twentieth century had revealed to statesmen that it was childish to attempt to control the actions of men. It is the souls of men which must be enslaved. For that purpose, a modern regime made use of scientific propaganda and of the malefic blessings of psychoanalysis and of television. But there was another way, and a better one; one which had existed for a long time: religion. Just as propaganda generally had only one purpose—to destroy the will to fight in one group of people, and to create it in another—so, too, religion had always preached resignation as well as holy war. Christianity, a religion which teaches free men to become slaves, was perfectly tailored to the enslavement of souls. It was the hypnotic of the masses, as Constantine the Great was well aware. An empire of contented slaves, guarded by foremen who were called confessors. A nation of frenetic believers, ruled over by a nonbelieving master.

The energy expended and wasted in faith, Grigori had reflected, must be harnessed, converted into action. But for what purpose? For the good of mankind, he answered vaguely. In fact, he could not have cared less about the good of mankind. Power was meant to be wielded, just as thoroughbred horses were meant to be raced, and beautiful women to be loved. As guns were meant to kill, and trucks to roll. Just as destiny was meant to be realized. Just as Scripture was meant to be fulfilled. It was of this that Grigori thought when he prayed, "Thy will be done." He thought of trucks rolling; guns killing; women loving; and horses galloping. And of the greatest possible power being wielded in all its plenitude.

Should he write of such things to Dobermann? Yes. It would sound convincing.

Comrade Professor, I will go even further. I confess to you that I dreamed of an omnipotent Church; of the exercise of complete control by priests over the whole political, economic, and social life of the nation. Now, thanks to you, I can see how monstrous such a notion was. It was not so long ago, however, that I looked forward to a hierocracy, albeit a communist hierocracy, in the likeness of that established by the Jesuits in Paraguay. It is said that those Roman priests kept the Indians in such perfect subjection that the latter thanked them even for a beating.

I realize now that this dream—a dream cherished today, as it has been cherished in all ages by almost all priests in every nation—is contrary both to the law of Christ and to common sense, to logic as well as to the good of mankind. Jesus himself said so, in so many words, when he instructed his followers to render to Caesar (that is, to the state) all that was Caesar's due.

You can see from the above, Comrade Dobermann, how far astray I wandered. Please believe that my confession is sincere. I am

telling you the truth as I know it
from my own experience.

Perhaps I'm being too
brazen. Well, so much the
worse. It amuses me.
And it does bear some
resemblance to "the truth
as I know it."
What about Alona? Shall
I also tell him about Alona?

Alona was at the root of the second, more insidious and vile temptation: the temptation to fatigue, to which Grigori had actually succumbed, although his fall was known to himself alone. For if he had killed Alona, he would have had a more glorious task to accomplish; and glory is an antidote against fatigue. Without Alona, he reflected, Ambrose would not have seemed so strong or so important. If Alona had died, death would have become Grigori's ally.

Why did I succumb? Grigori asked himself. And he answered: Because of fatigue. Of what was I tired? Of Alona. Spies and priests should never marry; not because they fear love—what a stupid reason!—but because they should fear that hateful lassitude which is the inevitable concomitant of conjugal life, and for which the other party is always responsible. Ambrose had indeed been killed; but it was Alona's fault.

Alona had not moved. She was still there, darning his socks. She was fond of working with her hands. She never read; but she was pleased when her husband, while she was sewing or knitting, read aloud the life of a saint or the explanation of a liturgical function. She has a body. And she has a soul. But has she a mind?

Grigori turned from his letter and glanced at Alona. She raised her eyes. She smiled, but it was a barely discernible smile, a parsimonious smile. She had cultivated the habit of hiding the great joy abiding in her heart. Her happiness was such that she became confused when she attempted to express it: "Father, I am so happy to work for you. So happy to have an advocate like you before our Lord. So happy to have been able to stop working at the factory, thanks to you. So happy to be loved by you . . ."

Did Grigori love her? Yes, as he loved a bed, a rifle, a landscape. Sixteen years earlier, in fact, when he had gone to see his superior—who was Grouztchik no longer, but who was not yet Nadson, but a man called Verniak, nicknamed "the Schoolmistress"—he had suffered a pang of regret. It is always difficult to rid oneself of a loyalty, whether it be to an automobile, a book, or a wife. And Grigori, on his way to Verniak's office to say, "The time has come to call for our runaway truck," had experienced the bitterness of a man who must kill a faithful dog which has gone mad, or sell a horse which is too old to work.

He had found Verniak in Grouztchik's old office. The chairs were clear of papers. Neatly ribboned files were stacked on his desk. The new chief wore enormous horn-rimmed glasses which somehow dwarfed his thin face, his pinched nose, and his stringy neck, which supported a celluloid collar.

"Please be seated."

The official tone.

Verniak was no stranger to the priest. He had met him on earlier visits, in another section of the same office where the Schoolmistress had been a subordinate official. At that time, he had worn striped shirts and soft collars. Obviously, it would have been inappropriate for Grigori to remind him now of those previous meetings; or to ask him what had become of

Grouztchik. It was rather a time to render an account and to plan for the future.

"Comrade Major, my mission is proceeding according to schedule. But, before it can enter into its second phase, we must undertake the liquidation which we have planned."

Verniak looked at the man in a cassock who had come to request the assassination of his legitimate wife. He pretended not to understand. "What 'second phase'?" he asked. "And what liquidation? Please express yourself more clearly. I have no time to waste."

Grigori began to explain, drily. "As you know, Comrade Major—"

"I know nothing," Verniak interrupted.

"If you will glance at my dossier—"

"Your dossier lacks precision, and shows signs of negligence—almost of guesswork. Whoever compiled it seemed to rely largely on intuition. I need facts. Tangible facts."

Grigori gave him the facts.

"If I understand you correctly," Verniak said, "I am to conclude that, for the past four years, one of our agents has been playing junior spy in a cassock. Is that correct?"

When he pronounced the word "cassock," his nose wrinkled, as though Grigori's clerical garb gave off an offensive odor.

Grigori attempted a further explanation, but Verniak cut him off. "Just a moment. Will you explain to me, if you can, precisely what benefit we will derive from your mission?"

The two men glared at each other across the desk. Only a year ago, Verniak's question would have made Grigori's heart leap with the hope that his mission would be canceled. But now, it did not. He felt obliged to defend his mission with all the means at his disposal, without knowing why. "A mission like mine," he began, "is intended to sabotage the sole enemy organization which we are required, by our constitution, to allow to prosper under our very noses."

Verniak's nose wrinkled again, as though it alone had been the subject of Grigori's metaphor.

"Young man," Verniak replied contemptuously, "I could answer that the Church is nothing more than a hodgepodge of outdated prejudices; a confraternity of cripples, maniacs, and old men; a structure so dilapidated and worm-eaten that, within ten years, it will collapse under its own weight. Nevertheless—"

The commanding officers whom Grigori had known had all been battle-scarred veterans; ferocious men, but men who welcomed ideas from their subordinates. He therefore interrupted Verniak without apology: "Comrade Major, it is precisely the purpose of my mission to prove otherwise. We do more than bury Christians. We marry them and baptize their children; millions of children."

Verniak raised a finger in a gesture of both warning and irritation. "Lieutenant," he said, "I would advise you to remember your rank, and not to expend your energies in thought when you have superiors who are better qualified than you for such a task.

"The Patriarch is an old fool, surrounded by a few scoundrels who jump with joy whenever they are able to gain the slightest material advantage from us. They ask for nothing more. The teachings of the Church, as you should know, are an opiate intended to paralyze the will of the people. All that we have to do is to close the opium dens, and the addicts will become normal people once again. All except the most addicted, that is, who will die. As you see, there is more than one approach to this problem."

"Comrade Major, I am afraid—"

"You are afraid?" Verniak asked in disgust. "You, an officer of this service?"

Grigori was thrown off balance by the stupidity of Verniak's question. He floundered, and then his temper rose. "You know very well what I mean," he replied. "Look at my service record, and then see if you can accuse me of cowardice. I was saying that I am afraid—yes, afraid—that the danger is greater than you think. The Church aims much higher than you think. She provides man with a complex of experiences which the state is incapable of equaling. And I am not referring to experiences which deaden, but to those which quicken and stimulate. The reason I was chosen for this particular mission was that I was especially aware of the danger represented by the Church. I—"

Once more Verniak's finger rose, meaningfully, threateningly. "Lieutenant, I, for my part, am also afraid. I am afraid that your excessive exposure to an ecclesiastical milieu has led you to a concept of matters which is as far removed as possible from Marxism. The fact, as demonstrated by our Marxist dialectic, is that the Church cannot represent the slightest danger to a regime such as ours. The Church is nothing more than a vestige. It is a few drops of pus at the bottom of an abscess. I will allow no more discussion, Lieutenant. I know what I am talking about."

Verniak was silent a moment, to underscore his point. Then he continued. "I am the first to admit that, in certain cases, it may be useful to apply pressure to an abscess in order to rid oneself of the pus more quickly. We shall therefore apply such pressure. But I confess that this idea of a twenty-year mission seems both ridiculous and dangerous, especially since it exposes you to corrupting influences over a longer period of time than our regulations can allow for, or than human nature can resist. I will therefore have to refer the matter to my superiors."

Verniak cleared his throat. His turkey neck quivered, rose, but his collar remained immobile as a rock.

"Now," he went on, "let us move on to this bizarre project

which you claim was approved by my predecessor. I am not required to accept your unsubstantiated word, but—"

"Comrade Major, if you will look at my record—"

"Yes, your record. The way that records were maintained before I took charge here— No matter. I was about to say that I am willing to accept what you say at face value. You are asking that we proceed to the physical liquidation of your spouse?"

The word "spouse" had an alien sound in the professional, communist vocabulary of Verniak.

"Yes, Comrade Major."

"For what purpose?"

"In order for me to become a widower."

"So I thought. But, tell me, if you become a widower, what will that accomplish?"

"I can then become a monk."

"Why have you not become one sooner?"

"The authorities would not grant permission. If you will look at my dossier—"

"Let us forget your dossier. Who are the authorities who would not grant permission?"

"The religious authorities."

"On what grounds?"

"It was the dying wish of a respected priest that I not be allowed to take the vows of a monk."

"What obscurantism!" Verniak sighed. "What prejudice! And you really believe, Lieutenant, that these savages represent a danger to our regime? Come now! But let us continue. Exactly what is the advantage of your becoming a monk?"

"Only monks can become bishops. The strategic situation of a bishop is so superior—"

"Tactical, young man, tactical. Don't begin to think of yourself as another Napoleon. Now, if you become a widower, I gather that you will automatically become a monk. Is that correct?"

Grigori hesitated. Verniak had put his finger on the weak point of Grigori's reasoning; a point of which Grouztchik had been unaware. "No," he answered. "It is not automatic. I remain a widowed secular priest, but—"

"But they can no longer refuse to allow you to become a monk?"

"Yes, they can still refuse, but—"

"Then I do not understand, Lieutenant."

"They can still refuse permission, but it is unlikely that they will do so. I can appeal to higher authorities, to the Patriarch himself. My monastic vocation will appear to have received the approval of divine Providence, since, at a given moment, I will have been deprived of a wife imposed on me by the will of men. Do you understand?"

Verniak smiled with that utter contempt of which only the most limited of men are capable. "No," he said, in a tone of satisfaction. "I do not understand." Then he added, in a different tone: "And I do not wish to understand. I understand only that your holy Church is a collection of swindlers and fools. It is beyond me how, in an age when we stand at the verge of conquering the universe, a man can still speak of 'divine Providence.' Here are your orders. You will take three weeks of leave, without your wife, either in the capital or in the South. I do not have the authority to cancel your mission; you will therefore resume it when you return. Perhaps you will be in a better frame of mind by then. Domestic life, young man, is not always easy; and short separations are often helpful. After three weeks of swimming or fornicating, and having to pay for it, you may feel differently about liquidating the woman who is your wife in the eyes of the law. I certainly cannot allow the facilities of the service to be used—"

Grigori leaped to his feet. "Comrade Major, if you dare make such an insinuation, I will request to be taken to your commanding officer immediately."

The two men glared furiously at one another. Finally, it was the Schoolmistress who lowered his eyes, and said in a low voice: "Lieutenant, you are dismissed."

Grigori hesitated, then drew himself to attention, clicked his heels, and saluted. Attired as he was in his cassock, the movements seemed incongruous, supremely insolent. For a moment, Verniak hallucinated a true priest, standing in his office, mocking him.

After a regulation half-turn, Grigori marched to the door, his cassock flapping about his legs. His hand was on the knob when Verniak recalled him: "Lieutenant."

"Comrade Major?"

"If any misfortune should befall your wife, I must tell you that I will hold you personally responsible and act accordingly. Understood?"

It was not a question which seemed to require an answer; and Grigori did not deign to reply. Verniak, however, insisted upon explaining. "It is possible that your wife may have an accident, or die of, let us say, mushroom poisoning, or even of cancer. No matter how she may eventually die, I will consider that you have been guilty of gross negligence in the performance of your duty. Now do you understand?"

Verniak had guessed, perhaps from the very insolence with which Grigori had clicked his heels, that the priest had said to himself: "If he will not help me, I will help myself."

Grigori had left Verniak's office in a disturbed frame of mind. If it was no longer allowed to kill anyone, what good did it do to have missions, or to give one's life to accomplish them? Grigori knew that Verniak's decision was not based upon humane concern, but rather upon an administrative spirit of contradiction; that is, he wished simply to prevent Grouztchik's plan from reaching fruition. Nonetheless, it was a crushing blow to realize that such considerations could outweigh the value of a mission to which a man was devoting his entire life. "I am condemned," Grigori had concluded, "to remain a mediocrity."

For months after his interview with Verniak, Grigori dreamed of murdering Alona. But he took no real pleasure in such dreams, for he was fond of Alona. She satisfied him; and he made her happy. Nonetheless, he reasoned, one must build dams and dig mines, even though they spoil the landscape. Still, Grigori feared the two masters he served. He might commit the perfect crime, but Verniak would know; and the service never lacked for proof or for witnesses. In the improbable case that Verniak either did not discover the crime or did nothing about it, it was entirely possible that the opinion of Nicephorus the Martyr—as he was beginning to be called—might still prevail at the Patriarchate. In that case, Grigori would remain a secular priest and a widower, and he would have gained nothing except holes in his socks and problems of the flesh. He would not even have the option of becoming a bad priest; for that would jeopardize his mission. And that was something which the service would never tolerate.

Grigori, therefore, had resigned himself, at least superficially, to waiting the sixteen years during which he was obliged to remain a priest; to endure rather than to act. But, in the depths of his soul, and without knowing it, he had resigned himself to a great deal more. On the day that Verniak had refused to have Alona liquidated, Grigori had lost a certain, altogether pagan, joy in living. Great forests which had been seeded in him and which, if properly tended, might have grown to unprecedented heights, on that day had been covered with salt. He had recognized that he would never be a bishop. That he would never conquer the Church at the level at which he wished to conquer it. That the sacrifice of his manhood, his youth—in other words, the sacrifice of what he still thought of as his life—would produce only a ridiculously small result. He had therefore come to accept a totally new concept of life, a gloomy and singularly pragmatic concept. He had begun to read, and to raise chickens. Hitherto, life to him had been a vast and luminous plane on which had appeared markings of his own design: his plans for making straight the way of the future. Now a "life" had been reduced to a structure of tiny pebbles, a structure which was in the process of crumbling because the concrete contained too generous a portion of sand. "Life" had become a word like other words—myopia, darning, stamp collecting, cigarette butts, and, in the final analysis, death.

It was thus that the second temptation had come into Grigori's life.

Death is like a tower at the end of a road. As the day goes on, shadows turn, details are highlighted, and it becomes impossible, from one hour to the next, for a man to recognize the tower toward which he is moving.

To Grigori as a child and as a young man, death had seemed a wide, deep, black word which referred only to others. It had been an incomprehensible word, borrowed from an alien tongue spoken by other men. Later, Grigori had both imposed death and risked it himself, frequently. It had thus assumed its most repellent physical aspect, and also its most serene. Grigori had learned the meaning of that strange word. It meant to have a bullet in one's guts; to step on a mine and be blown apart. It meant third-degree burns, and sometimes a third-degree interrogation. Grigori had thought that he knew the meaning of death because he knew how death was to be handled: it was to be avoided for oneself, and imposed upon others. "Death," at that time, had been truly a foreign word. A German word.

Once Grigori became a priest, death had assumed a new

mask. He learned that men feared death, or hoped for it, because they believed that death was a new birth. They had been taught that they would be born again into a world which was either good or evil according to whether they themselves were good or evil. It was thus, rather than by means of an exactly calculated scale of retribution for acts committed, that Grigori conceived the myth of Heaven and Hell. The idea of God presiding at the Last Judgment like a headmaster over a distribution of prizes was too grotesque; and Grigori rarely underestimated his enemies. Instead, each man returned whence he had come, the good to a good world, and the evil to an evil world. It might happen occasionally that there would be changes. Two people might exchange tickets, so to speak. Generally, however, there was a good reason why the word "good" was evocative of "goodness" and "happiness," and "evil" of "wrongdoing" and "suffering." There was an essence of goodness, and an essence of evil. And it was in this way that Grigori, without believing in these visions himself, explained to himself the beliefs of the priests and the faithful.

Even so, his concept of death had changed. Death was no longer a hole into which men tumbled, through either inadvertence or misfortune. Rather, it was a wall against which a man hurled himself in the belief that the wall was a doorway. "I am the way," Jesus had said. A wall in the night. But what if it was true that somewhere in that dark wall there was a secret panel? It could not be. The secret panel had been invented by men in order to console themselves. It was Grigori's professional duty to help men believe that that panel—or rather, that great door, that giant portal—truly existed, and to send them crashing against the wall in perfect tranquillity.

A compassionate man might have developed a taste for his work. But Grigori had not. He had nothing but contempt for such stupid hopes and primitive fears. When uneducated parishioners asked him whether it was true that in hell the damned spent eternity licking red-hot skillets, Grigori answered: "Of course not. The skillets are *white*-hot." Several times, he had invented extraordinary tortures, but these had not created much of a stir. He had been more successful when he merely described certain practices of the service when dealing with an especially recalcitrant prisoner. The more sophisticated among his parishioners objected to such stories. Then Grigori would answer, in keeping with the answer of the churches since they had to contend with scientific progress, that this must all be interpreted symbolically.

It amused Grigori thus to turn himself into a travesty of the devil. And, when he thought of his own death, he told himself: "Weighing one thing against the other, I must conclude that, if heaven and hell really existed, I would spend eternity licking skillets."

He had even gone so far as to ask the advice of his bishop on this point: "Your Excellency, if we admit that sinners really are doomed to suffer for all eternity, may we conclude that the spirits which torture them also suffer? Or do they derive a certain satisfaction from doing that for which they have been created?" The bishop's answer had been precise on only one point: God had created nothing for evil. The rest of his answer had been made up of confused and beautifully balanced sentences.

At that time, death had seemed so remote to Grigori that it lost all reality, like a star millions of light-years away from the man who sees it. He sensed dimly that, since he had escaped the dilemma of salvation because he did not believe in salvation, and since he had escaped the tortures of hell because hell did not exist, he would also escape death itself because he was now aware only of its religious, and not its physical, aspect.

Little by little, however, as Grigori grew older, as he saw sick parishioners waste away and die in a perfectly predictable way, and as he lost interest in his own life, he began to take a more natural and realistic view of death. Death became a part of his daily life, not only because he confessed the dying, prayed at the bier of the dead, and buried their bodies, but also because the life which he lived, limited as it was to the accomplishment of an unimportant mission, seemed to drag him irresistibly toward his own death. There was nothing he could do to prevent it. Formerly, he had been able to lay hold of an important idea, of a hope, of a course of action, and halt his downward progress. He had been struck, in reading the Gospel to his parishioners, by the words of Christ to Peter: "You are still mindful of earthly things." I, Grigori told himself, no longer think of earthly things. By earthly things Grigori had meant that green stalk which grows in every man and which baptism by water does not christen. It is an impious growth, at least starting at a certain age. Then the day comes when it must be cut down; unless life has killed it first. And this, Grigori sensed, was what had happened to him. He no longer thought of life as a shining plane. He no longer thought of earthly things. He thought of nothing. He hoped only vaguely for his mission to end. He chanted the liturgy, gave communion to the faithful, ate his cabbage soup with more noise than was absolutely necessary, meditated on the destiny of man, listened to the crowing of Petia the cock, regularly made love to his wife, and then fell into a sound sleep from which he was awakened each night by the sound of his alarm clock summoning him to his mandatory prayers.

It was during this period, of course, that the temptation of the serpent had made itself felt. Verniak had been promoted, and Grigori wondered whether his successor might not be more understanding on the subject of a runaway truck. Grigori became more energetic, almost gay; and for three weeks he lived in hope. Then, hope vanished, and he was consumed by a new rancor, one more bitter than that which had preceded it. It would have been diluted by the routine of everyday life if Ambrose, with the perversity which was his chief characteristic, had not chosen that precise moment to die.

In the parish over which Grigori presided, Ambrose occupied a special place. He was neither old, nor mad, nor truly poor, nor wholly uneducated. He was in business, and he operated at the fringe of the law, but always in accordance with it. He read few newspapers, participated as little as possible in the spontaneous demonstrations organized by the Party, and remained outside the mainstream of communist life without anyone ever troubling to call him to account for it. On the other hand, he participated actively in the life of the community, making reasonable and modest suggestions concerning drainage, school vacations, and mail delivery; and he reigned as an absolute patriarch over a large family with many complex branches. The public authorities themselves treated him with deference, for, on holidays, Ambrose sported a veritable fruit salad of decorations which made him an irresistible target for photographers from official publications. He had, in fact, been a war hero; but he mentioned that fact only to dismiss it lightly, as was becoming to an honest man and a tradesman. "Only once," he had explained, "did I do anything that everyone else did not do. And for that they didn't give me even the smallest medal!"

The fact that he had survived by what he described as a miracle had satisfied both his religious sentiments and his sense of humor. It had been an unprecedented exploit; but no medal. A suicide mission, and Ambrose had survived it. He blew to pieces sixty of the enemy and assured himself of eternal salvation. "But why, Comrade Ambrose," people asked him a hundred times, "didn't you receive a medal for that?"

He had answered: "Because, my friends, there was no one left to write up the citation."

"And why, Comrade Ambrose," they persisted, "was there no one left?"

"Because there were only twelve enlisted men still alive out of my whole regiment."

"How were so many killed, Comrade Ambrose?"

Then Ambrose would name a famous battle, one which will remain graven in human memory until the end of time. The curious would draw closer to Ambrose, hanging on his every word, raising their hands slightly as though they wished to place them on his arms or on his shoulders as a sign of respect. Ambrose, standing in their midst, never seemed embarrassed, never lowered his eyes modestly, never had to be begged to tell his story. He was proud of his exploit; and he seemed particularly delighted at the idea that he had received no reward for it.

Grigori was in his new parish only one day before meeting Ambrose for the first time. Ambrose presented himself at the priest's house at a fitting hour of the afternoon, toward evening. He knocked softly; and, when he had been admitted, he asked Grigori's blessing and made a sign of the cross to the ikon. He then greeted Alona, and remained standing until Grigori himself asked him to be seated.

"Well, here I am, Father," he began. "I've come to see what you look like, saving your reverence."

Grigori gazed at him without smiling. "It is not myself that you should look at, but my cassock."

"A good answer. You're right, of course. But, in a certain sense, you're also wrong. For if the cassock can make the man, it is also true that the man can unmake the cassock."

Ambrose loved to argue, as Grigori discovered, and he often embellished his arguments with proverbs and quotations.

"Do you attend services regularly?" Grigori asked.

"I never miss one, even if it means that I have to lose a sale to attend. But, by the same token, if I have to choose between attending service and doing a good work, I do not hesitate.

A good work is preferable, for while God sees into a man's heart, human beings are not so easily reassured."

"I see that you do not take lightly the salvation of your soul, and you are to be congratulated for it. This is a form of selfishness, so to speak, approved by the Church."

Grigori sometimes indulged himself in such double-meaning phrases, especially when he was dealing with uneducated parishioners. But, in this instance, he had been deceived by Ambrose's peasant accent.

"You are wrong, Father," Ambrose answered. "I couldn't be less concerned about the salvation of my soul."

"You surprise me. For once, self-interest and God's commandments are in agreement— But let us forget about self-interest. It is your duty as a Christian—"

Ambrose smiled with benevolence and contentment. "Shall I tell you something? The salvation of my soul is certain and assured, once and for all."

"I am shocked by your presumption! Have you never heard of the sin of pride? Don't you know that 'the man who wishes to save his soul shall lose it'? Aren't you afraid—?"

Ambrose waited until the new priest had exhausted his repertoire. "Father," he said finally, "I have a question to ask you. Is it or is it not written: 'If a man lay down his life for his friends, his soul shall be saved'?"

"It seems to me," Grigori answered, "that you are not altogether dead."

"Is that my fault? I did everything that had to be done in order to die, so that a dozen of my friends would get home alive and see their families and friends again, their wives, perhaps, or their children. Well, they got home, all right, but I was still alive. I could have concluded that my sacrifice was refused, but I didn't. There were sixty German corpses there to prove that I succeeded; and, what's more, I didn't receive even the smallest decoration for what I had done. Therefore, I have concluded that I am not of those who have received their reward in this world." And he had smiled, in self-mockery and at the same time, respectful, at least of the cassock.

Grigori was wary of men who went out of their way to provoke. It was not impossible that Ambrose had been sent by some police organization. Of one thing Grigori was certain, however: that Ambrose's military exploits were authentic. The details he supplied had proved that to the priest's satisfaction.

"I know your regiment," Grigori said. "I was in combat only fifteen kilometers to the north of you."

They had been comrades-in-arms; and, so true is it that enmity unites, that the two men were immediately drawn together by a warm mutual sympathy which even their membership in the same Church had not been able to create. They exchanged information on the parish, on the authorities, and on their hopes, at least for the immediate future. Within a few days, Ambrose, without receiving the title of church warden (for that could be conferred only with the approval of the civil authorities) began to exercise the functions of that office. He sold candles at a profit, piously carried the blessed bread, kept the floor of the church shining, polished the candelabra and the ikons, took charge of repairing the roof, the porch, and the cupola, and gave Grigori the benefit of his influence in his clashes with the Party and the municipal government. Grigori, in return, listened politely to many tellings of the story of the truckload of explosives and of the twelve friends who had lived to return home after the war. When Ambrose had too much to drink, the story was accompanied by tender tears as he thought of the boys he had saved. "I am a great sinner," he said, "and my sins are still multiplying. But when I appear before God, those twelve young men will intercede for me. They will hold the Book in their hands, and they will say: 'Is it written or not that if a man lay down his life for his friends, his soul shall be saved? Well, Ambrose gave his life to save ours.' They will be unanimous in that, I'm sure. Then God will say to me, 'Go in peace, good sinner.' "

When the first warmth of the friendship had cooled, Ambrose's insistence on always having the last word began to irritate Grigori. The priest sought means to spoil his friend's pleasure in always being right, and he soon thought that he had discovered a way. "What about the sixty Germans?" he asked Ambrose. "Do you think that they will also intercede for you?"

"The Germans died in battle," Ambrose answered, unperturbed. "They will go to heaven, so long as they committed no atrocities against defenseless civilians. What could they possibly say against me? I killed them just as they killed my officers and my comrades. They came with death, and they departed with death."

"But you," Grigori insisted, "killed them by trickery. You entered their lines carrying a white flag, and you had already lighted the fuse!"

"Father, it's hard to believe that you and I were in the same war. It's true that I had attached a white flag to the cab of my truck, but do you think they stopped firing? They only hesitated for a moment. Their fingers were not quite so steady on their triggers. They were asking themselves or their friends what to do. Thus, out of the rain of bullets aimed at me, there were only one or two drops missing. And, fortunately, those were the bullets that had my name on them."

"Let's admit," Grigori continued, "that the Germans will not blame you. What about their mothers? Don't you think they'll be there to accuse you before the throne of the living Christ?"

"I think it would be a serious mistake for mothers to complain to Christ," Ambrose replied gravely. "After all, Christ didn't have much pity even on his own."

Thus they argued for hours on end, and Ambrose always

got the better of Grigori, simply because his theological perspectives were at once so narrow and so certain.

Grigori, moreover, was certain that Ambrose was a good man. He was not the first such that Grigori had ever encountered; but, until then, Grigori had never suspected that goodness could be a stumbling block to him, traitor that he was. Some of his parishioners were good. That was their own business. The origins of their goodness were too lowly for Grigori to be disturbed. Ambrose's goodness, however, was different; it existed in combination with courage, patriotism, a cunning mind, and an inflexible will—all virtues which Grigori had always admired passionately. Ambrose never spoke an unkind word; yet no one ever accused him of cowardice. He was sometimes generous, but he asked for nothing in return. He reigned like a despot over his family; but his children, nephews and nieces and grandchildren all worshiped him. He was the protector of the poor, yet he did not wish to be honored for it, and he had a horror of excess in gratitude as in all else. "Thank you and good-by are two expressions that rhyme well together," he often said. And it amused him that they did not rhyme at all.

Though his faith was simple, Ambrose himself was not an ignorant man. He read the Bible and the bulletins from the Patriarchate, wearing the glasses which, because of his pointed ears, gave him a mephistophelian look.

So far as the things of this world were concerned, Ambrose was a convinced skeptic. When anyone spoke to him of politics, or economics, or the success of government policies, he only scratched the nape of his neck with a respectful air. Although his own morals were of traditional austerity, one of his favorite charities was to help unwed mothers. And, most remarkable of all, no one ever suspected him of being the unnamed father in any of these cases. The rigorous morality of his life, the heroic nature of his army service, the decency and modesty of his language, his habit of reading pious works without bothering to conceal the fact, caused some of the old women of the parish to begin whispering that Ambrose was a saint. Grigori was delighted when Alona, who acted as his intelligence agent, reported the rumor to him. Finally, he thought, I have found a way to teach Ambrose a lesson. And to Ambrose, he said: "Well now, Ambrose, is your canonization going according to schedule?"

Ambrose looked up, smiled, and reddened slightly. "It is sinful for you to make fun of those silly old women. They do not know that they are blaspheming. They are the poor in spirit."

Grigori said no more on the subject.

When it was discovered that Ambrose had cancer, Grigori hoped that his suffering would exhaust his gentle patience. But he was disappointed. Ambrose agreed to take certain medicines, and refused others, all with the greatest serenity. Toward the end, his body became an object of repugnance to most people; but Ambrose himself only made pious jokes about it. "Poor carcass," he said. "you've served me well in spite of everything. I can't blame you for being a bit too eager to turn into dust. After all, it's your destiny."

Grigori visited Ambrose with true priestly devotion. He sat on the bed, indifferent to the stench, and became an object of admiration throughout the parish. "Our pastor is a real pastor," the people said, "and not an ingrate." But despite the hours spent with his church warden, Grigori was unable to turn the conversation to the subject of death, or to the salvation of souls, or to any one of the points concerning which those who are about to die normally experience doubt or anguish. Instead, they had spoken of the future of the parish, of repairs to the church, of the children who must be given a religious education despite regulations to the contrary. "When I am dead," Ambrose said, "continue to hold services on Tuesday night. The authorities know nothing about it, and it gives a chance to those who like to go to church without being noticed. When I am dead, there will be no point in your continuing to visit the Therapontov family. They are not believers, and they only let you talk to the children because they owe me money. Let us hope that God's word has germinated in their little heads. When I am dead . . ."

Ambrose's deathbed advice made Grigori realize to what extent he had depended on his friend for his work in the parish. He resented him all the more for it. Ambrose's activities, for that matter, were covered in great detail in Grigori's files. The priest found it irritating that, thanks to his illness, Ambrose would escape the punishment he so richly deserved.

Ambrose grew weaker by the day. Surgical procedures had been unsuccessful; but Ambrose himself had never hoped to recover. At death's first whisper, he had answered "present"; and he had consented to treatment only to avoid scandalizing his family.

One morning, during the period when Grigori's hopes had been raised concerning his own future, Grigori learned that Verniak's promotion had changed nothing concerning Alona's fate. It had been decided that she would live. He was stunned by the blow, as though someone had brought an oar crashing down on his head or had stamped on his hand with a heavy boot. For an instant, and in an instant, his resignation and his self-renunciation vanished: "A lifetime wasted, a man condemned to mediocrity." Then, with bitterness in his heart, barely in control of his emotions, Grigori went to visit Ambrose.

Ambrose and his family occupied two rooms in an apartment they shared with other families. As soon as Grigori entered, he smelled the odor. In the first room, it was relatively faint, for the windows had been opened and the smell of orange peel frying on the stove diluted it. Ambrose's wife, two of his daughters, and his young son (who served Mass on Sundays) were busy with household chores. Several children—of indeterminate number and sex—were playing quietly in a corner.

They are waiting impatiently for his death, Grigori told himself, and his irritation increased by a degree. No, they are not waiting for it. They are keeping busy. They are acting as though death has already come and gone.

Everyone rose when Grigori entered the room. He raised his hand. "Please, don't disturb yourselves. I've come to see Ambrose." Within himself, he thought: not one of them has a heart. A splendid example of Christian education. Ambrose has done well.

Grigori was not unaware of the hypocrisy of his anger. But the cause of it was not the women or the pale boy with frightened eyes, or the children with their wooden toys, or even their attitude of waiting for death and being indifferent to it. He was angry at Ambrose himself, who remained confident and serene in the midst of his suffering and his own stench.

The second room was dark. The shutters had been closed and the heavy draperies drawn. The only light came from a candle burning before an ikon, from cracks in the shutters, from a small opening in the draperies. Otherwise, the room was in pestilential gloom.

The odor does not matter, Grigori said to himself. My nose will become accustomed to it as quickly as my eyes will to the darkness. But how can I instill bitterness into this man in the few hours that may be left before he escapes me forever?

Grigori bent toward the white sheets, toward the eyes glistening in the dark, to discern Ambrose's position in bed. He was half sitting, supported by pillows behind his back and under his heavy forearms.

"Bless me, Father."

Mechanically, Grigori blessed him.

"How do you feel, Ambrose?" He asked the question fiercely, with an anxious greediness, as though he himself, dark, bearded, and strong, were Death.

"Not well. Not well at all," Ambrose answered energetically, almost joyously.

Grigori sat on the bed and felt the unhealthy warmth of the body which would soon be cold. "I'm sorry to hear it," he said. It was true. Ambrose's Christian death would be a defeat for him. Yet, he had seen many men commend themselves to Christ with their last breath, and, as he had administered the last rites to them in the face of death, he had inwardly mocked them. Ambrose, however, was different. He was a warrior. He was sinking into oblivion while standing at attention, like a captain on the bridge of his ship. He had asked for none of the consolations of religion from his pastor, for he carried them all within himself.

Grigori searched for something to say and found nothing. Ambrose's death would be a failure both of the priest and of the anti-priest.

As Grigori's eyes became accustomed to the gloom, he saw Ambrose's jaws moving. "Are you eating?" he asked.

"I'm chewing on my tongue."

There was silence again. Ambrose began no argument on the theological significance of Jonah in the belly of the whale, or on the nature of the happiness of the poor in spirit, or on the sin which could not be pardoned. Grigori reflected, with an intensity equal to that which prevailed when he lay sleepless in his bed, in the quiet of a satisfied body. Who is this man? Who is "Ambrose"? If we admit as a working hypothesis the truth of Christianity, will he be saved? Who, exactly, will be saved?

This was a new question. He answered: The just will be saved, the good, and the ardent. The most difficult problem in Christianity is to know whether a man must have all three of those qualities simultaneously, or if only one of them is enough. There are times when gentleness and ardor are incompatible. In which category does Ambrose belong? His gentleness is so measured, his justice so limited, his ardor so pagan—will he therefore be damned? Who is damned?

This also was a new question for Grigori, even in the childish, essential form in which he enunciated it. He rested his hand on Ambrose's knee and answered himself. Those who are damned are the Pharisees, the weak and the violent—which is to say, the just, the gentle, and the ardent. Such are the contradictions in the Christian sect. Ambrose has killed men by the dozens. He has never pretended to be a martyr. And he is absolutely sure of being saved. Under these conditions, Ambrose will be damned.

Grigori felt a spark of hope. He bent toward the dying man, whose features were now barely recognizable. The white of the pillow, the ravages of age, both gave a strangely alien cast to the face already marred by the hand of death.

"Ambrose," Grigori said softly, "it is time for you to think of your reception in the hereafter."

Grigori felt no tremor in the knee under his hand. He felt only the round, bony kneecap and the tendons. Nothing more.

"Yes."

"Before we begin," Grigori said, "you must not only review your past life and the many sins you have committed, but, also and above all, you must examine your conscience; not for acts you may have committed, but for the way in which you judge such acts. As you know, a man who wishes to save his soul will lose it."

He waited rather nervously for Ambrose to contradict him. But there was no response. The dying man continued to chew.

"Let me talk to you less like a father and more like a brother," Grigori continued. "A brother who regards the salvation of your soul as a matter of personal concern to him. Have you ever considered that the certainty you have on this subject may in itself be sinful? After all, you are not an innocent child. In the sight of God, every man, no matter how pure he may be, is a mass of uncleanliness. And you, in spite of this, claim to be certain that you will enter the Kingdom of Heaven. Are you equally certain that there is no pride in your conviction?"

No answer.

"Ambrose, consider that our Church oscillates between two extremes: the pagans, and the Pharisees. Has it occurred to you that the way in which you worship—for instance killing sixty Germans in one stroke—may be tainted by paganism? Can't you see that your attitude toward your own salvation is that of a Pharisee?"

Ambrose answered, without quotations or hesitation: "God has promised."

Grigori's temper began to rise. The faith of this man was like a rock, a grain of wheat, an egg: closed upon itself, and rich within. "Is that sufficient reason for you to tempt God, Ambrose?"

Silence. After a few minutes, Ambrose whispered that he would like to confess his sins, take Communion, and then receive Extreme Unction. Grigori grasped the situation. Ambrose had passed the stage at which theological discussions with a specialist were of interest to him. He was therefore rejecting the expert and asking for the technician. Grigori answered: "I will have to come back later. I don't have the holy oils with me, or the wheat."

Grigori spent the day immersed in the routine of the parish, waiting for nightfall. He believed that a period of waiting would put Ambrose in the proper frame of mind, a technique he had learned in the service. If only Ambrose did not die. At least, not yet.

It was already dark when Grigori placed the articles he

would need into the shabby bag Alona had given him for carrying the sacred accessories: the censer, the stole, the ciborium, the golden spoon, candles, the Bible, a saucer of wheat wrapped in a napkin, the cruet, and seven small brushes. Carrying the bag, he went out into the street.

Grigori liked to walk after dark. There were fewer passersby, and his cassock was less conspicuous in the night. Only his cross swinging at the end of its chain, caught the light from shutterless windows and from the few lighted signs of the town.

Further up the street, there was a man dying, and dying in unique serenity. Unique, at least, in Father Grigori's experience. And I? Grigori asked himself suddenly. How will I die? Despite twinges of rheumatism, death seemed remote. I am only thirty-five, Grigori reminded himself. I have my entire life to live over a second time.

Hours had passed since Grigori's earlier visit, and the atmosphere of Ambrose's room was no longer the same. The odor was more suffocating, the heat more humid, both announcing the approaching end. Grigori asked that an oil lamp be brought. It was placed on the floor so as not to cause discomfort to the dying man. Immediately, terrible shadows danced on the walls of the room. Ambrose, still half reclining against his pillows, his eyes half closed, seemed in a coma; but when Grigori asked if he recognized him, Ambrose replied, in obvious irritation and in a perfectly clear voice, "Don't speak if you have nothing to say, priest. Hurry and get about your work."

The family left the room and closed the door. Grigori was alone with the enemy.

Ambrose's confession was the first matter to be disposed of. "If you do not feel well enough to answer," Grigori suggested, "blink your eyes for 'yes.' If your answer is 'no,' do not blink."

An expression almost of irony crossed Ambrose's face. He blinked immediately.

His nose cast a shadow which deformed his cheek. Grigori had the increasingly strong impression that the body of this man was on the point of dissolution; that the fortuitous mixture of flesh and nerves, lighted planes and dark openings, was about to resolve itself into chaos. But Ambrose's will was firm. His answers came, one after the other, without hesitation: yes, no, no, yes . . .

"Is there any sin," Grigori asked, "that you have concealed in earlier confessions and that you wish to confess now?"

Ambrose did not blink. His visibly yellowing eyes remained turned toward the priest.

"Do you feel that you are at peace with the Lord?"

An energetic blink.

"Do you feel any resentment at the nearness of death?"

The eyelids remained motionless.

"Are you sincerely contrite for your past sins?"

A blink.

Grigori sighed. He rose slowly. His square hand placed the end of the stole on Ambrose's head. The dying man closed his eyes and caught his breath, like a man who truly awaits the judgment of his God. It was believed, Grigori recalled, that God's mercy flowed down the length of the stole, like water in a pipe.

When Grigori spoke, it was in his priest's voice, grave, gentle: "May the Lord our God, Jesus Christ, in the grace and generosity of his love for mankind, pardon whatever sins you may have committed, my son." Grigori sighed once more, and then continued: "And I, unworthy priest though I am, by the power vested in me, forgive you all your sins, in the name of the Father, and of the Son, and of the Holy Ghost. Amen."

The priest removed his stole. Since he stood between the

dying man's face and the lamp, Ambrose's features, seen in the bright shadow, seemed to have regained their regularity, that primitive harmony which they had once possessed. Ambrose exhaled, and that expression of relief accentuated the look of peace on his face. Soon, however, the veins became visible on his sweat-covered brow, and he whispered, "Quickly!"

Grigori stepped back from the bed to the chest on which he had placed the covered ciborium. Once more, shadows danced on the walls, and Grigori heard Ambrose's almost imperceptible death rattle. He returned to the bed with the ciborium in his hand. In a loud voice, he asked: "Do you want me to ask your family to come in?"

Ambrose blinked, indifferently.

Grigori called out, and the family—they had been waiting for this moment—entered immediately in single file: the son, the three women, and the children. The boy stepped forward quickly with a napkin, fearful above all else that the sacred species might fall from his father's lips.

Grigori uncovered the portable ciborium and lifted its hinged lid. Ambrose's eyes were on his. Grigori bent over the bed and, at that instant, Ambrose's mouth flew open so mechanically, with a movement so similar to that of the ciborium's lid, that Grigori wondered whether it had not been caused by the relaxation of the muscles in death. The similarity between the two movements would have made him smile had he not been wholly occupied with his functions. Ambrose's yellow eyes could barely be seen behind his drooping lids. Was he already dead? Grigori hesitated for a moment. Then he saw Ambrose's brow wrinkle with impatience. He dipped the spoon into the man's open mouth, among his teeth, some yellow, others black and rotted, and a few of gold, and then withdrew it, slowly, with becoming solemnity. Ambrose's mouth snapped shut like that of a man whose greed had been satisfied. Again, Grigori almost laughed. Instead, he turned toward Ambrose's family with the look of a man who had just won a great victory. The boy, the women, the children, had not shed a tear. Instead, they had watched what took place with expressions which, to Grigori, seemed uncertain, divided as they were between respect for death and respect for the priest.

Grigori replaced the ciborium on the chest, closed the lid carefully—there was an audible click—and turned toward the small table on which he had placed the other accessories: the Bible, the cruet, the saucer of wheat, and the seven cotton brushes. He turned his head slightly, and Ambrose's son came forward. In his hand, he held a prayer book, and his lips trembled. He was not accustomed to singing, and he was afraid that his voice would break. He believed, no doubt, that a false note would render the sacrament null.

The rite of extreme unction began. The priest and the boy chanted in low voices. The three women, their hands folded on their stomachs, their heads bowed, remained motionless, without tears. The children had grouped in a corner, sniffing, whispering. The other room was filled with relatives and a large number of friends, and their moans and quickly stifled sobs could be heard in the dying man's room. Suddenly, the outer door of the apartment was pushed open and a coarse voice, the voice of the world, cried: "My God! It stinks in here!"

There was a chorus of scandalized reprimands, followed by an uneasy silence. In the sickroom, no one seemed to have heard the disturbance. The boy's voice had steadied. Grigori was chanting softly and modestly, but without depriving the liturgy of its pomp. Traditionally, seven priests were required for the ceremony, and Grigori regretted that there were not seven present so that the ceremony might be more impressive and better reflect the majesty of the Church.

"Lord," he prayed, "bless these oils so that, by their application, they may heal and deliver from all passions, from all impurity of soul and of body, and from all evil, so that your name may be glorified, Father, Son, and Holy Ghost. Amen."

Seven times were read extracts from the Acts of the Apostles and the Gospels; and seven times Grigori prayed that the holy oil might heal the body and the soul of God's servant, Ambrose.

Then the priest dipped a brush into the cruet held within reach by Ambrose's son and anointed the forehead, the nostrils, the lips, the palms, and the upper side of the hands. Ambrose lay quietly, consenting, yet a stranger, to what was being done to his body. It mattered little whether it was being honored or mistreated. He felt neither hope nor fear. He merely waited for his God to come down upon him in a different, less material form than the bread and wine he had just received. Thus his body, already decomposing and smelling of the grave, of no use to the soul which still inhabited it, would be consecrated, inside and out, to the God of its former master. At each anointing—there were seven, for Grigori took the parts of the six other priests who were not present—the priest prayed into the reverential silence which filled the room. No one heard the horns of the automobiles below in the modern, communist street, as the priest spoke the sacrosanct, almost magical formula: "Holy Father, healer of souls and bodies, cure thy servant Ambrose of the spiritual and corporeal ills which beset him, and make him strong once more through the grace of your Christ."

Grigori then placed the brush into the cruet and, taking the Bible with both hands, he opened it and turned it so that the open pages faced the floor. Slowly, he moved the book over the face of the dying man, as though it were a mask. The cotton brush had been a new one, and the oil had flowed generously from it. Ambrose's face, like Grigori's hands, glistened with the sacred fluid. Grigori was careful not to stain the pages of the book as he touched it to Ambrose's forehead, on which seven successive crosses had been traced.

After a final prayer, the book was closed, and the visitors were allowed to enter the room and kiss the hand of the man who was about to die. It was still warm, too warm; but, despite all the prayers and anointings, and despite the imposition of the Book, which symbolized the imposition of the hands of Christ, it would soon be cold as ice.

Grigori stood at the head of the bed and watched as the men and women filed past. Many of them were crying, and many of them (often the very same ones) left hurriedly after kissing, with obvious distaste, Ambrose's oil-soaked hand. Nonetheless, they had kissed it; and beyond their disgust Grigori read a thought which displeased him profoundly. "A good man is dying," they seemed to say, "and tomorrow we will be more alone in this world. He loved us as we loved him."

The ranking Party official of the region was also there, and he greeted Grigori with a timidity which surprised everyone. Grigori responded to the greeting of his comrade with a clerical bow.

Ambrose lay still, glistening with oil. When the procession of friends and relatives had ended, Grigori closed the door to the room and, turning his back to the bed, began to put his accessories in order. He could hear hushed voices whispering anticipatory condolences in the other room.

Suddenly, a voice spoke from behind the priest; Ambrose's voice, cracked but almost firm, colorless, but triumphant, as though already disembodied: "Would you kindly open the window."

For a moment, Grigori was seized by a grotesque panic. Had there been a miracle? Ambrose's politeness had lent a note of frightening reality to his request. Grigori turned.

Ambrose had not changed his position, but now his eyes

and his mouth were open. He was looking straight ahead, as though he thought the window were located there. "Well, open it," he repeated. "I would like some light, some air."

Grigori opened the draperies, opened the double window, threw back the shutters, and leaned out. It was dark outside, and a cool wind blew into the room. The flame of the oil lamp flickered, near the floor, then that of the vigil light near the ceiling. For the third time, shadows moved across the walls. Grigori turned toward Ambrose. With the window open, the light had changed. The oil on his forehead and hands glistened less than before. He was breathing with a slight rattle.

"Please, I beg you," Ambrose said, "open the window."

Then Grigori understood that there had been no miracle. He was strangely relieved. For a few minutes—perhaps even for an hour—Ambrose would feel better; then his agony would begin.

"I have already opened the window," Grigori replied. "Apparently you can no longer see or feel. Can you hear me?"

Ambrose blinked his eyes. His lips trembled. Was he able to smile? Grigori wondered. If so, it was in a spirit of amused fatalism. After several unsuccessful attempts, Ambrose was able to catch his breath. He spoke: "Too bad."

Grigori would have been willing to accept resignation; but humor, or what appeared to be humor, exasperated him. He sat on the edge of the bed, leaned toward Ambrose with a shocking question on his lips: "Ambrose, Ambrose! Are you not afraid of dying?"

Ambrose's eyes had been fixed on the ceiling. Now they turned slowly toward Grigori and stopped when they had reached his left temple. "Afraid?" Ambrose asked in an easily audible whisper. "Only the ignorant are afraid. I have read many books. I have read Saint Makarios. Saint Makarios of Alexandria. In a little while, my angel will come to comfort me. He will stay with me for three days, then I will go to heaven. I will see the Lord God. I will visit paradise. I will praise God for six days, and I will forget my suffering. But I will not forget my sins. I will go back to the Lord, and greet him. He will send me down again. I will visit hell and mourn the damned for thirty days. On the last day, I will return to heaven, and the Lord will give me a place according to my merits. So, there."

Grigori could contain himself no longer. He leaned closer, until his nose almost touched that of the dying man. He placed his hands on Ambrose's shoulders and began to shake him violently. "You fool!" he cried, "there is no heaven and no hell! There is no God! These are old wives' tales. In a few minutes, you will be dead! Your body will rot, and there will be nothing left. You will feel nothing, think nothing. You will no longer exist. I am not a priest, do you understand? I am a government agent, paid to spy on your religious activities! Do you hear me? Do you hear me?"

This was Grigori's great temptation, and he succumbed. The temptation of the priest and that of the agent had been the same; and, in a moment of weakness, he betrayed both missions simultaneously.

He drew back and looked at Ambrose, torn between a wild desire for the dying man to have heard him, and the most fervent hope that he had not. There was no sign of a reaction. If anything, Ambrose seemed weaker than before. Was it an illusion? No. His muscles were tensing, his body was beginning to arch. He was no longer breathing; he was gathering air in his lungs. Was it his death agony? Grigori drew back again. Had Ambrose understood? Was it the fear of death that had stiffened his body?

Suddenly, Ambrose's eyes were upon Grigori, and from his mouth there came a cry, hoarse but resounding: "My son! My son! Do not believe him! He is a false priest! He is a—"

He went no further. Grigori seized a pillow and, with both

hands, held it over Ambrose's face, just as, a while before, he had held the Book over his peaceful brow. Ambrose gave two quick jerks, then was quiet. Grigori pressed down for several seconds more, to be on the safe side. Then he rose, holding the pillow with which he had corrected his error. There was a drop of spittle on it. Slowly, the priest wiped it with the sleeve of his frayed cassock.

ACT V

It may please you to learn, Comrade Dobermann, that the man your arguments won over is not an intellectual minus habens, *but an excellent priest who, if he had been allowed to take vows, would have enjoyed a brilliant career in the Church. What more can I tell you? Now I know the truth. God does not exist. Religion is nothing more than superstition. The Church is an organ of exploitation. I can no longer continue deceiving our people. They must now look to the leaders of the Party for the spiritual guidance which they require, and I place myself entirely at your disposal to assist in undoing all the harm that I have done to mankind.*

I am, Comrade Professor, fraternally yours in Marx.

It was the bottom line of Grigori's mission. Twenty years earlier, in an intense spirit of simultaneous exaltation and repugnance, he had conceived of a different ending.

Now, both relieved and disgusted, he folded the darkened pages of his letter and slipped them into an envelope. Nadson had given him Dobermann's address, and he knew it by heart. He wrote it on the envelope, and moistened the flap with the tip of his finger as his mother had taught him so long ago. He turned to Alona. "Here is something to be mailed."

Alona raised her eyes. "Tomorrow? Right now?"

"Yes, immediately."

She stood, took the letter, and turned the doorknob. All her movements had a significance of which she herself was not aware. The following day, her husband would be gone, and she would never see him again. Poor Alona, Grigori thought. Foolish Alona. She did not even look at the address.

When she had gone, Grigori rose from his chair and cracked his knuckles. He felt as though he were on vacation. He should have visited Theodore, who was on his deathbed; and Anthony, who had beaten his pregnant daughter; and Tatiana, Irene, Anastasia. There seemed no purpose in it. He would not go.

Alona returned. The letter had been mailed. The last card had been played. The mission had been accomplished. Tomorrow, freedom.

Grigori spent the afternoon pacing the house, going out into the yard to see if there were any eggs, returning. Alona watched him in silence, aware of his agitation, but asking no questions. She never asked questions. Instead, she recited psalms, moving her lips silently. Grigori felt a sudden impulse to strike her. He opened a book. Dobermann would not receive the letter until the following day.

Grigori would not say his prayers that night. He had already decided. But, after supper, when Alona rose from the table and went to stand before the ikons, as she did every day at that hour, Grigori did not have the heart to persist in his resolution. It would be the last time, he told himself. Moreover, what explanation could he possibly give? He had already realized that he would never dare tell her the truth. Such was the power of a good woman. So be it. He would say his prayers.

They prayed. When their common prayers were done and Alona had begun to wash the dishes, Grigori continued alone, standing, kneeling, prostrating himself on the floor, mumbling words which he no longer understood. His thoughts were elsewhere. For the first time in more than fifteen years, the atheist prayed badly.

The prayers come, he reflected, without my thinking of them. How long will it take at the university for me to forget them? It will be pleasant not to have to go through this ritual every night . . .

He went to bed in a mood of bitter elation.

The next day was Thursday. Would he receive a summons from Dobermann that evening?

Grigori remained in the house that morning, pretending to work on his theological thesis. During the afternoon, he received a message asking him to visit Theodore. He refused. The family insisted, and finally he went, but resentfully. Theodore did nothing to improve his mood. The man did not want to die. He clutched desperately at life. By evening, he pushed his presumption to the point of feeling better.

When Grigori returned to his house, he found there had been no message from Dobermann. It was too soon to expect one, he assured himself. He had not allowed enough time.

That evening, the domestic routine was resumed. He discussed with Alona the events of the day, read her the life of a saint, and omitted, as he always did with a certain amount of ostentation, to lock the door. ("There is nothing to steal," he always said.) He prayed better than he had the preceding night; then, he went to bed and took Alona into his arms.

He awoke during the night, after several hours of sleep, for one of his meditations. His body was satisfied. The candle burned before the ikon. He heard Alona's deep breathing from the other bed and, occasionally, the crowding of Petia the cock. All these things he found conducive to reflection.

He thought of his letter. Were my lies as close as possible to the truth? he asked himself. Am I certain that I did not exaggerate or show too much zeal? Did I perhaps inject too much civilized humor, even though communists are incapable of understanding it?

He thought of his mission. I am, he recalled, an intelligence agent disguised as a priest. If I used those diabolical terms before a Christian, what would he think? That I am a contemptible, vile, filthy, twisted, immoral man. An essentially evil man. Am I? No. I am an officer. I could have had a brilliant career in the regular army. I am a man who uses his mind. I am capable of making decisions. I am a leader. I am capable of changing the course of events. I may appear to be contemptible, in the present circumstances; but I am not vile. Ten years ago, I killed Ambrose without any hesitation; and quite rightly, too. That is an indication of something. On the other hand, here I am, forty-five years old, and they want to make me a professor of atheism. Obviously, they regard me as a mediocrity. Am I one, maybe?

Immediately, age asserted itself, and Grigori told himself: Those who think that I am are idiots. Specifically, the idiots who are now at the head of the service. In Grouztchik's time, things would have been different.

Then:

I'm starting to prattle like an old woman. The service cannot be wrong, because the service is part of the regime, and the regime is infallible.

Twenty years earlier, Grigori had spoken the same words in all seriousness. Not a word had changed; but now they were uttered in irony. How paradoxical it is, Grigori reflected, that the Church, that bastion of error, has been responsible for the loss of my naïveté.

He frowned. It disturbed him to think that he was no longer naïve. It was not only a dangerous situation, but also, and above all, one unbecoming to a loyal citizen. To lose one's naïveté was somehow bourgeois, decadent, archaic. It was an unclean luxury—like adultery, or a French operetta.

Grigori turned in his bed, as though trying to find a position of greater innocence, but there was none. Once a man's eyes have been opened, he can never go back, no matter how strong the nostalgia for his lost purity.

When, exactly, he wondered, did I compromise with intelligence?

There was no way to tell. He thought longingly of the pink-cheeked killer he had been twenty years earlier. But his longing did not exclude an acute awareness of the irony involved. Lying in the darkness on his back, facing the candle-lit ikon, Father Grigori smiled. A man can lose his soul through foolishness, he thought. But the Church has saved mine. Then he slept.

No word from Dobermann came the next day. Grigori wondered what could have happened. Could the mail service have lost either his own letter or Dobermann's answer?

There was nothing on Saturday morning. Nothing on Saturday afternoon. A strange sense of relief mingled with Grigori's frustration.

I will have to give my farewell performance tomorrow, he told himself. He was no longer so much on edge. It was stupid of me to think Dobermann would answer immediately. Have I forgotten what bureaucrats are like? It might be a month before I hear anything.

Saturday night, as always, he went to church for the vigil of the sabbath. The church was dark, for Grigori never allowed more candles than were absolutely necessary, and the electric lights were unused. It saved electricity. Moreover, there was always an army officer or an official of some sort at services, obviously determined to remain inconspicuous. If there had been much light, he would not have come.

The sacraments were not administered during the vigils. It was merely a session of prayers, chanted in the ancient modes by two old women whose silhouettes were barely visible in the gloom.

With a slow step, dragging his feet, the censer in his hand billowing out clouds of incense, Grigori went around the church, censing all the ikons in turn. This is for you, Gabriel, Archangel; and for you, Saint Vladimir of Kiev. Then each of the faithful received a stroke with the censer. For you, my little dove; and for you, you old thief; and for you, my secret children, seed of the Church.

Through the window, Grigori could see the growing darkness. Within the church, the cracked voices of the two old women rose piously, effortlessly. There was no noise from the street. This, Grigori thought, is peace.

Fifty times in succession, the cantor intoned in his monotonous and nasal voice, "Kyrie eleison, Kyrie eleison . . ."

Like the strokes of a whip, Grigori told himself, as a shiver went through him. The flagellation of grace. Again. Again. Will I survive until the last stroke? Lord, have mercy! Lord—I am talking nonsense.

After the service, Misha, the altar boy, went to confession so that he might receive Communion the following day. He was eight and a half, and no longer a child in the eyes of the Church. He was not allowed to receive the Eucharist unless his sins had been absolved.

Grigori heard his confession behind a screen, in darkness.

A single candle burned in the great wooden chandelier made for fifty. The child whispered: "Father, I punched Boris in the nose. He bled. You should have seen him! Do you know why? Because he said it was bad to go to church!"

"Well done, my boy. You did the right thing."

Misha knelt, his large eyes on the priest who was his Saviour. Then he bowed his blond head and joined his hands around a candle. According to the custom, a bank note was wrapped around the candle. A very small bank note.

Grigori raised the hand which held the stole and looked down at the child; at the crown of blond hair; the childish nose protruding, the hands which, although still small, knew how to fight, and now were clutching a holy candle; the crossed thumbs. He lowered the end of the stole onto Misha's bowed head, like night falling upon the world, like grace raining down from heaven. "I, unworthy priest though I am, by the power vested in me . . ."

Unworthy? Grigori asked. Very unworthy. He asked again: Unworthy? Not as unworthy as all that.

It was done. Absolution was given, and the child rose to his feet, pure as on the day of his birth, pure as Adam in the Garden of Paradise.

"Thank you, Father," he said, and ran quickly from the church. A moment later, he was back, blushing. "Father, I forgot." He held out the wrapped candle. Grigori smiled and took the candle. The bank note was new, and it crackled under his fingers. Misha said: "Good night, Father." It was said in a respectful, but almost familiar, tone. Grigori, with the stole removed from his neck, was no longer more than a priest. He was no longer an archangel, come down on earth to reward and to punish.

"Good night, Misha."

Misha disappeared through the door. That night, he would sleep well and, in the morning, he would awaken joyfully.

Before the service, he would resist the temptation to slap his sister. Then he would go to the church. He would receive Communion and, throughout the day, he would think of himself as a winged angel. It would not be until evening, perhaps while he was playing in the street at sunset, that he might allow himself to fight with one of his friends; and then only if someone made fun of him or tried to cheat at marbles. Of such things was happiness made.

Naïveté, Grigori reflected, but naïveté of a different kind. Why? Because it was innocuous? No, that was too simple, too pragmatic an answer. There was another reason.

Grigori thought of these things as he extinguished the candles, put away the sacred books, and left the church, the key to which he carried in his pocket.

Next year, he told himself, the government will take Misha away from me and enroll him in a youth organization. Then they will teach him a different kind of naïveté. But what difference does it make? Next year, I will not be here. A month from now, I will not be here.

From a distance, he could see the lighted window of his small house. Alona was waiting for him. There would be no supper tonight. Not for him, because it was Saturday, and he must fast until after Sunday Mass; and not for Alona, out of a sense of conjugal unity. He was already slightly hungry; but it was such a familiar feeling that he had come to regard hunger as an old friend.

Soon, he reflected, I will no longer have to be hungry. Soon, I will be a free man. And, as he climbed the two wooden steps to his house, he smiled. Free! It was a term which had had meaning immediately after the war, when things had been less strict. Then, a man could find ideas, a place to live, women. But now, no one was free. A professor of atheism could have only one wife, and a proper wife, just as a priest could. He would be able to choose a young one, if he wished.

But would she respect him as Alona did? Would she be able to satisfy all his wants without irritating him by being too solicitous? Freedom, indeed!

Alona rose as he entered. He embraced her, holding her tightly against his chest, and kissed her as though he loved her. Then he pushed her away, feeling displeasure at his emotion and yet knowing that she would not take advantage of it.

They went to bed early, in their two narrow, parallel beds.

Grigori's waking thought on Sunday morning was of Misha, who, like Grigori himself, had had no supper the evening before and would have no breakfast that morning. And who, like Grigori, would receive Communion. For the child, the days on which he received Communion were feast days; not explosions of gladness like Christmas and Easter, but quietly joyful nonetheless.

The purity of that autumn morning, partly cloudy but bright, a slight chill in the air, reflected the supreme purity which would shortly descend upon the earth. Grigori thought of Misha again as he dressed, washed his face, dipped his beard in the iron basin, and then brushed that beard which, in a short while, would itself become an accessory in the liturgical mysteries.

In other circumstances, I would have been a boy like Misha, Grigori told himself. If I had been a believer, I would have broken many noses to defend the faith. Still, the idea of breaking noses for the faith is, from a Christian viewpoint, sinful. As obscure as the Bible is on many points, there is one thing that is quite clear; and that is the principle of non-resistance to evil which nevertheless we adopted from the Hindus. It's for that reason, of course, that Christianity—as Engels said—is a religion of slaves, a religion unworthy of the virtues and the heroism that it has created. The crusaders were bad Christians because they were real men. Misha is a crusader. If everything I wrote to Dobermann were true, I too could have been a crusader who, at the end of a life rich in Christian exploits, recognizes that there is a contradiction between his courage—that is, his virtue—and the weakness inherent in the religion of Jesus. I wonder if that realization would have made me fall into despair. I think not. I would have made use of courage all my life, and, if it turned out that I had done so in an unworthy cause, what difference would it have made? After all, Christ is not served by the sword; and the crusader who displayed his virtue rendered poor service to a cause which deserved exactly the kind of service that it got.

What decadent nonsense! I wouldn't be surprised if I were turning into a humanist. What has happened to the respect I had for our regime because it was able to transcend time? Less than three days ago, the idea of twenty-year missions was the most exciting thing in the world to me, even though I knew that things had changed enormously between Grouztchik's time and Nadson's. Well, none of this is important. If Nadson called me two weeks from now and said, "You will remain a priest for the rest of your life," I would be able to say, "Amen." What power would I have as a professor of atheism? But as pastor of a parish, I have supernatural powers; and, by God, I make use of them.

Grigori was displeased at having indulged himself in such pointless interior discussions. Part of the morning's joy had disappeared. Part of it, however, remained: the joy he felt as a child when his mother said, "Today is Sunday."

Grigori seldom thought of his childhood, but today memories of it bubbled forth from somewhere within him. He saw two faces. One was his own, horizontal on a pillow; the other, that of his mother, bent toward him. They were turned toward each other as toward a mirror.

Priests. His childhood had been peopled by clandestine

priests. There had been one in particular— But no, Grigori admonished himself. I won't think of that. I've been a priest long enough for me to be able to forgive him. I? A priest? Forgive? I can see that it really is time for me to take off the cassock; it's beginning to fade on me.

He smiled. His little joke had worked, to the extent that it disguised the interior anguish which he had glimpsed.

He left for church so as to arrive in time for the ten o'clock service. His walk through the streets was even more disagreeable than usual. Young rogues, wearing armbands, threw mud at his back. As the mud struck him, Grigori was suddenly conscious of all the humiliations he had suffered over the past twenty years. The accumulation of them was like a great burden which had without warning been placed on his shoulders, and he buckled under the weight of it.

I did not know I had suffered so much, he told himself.

It had always seemed so natural for him to suffer in the pursuit of his mission that he had never thought to weigh those sufferings. Today, however, he experienced an unaccustomed surge of revolt. He had been placed in an impossible position. He had been ordered to write to Dobermann that he was giving up the priesthood. And, at the same time, he had been ordered to continue his priestly duties.

Good God! he wondered. Is it possible that I misunderstood my orders?

A cold sweat covered his body, just as had happened when, as a young officer-candidate, he had been ordered to report to the colonel.

That cannot be, Grigori told himself. I understood them perfectly. What's wrong with me then? A case of nerves?

In order to calm himself, he began to think of the service he would perform in a short while: the succession of arbitrary gestures and mysterious formulas which would bring such consolation to the sixty-or-so persons of his congregation.

They are my men, he told himself. But I am theirs, also.

Grigori's church was a small wooden building surmounted by a cupola of faded gold. Over the portal was a discolored painting. The porch was uneven. He climbed the slanted steps, put the large key into the lock, turned it, and entered. Immediately, he felt surrounded, like the hero of a detective film who goes home to find his apartment filled with gangsters, or police. "Close the door," they say to him. "And we'd advise you not to try any tricks."

Grigori, in his church, was surrounded by Saviours and saints who looked down on him from all sides. The most important of them were directly opposite, on the ikonostasis: the Saviour, the Virgin, Saint Nicolas, Saint Michael, Saint Gabriel, a second Saviour with his twelve Apostles—the heavy artillery, as it were. Nearer, lying in wait behind the funeral table and the great candelabra, were another Virgin and a crucified Saviour. On the flanks were the cavalry and the infantry of heaven; the warrior saints for whom Grigori felt an unabashed sympathy: Saint Vladimir, Saint George, Saint Alexander Nevsky, and Saint Olga, a true Christian, who burned whole villages and their inhabitants to avenge the death of her pagan husband —an edifying story if ever there was one. It was by such means, Grigori told himself, that Christianity had been imposed on the world. There were the philosopher saints, for whom Grigori felt nothing. And the martyrs, whom he detested, and whose eyes always seemed to look away from one. Grigori usually managed to bypass the martyrs when he censed the ikons during the liturgy.

Ah, the martyrs! he said to himself. They let themselves become martyrs! The fools! And my mother? Wasn't she a martyr too, perhaps? Why shouldn't she have an ikon like the others?

Behind him, over the door, there was still another Saviour, his arms outstretched; and, on the window frames, door frames, and banners, another regiment of saintly images.

Grigori was transfixed by those golden stares. He crossed the church slowly, inhaling the familiar odor of dust and incense. He stopped before the Royal door, on the carpet of pink jute, and said the mandatory prayers asking God to give him the strength and the purity necessary to celebrate the mystery of the Mass. Grigori did not pray in a way that some Christians would have thought proper. There was no life in the words he pronounced. They went through his mind, one after the other, as though he were reading a text attentively. Grigori did not send his prayers heavenward, like so many rockets, because he was certain that the one to whom they were directed did not exist. Between prayers, the thought came to him that his orations were like mortar shells aimed at an unseen target. "Just drop the shell into the muzzle and don't worry about the rest."

But maybe being attentive was enough.

He was alone in the church; and yet he prayed and performed all the ritual gestures with meticulous care. He went to the small ikons of the Saviour and the Virgin hanging by pink ribbons on the frame of the Royal door and, lips puckered like those of a child, he kissed them piously one after the other. Then he turned toward the nave and, bowing, asked the (absent) faithful to forgive him his faults and to pray for him.

He entered the sanctuary, where there reigned a tranquillity which was familiar rather than solemn. He looked at his vestments, hanging on the patera, and said to himself in mingled certainty and astonishment: They are mine. I am the priest of this church! Who could believe it?

Three times, despite a pain in his back, he prostrated himself before the altar, reluctantly but piously. He kissed the altar and the metal sheet which covered the Holy Book. Then he began to vest for the Mass, putting on the sacerdotal ornaments and the honorific accessories the use of which he had been awarded for services rendered: the glaive and the scourge, both of them pieces of brocade symbolizing the sword of the Lord. Later, he would put on the miter, a crown of paste stones given to him by his congregation. As he vested, he recited verses from the psalms explaining the significance of the vestments and the virtues which they represented. Finally, he washed his hands in the small basin which Misha had laid out; and a flash of bitterness passed through him as he thought: "Never before the Royal door."

Grigori had now separated himself from the world. His chasuble isolated him like a high wall, like the cloud of Christ's Transfiguration. He was no longer a man. He was the instrument of God.

He turned toward the Table of Sacrifice at the left of the altar. It symbolized both the cave in which Jesus had been born and the Golgotha on which he had sacrificed himself. Five loaves of bread had been placed there by the church warden before dawn that morning. There were five because Jesus had fed five thousand persons with five loaves of bread. Each loaf was divided into two parts to commemorate the two natures of the Man-God. The upper part of each loaf bore the imprint of a cross and an abbreviated form of the motto "Conquer in Jesus Christ," which Grigori found agreeable because of its martial tone if not because of its meaning.

Grigori took the lance, cold to the still damp flesh of his hand, and plunged the blade into the first loaf, cutting a cube of bread from it in commemoration of the Lord God and Saviour, Jesus Christ. He took the cube into his hand. It represented the Lamb, and Grigori, in separating it from the rest of the loaf, repeated the prophetic words of Isaiah: "Like the calf led to the sacrifice, like the spotless lamb sheared in silence, he has not opened his lips, and he suffers in humility. Who can tell what is his nation?"

Grigori, in whispering the sacred words, replied within himself: In silence! In humility! You and I have nothing in common, Jesus of Nazareth.

Looking with irritation at the Lamb, Grigori placed it on the paten and cut it lengthwise and widthwise; then, furiously, he plunged the lance into its right side, in memory of the wounding of Christ on the cross.

"So much for you, Lamb!" he said.

He went back to the ciborium, into which he poured water and wine, symbolizing the water and wine which had flowed from Christ's side.

He heard the faithful entering the nave and taking their places, exchanging whispered remarks. An old man's feeble voice—that of the choirmaster—began to chant the prefatory prayers. To Grigori, these sounds seemed very distant. He was alone in the sanctuary; alone with the Lamb, as with an enemy on the field of battle.

The enemy, however, grew in numbers as Grigori himself created new ones by cutting a piece from the second loaf and placing it to the right of the Lamb, in honor of the Virgin, Mother of God. From the third loaf, there were nine pieces taken, in honor of the nine orders of saints: John the Baptist, the prophets, the Apostles, the Fathers of the Church, the martyrs, the holy men, the beggar saints, the grandparents of God saints Joachim and Anne, all the saints and Saint John Chrysostom. The nine pieces were placed to the left of the Lamb, in three rows. A piece was taken from the fourth loaf, in honor of the living; and from the fifth, in memory of the dead. The two pieces were then placed at the feet of the Lamb, one above the other. In the same place, he deposited the pieces cut from the loaves of those of the faithful who had asked him to pray, during the Mass, for their relatives and friends. The names of those to be mentioned had already been inscribed on a list which Grigori would soon read.

Thus the Communion of Saints was symbolically realized.

The Lamb, transfixed, was face to face with the priest, at the head of a mystical army. "Conquer in Jesus Christ!"

Grigori placed a metal star over the pieces of bread. Misha had entered soundlessly and was blowing upon the charcoal and incense in the censer. Grigori held out his hand without looking at Misha, and the altar boy, after kissing the outstretched hand, handed him the censer. Grigori took it, but raised an eyebrow; for Misha was late, and had not yet put on his cassock. The boy blushed. Grigori censed the star and the three pieces of cloth which he placed upon the star and then the chalice. He censed the star and chalice together, three times, in memory of the Three Wise Men. He offered thanks to God for having established the Eucharist, and asked the Father to accept the heavenly sacrifice of the sacrament about to be offered, to be mindful both of those who offered it and of those for the sake of whom it was offered, and to make Grigori, the unworthy priest, worthy of celebrating the divine mysteries.

Grigori saw no irony in such words. Does anyone believe in every assignment that he is given? he asked himself.

The true Mass was now about to begin. Grigori opened the Royal door, then bowed to the congregation. He felt himself to be even more tightly surrounded than when he had entered the church. Not only were the saints all around him, threatening him with their weapons, books, and banners; not only were the angels diving down upon him from the ceiling; not only was the Lamb, with his army of pieces of bread, attacking from the rear; but now, in front of him, sixty living beings, representing humanity, moved toward him and pushed him toward the altar by their prayers and signs of the cross and prostrations. This field of praying faithful, this forest of crosses traced by human hands—strange hands, made rebellious through humility; frightening hands which, in their measured movements from forehead to chest and from right shoulder to left, crucify their owners—this outpouring of childish fervor awakened in Grigori a feeling almost of terror. He looked upon those shining eyes, upon those ritually folded hands, and said:

"Peace be with you."

With his own hand, his guilty hand, he made the sign of the cross, not on himself, but over the people. By that sign, he conferred peace upon them; and, at the same time, he thought: May your kind of Christ be with you. You deserve nothing better.

The mixed choir—six women and three men, all with cracked voices which, nonetheless, possessed a harmony all their own—responded:

"And peace also to thy spirit," which was to say: "May your own Christ be with you."

Grigori entered the sanctuary and thought, while praying: My own Christ is not a poor wretch. If ever we meet, he'll have a few things to say to me, and I expect I'll get the worst of it.

As the choir chanted the Beatitudes, Grigori took note that each of them excluded him, rejected him categorically. None of the states of blessedness enumerated by the Gospel bore the slightest relationship to himself. He was not poor in spirit, or a peacemaker, or persecuted for the sake of his faith. What place could he have among those miserable beings, those cripples, those martyrs? Where would he stand in that gathering of believers among whom Christ the King worked his miracles?

I, Grigori told himself, belong to the other side.

He did not regret it, but neither was he proud of it. He simply acknowledged the fact, and then continued with the liturgy.

When the moment came for him to show the Gospel to the people, Grigori took the Book into his hands and held it before him, to symbolize Christ going forth to teach the world. An unexpected thought came into his mind: I am carrying Christ as the donkey carried him on Palm Sunday.

He read to the people from the Book—the Book in which, he recalled, there was nothing applicable to himself. And yet, he reflected, I am a Christ-bearer, like the donkey.

The people listened as he read, their heads bowed in reverence. The only man among them who did not believe in God was, for them, the voice of God. I am, Grigori told himself, the man whom their Christ has repudiated from all eternity.

After the reading of the Gospel, there were new prayers. Then, as the remainder of the service was open only to those who had been baptized, the priest solemnly announced, in a pompous and menacing voice: "The catechumens must leave! The catechumens must leave! Guard the door!

No one moved, for everyone had been baptized, but it amused Grigori, as he prayed, to think that he, of all men, had the power to eject the non-baptized from the church, just as, on the day of the Final Judgment— What foolishness! he told himself.

Grigori would willingly have lingered over these problems, but there was no time. The liturgy, like a military action, could not be postponed. The liturgy of the faithful had begun.

Grigori, in the sanctuary, uncovered the ciborium and prayed to be made worthy of the bloodless sacrifice of the Mass. He prayed like a reasonable man, without ecstasy; like a priest who believed in the rite which he was performing. He prayed, in the same way, for the faithful to receive the grace of taking Communion without sin.

The choir sang with gentle emotion: "We who mystically represent the cherubim sing the thrice-holy hymn to the life-giving Trinity. Let us put away all worldly cares so that we may receive the almighty King, attended invisibly by the angelic hosts. Alleluia."

Grigori took the chalice into both hands and went down into

the nave. At the sight of him, the faithful fell to their knees. He was torn between foolish pride at the fact that dozens of persons had prostrated themselves before him, and resentment because it was not to him they kneeled but to the sacred cup which he carried in triumph.

What am I, he asked, compared to these drops of water and wine?

The sudden thought that the chalice might truly contain God soothed his anger; for, in that event, his humiliation would be less. Above all things, Grigori respected power.

With deliberate solemnity, and very slowly, he prayed for the Patriarch and all the clergy, so as to enjoy as long as possible the spectacle of the knees bent and the heads bowed, of that willing self-abasement, of that voluntary abdication of the human will. His eyes rested upon Alona, who was kneeling to the right, her eyes alight with anticipation.

These men and their God are like Alona and me, he thought without tenderness.

Slowly, he regained the sanctuary and intoned:

"Let us love one another . . ."

But I love no one, he remembered.

Three times he prostrated himself before the altar, on which rested the negligible material weight of the bread and the wine, whispering devoutly the words of love: "I will love thee, O my Lord, who art my strength; thee, O my Lord, who art my help and my refuge."

Grigori kissed the paten, the ciborium, and the corner of the altar, thinking: No, I do not love you. You are stronger than I. For twenty years, I have waged war against you, without being able to do you harm. No, I do not love you. I do not love your gentleness, your renunciation of self, your charity—your slavelike virtues. I do not love your parables, your sophisms, your heritage. I do not love your doctrines, for you teach how to save oneself—the most despicable of teachings. I do not love the melodrama of your birth in a stable, or of your death on a cross. I love nothing about you. I despise the Spirit which you send, the Church which you have founded, the priests who hide in houses and cause the deaths of the foolish women who conceal them. There is nothing about you of human reason or human courage. You are a paradox made flesh. I reject you."

Now, if there had been a deacon present, Grigori and he would have exchanged a fraternal embrace and the words: "Christ is among us."

"He is among us, and he will remain forever." But, since there was no deacon, there was no one to embrace, and Grigori spoke the ironic words himself.

The sacred liturgy continued as inexorably as a symphony, as a syllogism, as a military offensive. The movements already played, the positions already seized, were over and done with, and Grigori felt an inner astonishment at the determinism of the liturgy. No one had the power now to prevent that which was ordained to happen, whatever that might be. He himself had not the time to reflect on the precise nature of that event, but he sensed that the ineluctable forward movement resembled that of childbirth. Once the labor pains had begun, who could prevent the child from being born? Therefore, he continued.

The Credo thundered through the church, chanted by the faithful with the concentrated energy of those who, for all the mystical safeguards with which they might one by one surround themselves, were conscious that tomorrow they might die.

"Let us bring forth the holy sacrifice in peace," Grigori chanted, and the choir's response explained the nature of that sacrifice: "The mercy of the world, and the offering of our praise."

Grigori turned toward the people and spoke the apostolic greeting:

"May the grace of our Lord Jesus Christ, the love of the Father, and the unity of the Spirit, be with you."

Then, with sudden inspiration, and emphasizing the holy words with a proud gesture of his hand, he commanded, "Lift up your hearts!"

The Last Supper was about to begin.

The gates of the sanctuary were closed, and Misha was Grigori's only witness. The priest prayed a triple, secret prayer. He gave thanks to God in his three persons, first for the infinity of his perfection, second for his love of mankind, and finally for his willingness to accept the service of humans although the powers of the heavenly spirits were his to command. "Let them shout their canticle of victory," Grigori prayed in a loud voice, "in songs and cries, in calls and words."

No sooner had he pronounced the formula than Grigori imagined that the sanctuary, the church itself, was filled with the vision of Ezekiel and of John. It appeared before his eyes, as it did every Sunday when he spoke the symbolic words evoking four mysterious creatures. "Songs" brought forth an eagle, which came to rest with beating wings near the altar at which Grigori presided. "Cries" produced a bull, which stood facing him. "Calls," a maned lion. "Words," a human figure—a virgin or a youth—who took his place at the holy table.

What a menagerie! Grigori thought.

In strangely harmonious concert, and in keeping with this prophetic vision, the four nonexistent creatures caused the praise of the Lord to resound: "Holy! Holy! Holy! Almighty God!"

And the choir: "Lord God of Hosts, thrice holy, full are heaven and earth of thy glory!"

In order to associate the song of the angels with that sung by the Jews when Jesus entered Jerusalem, the choir added: "Blessed be he who comes in the name of the Lord. Hosanna!"

Grigori, meanwhile, stretched out his hands toward the altar. The menagerie had disappeared, but the sound of the chanting remained like the points of the compass, like a trail leading from the infinite to the center of the ciborium. The walls of the sanctuary, like those of the church, had disappeared. Grigori knew very well that they were still standing; but, at the same time, he knew that they no longer existed, and that he was standing at the summit of a hill which, every Sunday for seventeen years, had grown higher and higher, and upon which today blew the four winds of space. For a moment, he wondered whether there was a draft—

There was silence for a moment, then Grigori chanted in a devout and simple tone, free of all grandiloquence: "Take and eat, for this is my body, broken for you in expiation of your sins."

Behind him, invisible, a forest of hands rose and fell in the sign of the cross. For every tree, there was a wood-cutter.

"Take and drink all of this, for it is the chalice of my blood, that of the New Testament, which has been shed for you and for many unto the remission of sins."

He did not see them, but he knew that the signs of the cross were made, some formal, some careless, some wavering, some small, some large, just as they had been in the arenas of Rome, with the smell of wild beasts and resin.

Now the transubstantiation moved quickly toward its climax. With his hands in the form of a cross, Grigori raised the ciborium and the paten above the altar, recalling the ancient story of the drama played out for the love of mankind: the cross, the tomb, the resurrection. He recalled, in anticipation, the Second Coming. And he offered the gift of the sacrifice to the Father, saying: "We offer to thee that which is thine; we who belong to thee, in obedience to thy command and in the love of thy action."

What lover could speak with such passion? How strange that men loved so strongly an object so unlovable: Jesus.

Behind the priest, the people were kneeling. He heard the floor creaking, the heavy shoes of the men scraping the floorboards, and the groans of the aged.

The choir sang: "We praise thee, we bless thee, we thank thee, O Lord, and we pray to thee who art our God."

Three times, the priest invoked the Holy Ghost by virtue of the new covenant. After all, God was obliged to keep his word.

He traced a cross over the paten; another over the ciborium; and then a third, for the two elements united. His gestures were slow and becomingly reverent.

It was done. The molecules of wine had become blood; those of bread, flesh.

Grigori fell to his knees and prayed intently for the efficacy of the Eucharist. When he rose, he discovered, without surprise, that Christ was there, on the altar.

Ah, so you've come.

It was not a gracious welcome, and it was spoken in an unpleasant tone, as though to say: Why didn't you stay where you were? We'd be much better off without you. But, since you're here, we'll have to make the best of it.

The liturgy continued with a prayer to the victorious saints, a special prayer to the Mother of God, and a prayer for all the faithful.

That sly Alona, Grigori reflected with gentle irony, has been right all along.

Now the living and the dead were united in the prayers of the liturgy.

Oh, Mother, said Grigori, so you are here too.

The element of surprise was somehow lacking. This was a service like any other, and it bore no resemblance in any respect to the adventure on the road to Damascus, when God had fallen upon Saul like a highwayman upon his victim.

All this time, Grigori told himself, I thought I was shooting with blanks, and the gun was loaded with real bullets. Everyone knew it but me. Otherwise, why would these people all be here?

No wonder I was unsuccessful in making Ambrose lose hope. He *knew;* and he knew that he knew.

"May the blessings of our great God and Saviour Jesus Christ be with you. Amen."

With all of you. Including the communist church warden. Of course: He was a comrade!

It was time to pray for the grace of being able to receive Communion without committing sacrilege—a rather delicate undertaking.

Why should I be concerned? Grigori asked himself. I certainly haven't omitted any of the mandatory prayers. I've prayed like any priest; and, certainly, I'm better than most of them. And there's no doubt, is there, that I was validly ordained?

He was aware that there was a sophism somewhere in his reasoning, but he had not the time to think about it, and he hoped that God had no more time than he. The timing of the liturgy was as strict as that of a trapeze act.

Our Father, which art in
heaven,

I never knew my real father.
I know this one, and I'm not
sure that I care for him.

hallowed be thy name;

It is sufficient to say "his
name." He is the one who names
his creatures; and, in pro-

nouncing his name a man becomes as strong as he. Yes, he is strong but with an inverted strength. That's cheating.

thy kingdom come;

And so, I will be carried, with my hands and feet tied, onto my own Golgotha. But I will win—according to your own rules, if not according to mine—because in punishing me you are being untrue to yourself. In other words, you and I will both lose, each of us in his own way.

thy will be done on earth as it is in heaven.

Your will, and not my own! I know that yours will be done in the end, but not before mine is crushed. And if you crush me, you will be playing false to your own rules, for you pretend to be a merciful God.

Give us this day our supernatural bread,

If by "bread" we mean grace, I must say that you haven't

exactly spoiled me. Are you
going to have a nice surprise
for me today? Thank you in
advance.

and forgive us our debts as
we forgive our debtors;

Our debts of love, naturally.
No one loves me, and I
love no one. So we're even,
aren't we? No. I forgot about
Alona. What bad luck!

and lead us not into
temptation,

When have you done anything but
lead us into temptation? Isn't
it leading us into temptation when
you offer yourself to us naked,
helpless, begging us to scourge
you and spit upon you?

but deliver us from
the evil one.

Yes, deliver us, if you can.
Disentangle us, by all means. Lay
hold of us by our hair and pull us
out—even if it breaks our necks.
But you, who weren't even able
to come down from the cross, how

could you raise someone else up
to it?

*For thine is the kingdom,
and the power, and the
glory.*

Here are words that I would agree with, if they meant what they are supposed to mean rather than the opposite. My God, what do I have in common with you?

Grigori took the body of Christ into his consecrated hands, elevated it above the paten, and said:

"Holy things unto the holy."

Behind him, Grigori heard Misha close the Royal door and draw the curtain. The altar seemed to darken, resolutely to cut itself off from the rest of the world. Once more, Grigori was alone with his God and the boy; another trinity. The choir chanted, "One is holy, one is the Lord, Jesus Christ, for the greater glory of the Father. Amen."

Grigori held the Lamb above the altar and looked at it intently. You're on the cross now, Master! What a disgrace! How wrong I was in choosing you as my sovereign. Poor God! You had to become man to buy back your own creatures after they escaped from you. I almost feel sorry for you.

He placed the Lamb on the paten and, as though to punish it, he broke it into four pieces. The fragmented Lamb lay helpless.

Good, Grigori thought. It's only right that you suffer, since you weren't able to control the world that you created.

Not for an instant did Grigori doubt that it was the body of Christ that he broke. In his deepest being, he was one with the

Pharisees who had been so concerned with the law two thousand years before; one with the disciplined Roman legionnaires who had done their duty and put this man to death, this Jesus, this God who was a misfit, Christ.

Never had a Mass been celebrated in such rage, or in such faith.

He placed a quarter of the broken host into the ciborium and poured warm water over it. Misha had heated the water beforehand, so that, like blood, it might be warm.

He took another quarter of the Lamb and devoured it. He drank a swallow of the blood and sucked the rim of the chalice with his lips, as though the cup were an open wound in the side of Christ.

The two remaining quarters he broke and placed in the ciborium so that the congregation might take Communion also, by virtue of what was called the bloodless sacrifice, though, in fact, it was no less bloody than the sacrifices of pagan antiquity. Jesus was a man, and it was his blood which the people were to drink.

Grigori opened the double gates of the Royal door and saw men and women coming toward him, their hands crossed over their breasts, their faces solemn but avid for their share of this strange, unworldly, but nonetheless savage sacrifice.

The children came first: the very young, who opened their gap-toothed mouths and their milk-white eyes and looked as though they remembered. But what did they remember?

Misha came next, transformed, for the moment, into an improbable angel.

The rest of the congregation followed: the young and, above all, the old. Each came in turn, not like sleepwalkers lost in their dreams, but like hungry soldiers filing past the mess counter for their regular, unvarying meal.

It is I, Grigori, who am feeding them.

He was vaguely moved. Ancient legends came to mind; stories of sacrifice and military valor.

It is too late for me, he told himself. But these people—they love it so much . . .

He watched them return to their places among the congregation, as though transfigured by satiety.

After the Communion, Grigori was eager to end the service. In the sanctuary, he hurriedly placed the pieces of blessed bread—representing the saints, the living and the dead—into the ciborium, and thus consecrated the union of Christ with his Church. For the last time, he turned toward the people, the ciborium in his hand, and everyone knelt in a sudden gesture of universal thanksgiving. He then carried the ciborium to the Table of Sacrifice, and returned to stand before the congregation.

It was time for Grigori's sermon; but he felt that he had not the strength to preach. He spoke a few words in explanation of the Gospel he had read earlier. He finished quickly, for he wished to return to his house, to Alona at home. Yet he waited until the people had filed past him once more to kiss first the crucifix which he held out to them, and then his hand. Grigori thought of those statues in the church of Rome which had been worn by the kisses of the faithful.

They will wear out my hand, he told himself. No, they won't. I have only a few weeks left.

Misha distributed to the people the small pieces of blessed bread which had remained after Grigori had extracted the fragment which became the Lamb.

There was a last prayer, and the service was over. The parishioners left the church, talking contentedly among themselves. The liturgy had been played out.

I finished early today, Grigori observed.

Misha had already removed his handsome brocaded vestment. Grigori hurriedly consumed what remained in the ciborium and then removed his own vestments.

He left the church. He found several parishioners waiting. Some had questions. Some asked to be allowed to visit him, and others had brought eggs for him, and meat, and kvas. "Yes, yes, certainly . . . By all means, come . . . Please give it to my wife . . . Come this afternoon."

Before leaving, he blessed them, and he raised his forearm in a swan's-neck movement: "In the name of the Father, the Son, and the Holy Ghost. Amen." They kissed his hand again.

Alona had already returned home and was preparing lunch. She was an excellent cook, and Grigori was hungry. This would be a good meal. There would be borsch.

Somewhere in his mind, there lurked a problem which he found difficult to identify. Oh, yes, this business of Christ showing up this morning. Well, we'll see. In any case, there's not much I can do about it. I think that I've always known . . .

He walked in the street, and the usual problems presented themselves. Should he step aside or not? Somehow, he reflected, these things are no longer important.

There was a low black automobile in front of his house.

As he drew nearer, Grigori heard the muffled sound of its engine.

EPILOGUE

Since that Sunday—how long ago was it?—Grigori had never prayed. He felt no need of it, and the habit had been broken.

He did not pray. But, lying on his cot, he meditated, and his meditations were those of a man at peace. Only one discordant note made itself heard, a note which intruded with increasing frequency: the borsch which he had not eaten. It would have been so good. Grigori regretted it with great intensity. And, in the background, there was also the consciousness of Alona's disappointment when she had been left with her lunch on the table.

They could have let me at least taste the borsch, Grigori grumbled to himself.

These stabs of regret, as frequent as they had become, were only momentary pangs. The rest of the time, when he was not being interrogated, Grigori meditated. Or, more accurately, he gave himself over to contemplation. His eyes had been so burned by glaring floodlights that he could hardly see, and he was incapable of distinguishing colors. His limbs and sexual members ached inwardly from the electrical shocks to which they had been subjected. There was a constant rumbling of pain in his chest. And yet he lay and contemplated creation in a spirit of somber, medieval simplicity.

They've gone a long way in improving their methods, he reflected, since I was in the business. Now they no longer leave marks on their customers. The blowtorch, obviously, is outdated.

As a technician himself, he could not repress a faint admiration for the proficiency of his successors.

They know their job, he conceded.

The perfectibility of human skills seemed to him a way for creation to glorify the Creator. There was no limit to the heights mankind might scale. Man progressed, and no matter how harmful that progress might prove to be, it reflected honor upon God.

An improbable comparison returned again and again to his mind: a holy Mass, and a torture session. The two were so completely the opposite of each other that their very opposition engendered a similarity. The one was an act of love and harmony: chants, kissing of the altar stone and of the priest's hand. All these things had a well-defined purpose, which was to extract from Christ an avowal of his love: the Eucharist. The other was an act of constraint. There was violence, and there were screams and insulting and painful acts. And these things, too, had a well-defined purpose: to extract from the victim an avowal of another kind. Like a hinge between these disparate things, there was the cross.

Grigori's thoughts, mixed with memories of his childhood and youth, were on a level different from that occupied by his dominant sensation, which was fear. But even the fear which had paralyzed him in those first days was now becoming a part of him, in such a way that it no longer paralyzed him. Grigori was becoming a slave who no longer feared to be beaten; for fear is predicated upon a doubt, and Grigori no longer doubted that he would be beaten. He had become accustomed to fear as he had become accustomed to uncleanliness, to the stench of his cell, to the stinking filth with which his own body was covered, for in addition to everything else, he had vomited on himself after some of the interrogations. Now, even when he heard footsteps in the corridor and waited, with chattering teeth, for number 665 to be called, he continued to contemplate the world with ironic and stupefied detachment.

My stomach is growling, he told himself. It usually grumbles. The lieutenant who interrogated me this morning obviously had a hangover. I wonder if he had a good time last night. I hope so. He's not so bad . . . The captain, however, has yellow teeth. I wonder if he doesn't brush them, or if he's coming down with something . . . I see that I can't move my fingers any more. They tingle, as though they were covered with ants. How funny! Ants on my hands and lice in my beard. The one weak point in this prison is sanitation. The first thing I'd do would be to have everyone shaved.

Grigori had quickly renounced all hope, just as, when first in the seminary, he had renounced all temptation.

Above all, he told himself, I must be on guard against a rekindling of hope.

In the certainty of misfortune, Grigori found peace. It was not that he wished to become a martyr or a hero. It was rather that he knew precisely what to expect. He was certain of the worst. And, in that sense, the worst was good. Good, because it was somehow reassuring. Whenever Grigori saw his torturers, he experienced a feeling which was akin to disgust and, at the same time, to relief. It was a sense of friendship, not unlike the feeling that a man experiences at the perception of his own body warmth, or of his own filth. If Grigori still felt fear, it was fear of only one thing: the chance that he might be transferred to another prison before he died.

Grigori had no relations with the inhabitants of the neighboring cells. The first few days, they had knocked on the walls, using the old prison code. The man to Grigori's right continued to do so. But Grigori did not reply. He remained an officer unjustly accused, a servant of the regime whom the regime had repudiated. He had nothing in common with the guilty men to his right and to his left. In the torture chamber, he was, and remained still, the associate of those who tortured him rather than that of the victims who had preceded him and would follow him. This did not mean that he expected favors from his superiors, any more than his faith in God meant that he expected to save his soul. God existed. The regime existed. Everything that existed was good. Evil existed; and, in that sense, evil was good. It was good, so to speak, at its two extremes: it was pleasant for the one who whipped, and edifying for the one who was whipped.

Disconnected images raced through Grigori's mind, or at least through what was left of it; for the treatment to which he had been subjected had affected his nervous system, and he was no longer himself. He lived in a stupor, but perhaps it was a stupor which itself was lucidity.

His mother. The priest hidden in her house. At dawn one morning, the commissar had come to arrest both the priest and the one who had hidden him. There had been armed men with the commissar, and their flashlights had reflected simultaneously from the ikons and from their submachine guns. A child's decision: I want to be a man with a gun. Alona. Her buffet full of ikons. He thought of her way of kissing him: always timid, no matter how passionate she may have been. She kissed relics . . . He thought of Nicephorus and the enigmatic decision which had preceded the man's death. Why had he wanted Grigori to become a priest? . . . Petia the cock, crowing in the yard, joyfully beating his hens . . . He hated the priest who had let himself be taken by the men with guns without resisting, without striking out, without even screaming, his hands tied behind his back and his knees trembling . . . Alona. The borsch; that marvelous borsch which Grigori would never taste.

At the thought of the borsch, with its cabbages and beets

and, perhaps, a bit of meat, Grigori's eyes invariably filled with tears. Then the cycle began again.

Alexander with the doorknob in his pocket . . . His mother's final farewell: "May Christ watch over you, my child!" It would have been more fitting for her, the victim of Christ, to shake her fist at the heavens . . . Misha, and the other altar boys who had preceded him, all confused in Grigori's memory. Misha opening his mouth greedily for the Eucharist . . . His army friends during the war. They had had everything in common: honor, black bread, smelly feet. Grigori's memories of combat had disappeared, or at least they no longer evoked the same nostalgia as before. It had been a good time in his life, of course; but it had been a time of childish things, and it was no longer important. The battles he remembered as important were those he had fought at the age of twelve; fights with other children in the neighborhood.

Grigori rarely thought of his priesthood. He was simply a man who was being punished; an officer of the regime being prosecuted unjustly. Once or twice, however, he looked at his dirty hands and reflected on the unbroken succession which bound him, through the imposition of hands, to the Master who had lived two thousand years before. There was bound to be some loss of energy. Nonetheless, some strength must still remain in those squat fingers, in those square and deeply lined palms, which had received the mission of binding and loosening.

A lot of good it does me, he thought.

And then he thought: My hands are filthy. And I'll never wash them before the Royal door.

The thought was almost as painful to him as the lost borsch.

When Grigori came abreast of the automobile, two men appeared on his left. They had been hiding in the bushes along the sidewalk. Grigori was caught between the automobile on one side, and the men on the other. Immediately, the driver opened the car door. "Get in, priest," the younger of the two men said.

The man who spoke was a tall, sturdy, blond youth. His open collar showed prominent clavicles and well-developed neck muscles. His athletic body was only partly disguised by a black sweater. He held his fidgeting hands behind his back, as though ready to push himself forward with them. His face was bony; his expression, one of impatience; his eyes, too bright, and malevolent. Grigori was able to place him immediately; a daredevil officer, slightly more intelligent than the average, who had been transferred into the secret service without having any particular qualification for such duty.

The other man was dark, of medium height, and fat. He wore glasses with deeply tinted lenses, and his dark coloring and black hair made him look like a Turk. He seemed alert, ready for action and, at the same time, conscious of details. He had been born to do the work that he was doing.

Grigori's first response was that of the officer. The second was that of the priest. Who were these men? What were their spiritual profiles? What was written next to their names in the dictionary of souls?

There was no mystery about the blond. He was a violent man; but, in his case, violence did not presuppose purity—as it so often did. And, immediately, Grigori's professional mind intervened: How can I save his soul?

There was no easy answer. There are not many policemen in heaven, Grigori said to himself, because there are so many temptations in their line of work. But the secret service, at least so far as temptation is concerned, was a police agency raised to a high degree of perfection, as Grigori was well aware. There were two ways to go about it. Either there must be a sacrifice so great, so pure, so generously accepted that it would wipe out all sin. Or there must be the love of a woman;

a surgical love, of the kind which moves a man to strip off his skin with a knife.

And the other man, the dark, calm one?

There were three ways of being saved, Grigori reflected. By faith, by hope, or by love. Such a meticulous man was probably incapable of love. And, since he was also a narrow man, he was undoubtedly impervious to faith. There remained hope. Perhaps this man was working for the future. Perhaps he was convinced at least of the transitory usefulness of his work. Perhaps he was not wholly committed to his work, and he secretly hoped that one day there would be no need for it. It was not probable. It was more likely that he would lose his soul in the line of duty; would damn himself by being conscientious and competent and painstaking in work which was worthy of damnation.

Grigori looked at the two men and thought: "I am probably looking at two damned souls."

The thought irritated his professional conscience.

He met their eyes with assurance, and, at the same time, with that fear of the arbitrary of which men under certain governments are never free.

"Who are you, citizens? What do you want with me?"

The younger man, without answering, pushed Grigori with such violence that the priest stumbled backward against the foot of the dark man and fell through the open door of the car into the back seat. His first impulse was to defend himself; but his muscles had atrophied through disuse. The blond youth grasped Grigori's arm and held it behind his back; then the other man seated himself beside Grigori, and the car began to move.

Grigori's first thought was that there had been a mistake. I must tell them who I am, he thought. But what if they do not belong to the same service?

"Did Professor Dobermann send you?" he asked.

There was no answer. The dark man pulled a blindfold from his pocket and said, "Don't move."

Grigori did as he was told. His anger had already cooled, and he was convinced that he was the victim of a misunderstanding. In this kind of work, however, misunderstandings usually had tragic consequences. The thing to do was to set things right again. And, for that, he must remain calm.

"Citizens," he said, as the blindfold was being tied around his eyes, "I'm certain that there's been a mistake. It's true that I'm only a village priest, but I can tell you that I'm not entirely without influence. I'm a former officer, and some of my friends from the army now hold important positions. I'd advise you to take me to your superior officer as soon as we arrive."

Silence.

The blindfold did not disturb Grigori unduly. He knew that, somewhere in the vast machinery of the bureaucracy, something had gone awry, but he would be able to explain himself satisfactorily. Nadson would have had to be telepathic to have learned that, less than an hour before, Grigori had come to believe in the existence of Christ. Grigori thought he knew the most probable explanation for what was happening. His letter to Dobermann had been lost. Nadson was angry at what he thought was Grigori's disobedience of an order, and, like most intellectuals, had overreacted.

The expression, "the existence of Christ," Grigori knew, was inadequate. He was certain that, in a sense, the atheists were right, and that the God they denied did not exist. He therefore had no intention of giving up his mission. But, in another sense, the Christians were also right, and God *is;* for his name itself meant "I am." If God did not exist, there would be no one to say, "I am."

All this is much too subtle for Nadson, Grigori told himself. To Nadson, I am just an agent who has accomplished his mission.

He would have to see Nadson. The name would probably serve as a password of some sort.

"I want to see Comrade Nadson," he said.

Silence.

"Do you know Comrade Nadson?"

Silence.

Grigori hesitated. His arrest might be a final test. Certainly, if he told these men who Nadson was, he would be leaving himself open to a charge of high treason. Perhaps they were attempting to ascertain whether seventeen years of being a priest had made him forget the regulations of the service.

The automobile made turns and detours to eliminate any possibility that Grigori might know where he was going. This was routine. Grigori yawned. He had not eaten since the day before. Poor Alona. Had she seen the automobile? She must be worried.

After he had been in the automobile for an hour, Grigori sensed that they were in the open country. Then, after a sharp turn, they stopped.

"You can take off the blindfold."

He was in a concrete garage.

"Hurry up."

There was a corridor, a staircase, and then an interrogation room.

His two abductors stood stiffly at attention. "Here is the priest."

Against the sunlight, behind a metal desk, Grigori saw insignia glistening on a man's shoulders. A large man, in combat uniform but wearing all his medals, rose from his chair. Grigori, in his cassock, drew himself up to attention.

"My respects, Comrade Colonel," he said.

The colonel squinted at him. He had an enormous beast's snout for a face and he emitted a series of rumbling noises.

"You bunch of charlatans," he said, and then fell back into

his chair, sniffed with all his strength, put his elbows upon his desk, lowered his head into his hands, and fell silent.

The three men at attention did not move, or breathe, or blink. A minute passed. Suddenly, the colonel's fist crashed onto the desk.

"You animals!" he shouted. "Are you going to begin?"

There was a time when Grigori would have been impressed and frightened by such antics. Now he found them ridiculous. As an attempt to put him into what was considered a proper frame of mind, they failed miserably.

Grigori stepped forward, came to attention again, and looked into the colonel's bloodshot eyes. "Lieutenant Grigori . . . reporting, Comrade Colonel."

The colonel glared back at him, "Animal," he repeated, this time in a low voice. "Imbecile. Idiot. Stupid civilian. Filthy pig. Phony priest. Think, man, think! You have nothing to lose. Don't try any of your tricks. Think!"

Between his irregular, widely spaced teeth, Grigori saw yellow bubbles of saliva.

Grigori knew this man intuitively, as he had known the two others. He was a rear-echelon officer, by nature incompetent, who had been transferred into the secret service because it was the only way to get rid of him. He possessed an astonishing gift for collecting medals which he did not deserve. He was, in a word, the classic survival artist, with this difference, that he spoke one or two foreign languages very badly and thus had been able to work his way into the service. Such was the judgment of the officer Grigori on the colonel.

Grigori the priest, however, judged differently. This man, he told himself, is so lacking in intelligence, in understanding, in heart, in everything, that it would be unjust to condemn him. He is one of the poor, in every sense of that term except the most superficial one. He says, "think"; but he does not know even the meaning of the word.

As Grigori the officer and Grigori the priest were debating, Grigori the man felt sweat pouring over his hands, his forehead, his chest. He realized that, as the first order of business, he must clear up the misunderstanding.

"Comrade Colonel," he said. "I would like to see Comrade Nadson."

"Nadson, that stupid civilian! My job here is to try to straighten out his mess. What do you want with Nadson?" As the colonel spoke, he spat out tiny drops of saliva.

Grigori hesitated. There was no proof that he was really in the hands of an official service, face to face with a real army colonel. It might be a semi-official agency; or the colonel might easily be—it sometimes happened in the service—a noncommissioned officer in disguise. If so, it would be treason for Grigori to speak of Nadson.

"You are all idiots!" the colonel roared. "You bring me this peasant, and you haven't even conditioned him! I'm going to take a nap; and when I wake up, I want him to spit, by God! To spill his guts!"

The colonel rose and hastily gathered up the papers on the desk. His frown, his puffed red cheeks—all these were part of a carefully staged scene, Grigori knew. The nap was also fictional. And yet, Grigori's knees began to shake uncontrollably. "Comrade Colonel," he stuttered, "there must be a mistake. I'm not a priest. I'm an agent employed by Comrade Nadson. Everything that I've done, I've done in the line of duty. If you will only—"

"You should know that you're not here as a priest, but as a lieutenant." The colonel spoke with exaggerated politeness. "What do I care about priests? But a turncoat officer in my own army—I know how to deal with such people." He raised his finger in the form of a stake, eloquently suggesting impalement.

"But Comrade Colonel! I'm no turncoat! If my letter to Dobermann has been lost—"

There was a new roar from the colonel. "Be quiet! Don't make me laugh with your lost letters! Our Minister of the Post knows his job. And I note that you have insinuated he is incompetent. How did a leftover from the old regime like you manage to get into the service?"

Grigori was unaccustomed to such language. "Comrade Colonel," he replied angrily. "I am not a leftover from the old regime, and I demand the respect due to the uniform I wear!"

The colonel signaled Grigori's two abductors to take notes, and they scribbled furiously in their notebooks.

"I am an agent on assignment," Grigori continued, in a voice that seemed strange to him, "and anyone who interferes with my mission is liable to prosecution before a military court. I have followed my orders to the letter, and my letter to Dobermann—"

"Are you still talking about that? I have it here, your letter to Dobermann! What am I supposed to do with it? Dobermann is nothing but a—a *civilian!*"

Grigori was confused. He looked at the three officers, one after another. As soon as he had stopped following the logic of the situation, he had grasped its metaphysical implications. He knew that he would never leave this place; and, with that realization, indifference settled upon him. But only within himself. His body was increasingly in the grip of fear.

"But, Comrade Colonel—"

"But what? Let's hear your explanation."

No words came to Grigori's mind. He knew that he was being subjected to "conditioning" of the grossest kind, and he was incapable of reacting. He opened his mouth, and then closed it again. He knew beforehand that he was beaten.

The colonel sat down again, heavily. He resumed his former position, his forehead resting on his hands.

"Begin," he ordered.

His two subordinates stepped forward. Grigori felt them coming behind him. He rushed forward toward the desk, pleading. "Just tell me what you want to know! I've submitted a report! Everything is in my report!"

The colonel did not raise his head. The two men moved forward another step. So did Grigori. He placed his hands on the colonel's desk and saw that they were trembling as they had never trembled before. "Comrade! Comrade!" he shouted. "All you have to do—all you have to do is decode my report—"

The colonel's short gray hair glistened with sweat between his fat fingers. His fingernails were dirty. Grigori felt hands gripping his arms. "Comrade Colonel!"

The two officers tried to pull Grigori backward, but he clutched at the sharp edge of the metal desk. The officers cursed, but Grigori held. The colonel did not move, did not speak; but it was evident that he was displeased. Before long, someone would pay for that displeasure.

The officers tugged harder, and the desk moved forward. The colonel moved his elbows, as though to hold on to it. It was obvious that he was on the point of exploding. The younger of the two officers brought his fist down, hard, on Grigori's forearm, and the priest was forced to loosen his hold.

The colonel spoke with perfect calm: "Put him in uniform."

They still use the same expression, Grigori noted. The familiar term served to restore his composure. He almost smiled at the thought of nudity as a uniform. He was surprised at only one thing: they had not started beating him. This was disturbing. It showed an absence of spontaneity, and a devotion to method and discipline among these agents, which promised ill for what was to come. It was possible that they wished merely to avoid marking him; and that was a good sign. It was more likely, however, that they did not want to risk an accident. A simple kick in the stomach could kill a man.

During the first interrogation session, not a single question was put to Grigori. He was insulted, shamed by the high moral tone adopted by his tormentors; and, as he lay on his back, his head dangling over the side of the table, he was acutely aware of the electrical current coursing painfully through his body.

He offered no resistance. He sighed, wept, shrieked. He begged to be told what it was they wanted of him.

"Dirty fascist! You know very well what we want. Filth! Traitor to your country and your Party!" the blond lieutenant shouted.

The dark captain murmured gently: "You were given an exceptionally careful political education, comrade. You can't imagine how painful it is for us to know that you've gone so far astray. Surely you know that perseverance in one's mission is of the greatest importance; and you, you—well, what you have done, comrade, is hardly in keeping with the best traditions of the service. Such a lack of awareness! The fact that you are a man of proven ability only makes your failure more despicable."

"Scum!" the younger officer shouted. "Filth! You disgust me! You've disgraced the service! I'm not allowed to touch you right now, but don't worry. I'll make up for it later. I know how to deal with trash like you!"

The colonel sat silently holding his head in his hands. From time to time, he gave an indication of impatience, and then the current was increased; or an indication of satisfaction, and then Grigori's interior agony ceased.

Occasionally Grigori heard himself crying out rhythmically, like a woman in the act of love. From the very first moment, he had abandoned all thought of dignity, all semblance of resistance. There was no room for pride. He was in the hands of his tormentors, and he was like putty, able to be shaped and reshaped according to their whim. Like an animal on the vivisectionist's table, he felt neither rebellion nor hope, only naked pain.

The stratagem might have succeeded with the younger officer, and certainly with the colonel. But the dark captain was alert. During the third session, he walked to the colonel's desk and whispered into his ear. The senior officer seemed on the point of suffocating. He ordered the current to be reduced, and then addressed Grigori in a pleasant tone: "Well, priest. What day of the year have you chosen for your feast? You know, of course, that they're going to canonize you as a martyr."

Then he concluded: "I've just about decided that our friend here doesn't have anything to confess. I'll have to write a report, of course, but it's quite possible that in a few days . . ."

Grigori was perfectly aware that a trap was being laid. It was their intention to torture him by rekindling hope. They wished to explore and destroy every possibility of resistance so that, on the day that they began the actual interrogation, he would have been stripped beforehand of any means of defense. But what if it was not a trick? What if the colonel was really convinced of his innocence? How could he smother the tiny spark of hope which, in spite of everything, still glowed?

Then, suddenly, from a corner of Grigori's mind which he had not thought to search, a remedy presented itself. It would be enough for him to say, without saying it to anyone in particular, like reciting a line to an actor offstage:

"Your will be done."

Instantly, hope died; and with its death came salvation.

For twenty-four hours they allowed Grigori to remain in his cell undisturbed, so that he might nurture the seed of hope which they had planted. The fourth session was especially brutal, as Grigori had known it would be. They even slapped his face, to see what his reaction would be. He did not react. He repeated within himself:

"Your will be done."

Certainly, Grigori concluded, it was not a prayer. It was a technique. But a technique that worked.

It was not until several sessions later that questions were mingled with the pain and the exhortations of his torturers. The letter to Dobermann played a large part in the list of charges which had been drawn up. Parts of it were quoted, and always in an accusatory manner. The prisoner was led through a labyrinth of questions, in which he knew there was a trap at every turn. Yet he had nothing, absolutely nothing, to hide. The only possible explanation was that someone had slandered him. Even the report, over which he had labored so diligently, was considered a crime: "A shameless fraud," they said. "An incredible intellectual perversion." It was "filled with bourgeois and reactionary attitudes." And, they shouted indignantly, "You pretend to be innocent? You who wrote this thing? You are a throwback to the Dark Ages! A pervert! A disgrace! You should be liquidated. And," they added, "with this letter to Dobermann and your report, we can have you shot without a trial."

It was not until all the quotations from his letter had been read to him a hundred times, when he had lapsed into a stupor, when all hope had vanished, when he had found unexpected peace in the midst of his torment, that Grigori understood.

"'For every sin there is mercy,'" read the blond officer. "You are a traitor to communist society!"

"'Mea culpa,'" the dark officer murmured. "What an unfortunate expression!"

"'The sin into which I have fallen.' Indeed! How could you fall any lower than you have, you filthy pig?"

"'My Calvary,' it says here. You've apparently adopted the

vocabulary of superstition. Calvary, dear Comrade, is not a dialectical concept.

"You wrote: 'There are no fanatics at the Patriarchate.' What does it take to convince you, stupid?"

"According to you, priests lead a life of poverty. Don't you know it is contrary to our Constitution even to insinuate such a thing?"

"You admit that you secretly taught superstition to our children! Corrupter of children! Jesus-devil!"

"You yourself confess that you were a good priest. This can only mean that you were a bad communist. Don't you realize that it is the duty of a communist to be perfect? And I must tell you that your comments on Jesus' method of recruiting followers disturb me a great deal. Even when you criticize the methods of the contemporary Church, you betray an unlawful interest in the wellbeing of the eternal Church. . . ."

"Scum of the earth! You say that the Party's followers are not enthusiastic and that they don't give of themselves! You must be an agent of the imperialist powers!"

"It seems to me, comrade, that your analysis of the situation which prevails between the Church and the state is inspired more by the Grand Inquisitor than by Marx. I find, in fact, that you have really taken to heart the interests of the Master that you created for yourself."

"You even speak of this letter as a 'confession.' Do you remember the first day you came here? You demanded that we show you the respect due to your cassock!"

"The ending of your letter was written in a spirit of obvious irony, comrade. And what can possibly be more reactionary than irony? I might add that the expression 'Fraternally yours in Marx' seems to me to be completely out of place. I might even say that it is blasphemy!"

These were the things they said to Grigori during the second stage. During the first, they had accused him of having told

Dobermann, on the one hand, that he had been a good priest, and, on the other, of having lied to him by not telling him about his true mission. These fabricated accusations were designed to confuse the prisoner. The second stage was more real, but still only a preparation. By then, Grigori thought that he had caught the drift of the accusations, that he was suspected of having developed a criminal loyalty to religion. And he defended himself accordingly. "What about my report?" he asked. "It gives the names of all those who—"

The report seemed to Grigori to be a masterpiece. In it were the names of the overly devout laymen of his parish; the parish leaders who organized catechism courses for the children; the bishops who, in the security of the confessional, had accused themselves of hating the Chief of State; the Party officials who had brought their children to be baptized. But when he spoke of his report, his torturers merely exchanged glances, smiled, and immediately increased the current which sparked through his body from his genitals to the nape of his neck.

Finally, one day, the colonel looked up from his desk. He had sat there, at every session, his head in his hands, without speaking a single word. Now, he placed his hands flat on the desk and, for the first time, he seemed to notice the presence of the man whom, for days, for weeks, he had heard cry out in pain. Instantly, his two subordinates fell silent, and the current dropped to zero.

"My friend," the colonel said not unkindly. "I made up my mind about you some time ago. You were still wet behind the ears when they sent you on this mission. What they should have done was to send a man of fifty; not a greenhorn of twenty. That's all I'm going to say about the service. This is autocriticism if I've ever heard any. The priests were too strong for you—which doesn't surprise me. They corrupted you and you didn't even know that you had been corrupted.

Now you are paying for it. That is, after all, only fair. Now you're going to have to make up your mind to tell us exactly how they operate, and who is at the head of the conspiracy. The Minister thinks it's the Patriarch; but the Minister is an idiot. I know it's not the Patriarch, and you and I are going to prove that it's not. So now, tell me his name."

"Whose name, Comrade Colonel?"

"You know very well whose name. The leader of the priests who want to overthrow the regime."

The interrogation continued uninterrupted for twelve hours. It was the most brutal session that Grigori had yet had to endure. By the end of the first hour, he had given ten names; and it had been pointed out that he had lied in all ten cases, that this bishop, this deacon, and that candle merchant could not possibly be the head of the conspiracy. Whenever the current was decreased, Grigori attempted to clear his head and explain: "There is no conspiracy. You know very well that I gave that name only because of the electricity. You know that there's no secret conspiracy."

Once, the colonel had laughed uproariously. "No conspiracy? For forty years we've been trying to destroy the Church, and we've never been able to do it. And now you tell us there's no conspiracy? What do you take us for? Double the current!"

In twelve hours, Grigori lost consciousness four times. Each time, they revived him by throwing water on his face, and then the questioning began again.

As in a dream, Grigori heard the blond officer say to the colonel: "You know, I have to admit that these priests really know how to keep their mouths shut. We'll have to find out how they do it. It could be very useful when our men are captured. Wait a minute. He's regaining consciousness."

Grigori opened his eyes and saw the faces of the three men looking down at him; three inhuman faces devoid of love. The puffed, leonine snout of the colonel; the pale, cruel mask of the blond officer; the impassive, watchful countenance of the dark officer.

"He must think that we have no method except electricity," the dark officer said, hardly moving his thin lips.

"You're right," the colonel replied. "We're being too nice about this. I haven't even eaten for twelve hours. Let's use the blowtorch on him, and if it leaves marks on him—well, it can't be helped."

"Unless, of course, he wants to tell us the name of the chief conspirator," the dark officer murmured.

The blond bent over Grigori, his nostrils narrowed, two fingers extended toward Grigori's open eyes. "Let's go! Talk! What's his name?"

Grigori heard himself say, as though from a distance—it was difficult for him to move his lips: "His name is—"

With a great effort, he raised his head and turned toward the three men leaning over him. I'm going to play a good joke on them, he told himself. He could see that they were waiting attentively. They had understood that he was about to tell them something. The colonel was already anticipating the pleasure of proving the Minister wrong. The dark captain saw a medal already glittering on his uniform. And the blond lieutenant would shortly be a captain.

Grigori spoke in a voice which had regained something of its clarity and strength. "The head of the conspiracy," he said, "is called Jesus of Nazareth."

Grigori lay on his cot, a soul in a rag of a body, meditating with open eyes.

One part of his mind was aware that, during the last interrogation, the colonel had decided to ask his superiors for written orders. Once he received them, the interrogations would probably be carried on in a different fashion. It was probable, for example, that the threat of the blowtorch would turn out to be more than a threat. It was with this in mind that Grigori had smashed his soup bowl that night, and, when he handed the pieces to the guard, had kept a large, sharp fragment, which he hid in his mattress. Now he removed it from the soiled straw and looked at it. It was his key to freedom; a good, keen edge which could easily slice through the arteries in his wrists.

There's so little life left in me, he reflected, that it shouldn't be hard to get rid of it.

He held the fragment against an artery. But then, suddenly, he smiled. You'd like me to kill myself, wouldn't you? he asked. Like Judas? That would simplify your problem, wouldn't it? Well, I'm going to disappoint you. I'm not going to kill myself.

He dropped the sharp fragment and it fell to the floor with a clatter.

That night, for the first time, Grigori listened as the rhythmic strokes of the prison alphabet echoed from cell to cell. Someone knocked on his wall, methodically, repeating the same sounds which Grigori had heard night after night for an indeterminate, measureless time, but without understanding.

He listened, counted, calculated, and decoded: PRIEST . . .

The knocking continued: ANSWER

"Priest, answer!" Grigori's neighbor began again: *"Priest, answer! Priest, answer!"*

He had been transmitting this message for weeks.

In the darkness, Grigori smiled without pleasure. He began to knock on the wall, carefully computing the proper number of strokes for each letter of the alphabet: WHAT DO YOU WANT?

The unknown neighbor, with the rapidity of an expert, replied: CONFESSION.

Grigori beat the wall with his fist to make his neighbor repeat the message. It came again: CONFESSION.

For the third time that night, Grigori smiled. It was the smile of a hunter tracking his prey.

He answered, slowly: GO AHEAD.

Even after he had painstakingly pounded out the formula of absolution through the wall, Grigori felt no exaltation, no ecstasy. Not even pity. There was bitterness, like that of a chaste and sensitive young man who finds his first woman before he is ready. Fishers of men? Perhaps. But Grigori was not one of those fishermen who measure carefully every miserable fish they catch. No. He was a reluctant fisherman, thrown by destiny into a leaking boat and equipped only with a rotten net. He resented the unknown neighbor with his considerable burden of sins. He felt almost angry at having had to grant him absolution. He would have preferred to catch nothing, for he had the feeling this was the beginning of new problems. He knew that, in a certain sense, he had allowed himself to be transformed into a priest by a man he had never seen.

This has been the first time that I truly acted as a priest, he reminded himself.

He knew that it would not be the last. If he had had the Eucharist with him, and if it had been capable of passing through walls, he would have felt obligated to give Communion to the traitor next door—or the ex-traitor, since he had been absolved. He no longer smiled his hunter's smile. He felt that, far from being the hunter, he was the wolf or the fox caught in the trap, with the hunter not far behind.

It was a restless night.

Why did I let myself get involved in this sort of thing? he wondered. That was really all I needed. Well, let's think this thing out. Apparently, I am a Christian priest. Today, at least, I carried out that assignment. I suppose I should be in seventh heaven, among the cherubim and seraphim; but here I am, worrying about it. It's another example of the paradox of Christianity. Jesus remains on his cross, his hands pierced by nails, and yet he would like to find a way not to drink of his chalice. There's no joy in it, and certainly no cherubim.

Well, let's see. Tomorrow I'll probably get a taste of the blowtorch. Or, in the terminology which I'll now have to use, I'll have a taste of martyrdom. I suppose I'll be expected to shout, "Hosanna!" The truth is, I don't even have the strength to say, "My God, why hast thou forsaken me?"

Somehow, all this seems too simple. Christ has thrown his net over my soul. I'm caught in a vicious circle: temptation, sin, punishment, expiation, salvation. Then it begins all over again. I've sinned against the Holy Ghost; therefore, I must be punished; and, in being punished, I am saved. People say that the ways of God are unfathomable. In my case, I'd say that they are too obvious.

Let me try to look at it honestly. If I protest, isn't it only because I'm afraid of the blowtorch? In my human weakness, I would rather get damnation than the blowtorch. What was that silly idea I once had about a beginning and an end? Didn't it all really begin the day that that frightened, bearded priest asked my mother to hide him? And isn't the end right now? Or tomorrow, with the blowtorch in my eyes?

Grigori tried to find peace in a proven technique. Your will be done, he repeated over and over again. But he was unable to say it with all his diminishing strength, with all his frayed nerves.

Yes, certainly, he thought, let it be done. I accept martyrdom, of course; but I can't be enthusiastic about it. The truth is, I'm afraid. Very much afraid. The idea of joining my suffering to yours does not help at all. You've already been through your suffering, and mine is yet to come. And will I be happy with you when they're all done with me—all clean and warm, in the bosom of Abraham?

I know that, according to Christian mythology, this blowtorch is the greatest grace you can confer. I know that I should be grateful to you for making me suffer so that I can atone for my sins. I know that the fire of the blowtorch will save me from the fire of hell. Still, I'm weak, and I must tell you that I don't find the bosom of Abraham as tempting as I should; especially not when I think of the price I'll have to pay for it. I can cry out, "Jesus, have mercy on me!" as much as I want. I still know that it's precisely because you do have mercy on me (that is, my soul) that you will allow me (that is, my body) to be consumed over a slow fire. All these paradoxes! I wish you would at least let me sleep.

Sleep did not come. Grigori's neighbor, for the first time in weeks, was silent. He was at peace. Perhaps he slept. Biblical passages concerning sleep raced through Grigori's mind, but none of them seemed to fit his case. Jesus told his disciples to watch and pray, and they went to sleep; but they had not been just absolved, and they were standing on the threshold of death. They slept because they were sleepy. But perhaps the man in the next cell was awake, savoring his new-found innocence.

What about me? Grigori asked. Who will give me back my innocence?

A terrifying thought entered his mind: I will die in a state of sin.

He sat upright on his cot and said aloud into the darkness: "Do whatever you wish, but send me a priest!" Then he fell back, held fast in the trap. A priest could not absolve himself; and communist prisons did not provide chaplains. Would martyrdom be sufficient to wipe away his sins? Only if he accepted martyrdom willingly and generously, like the good thief.

I know, Grigori told himself, that at the very end, something in me will say "no."

He therefore forced himself like a man entering into a binding contract, to say: Yes, Lord, I accept the blowtorch in my eyes in exchange for your forgiveness.

He pronounced the words one by one, carefully, in a low but audible voice, without mental reservations, in good faith, yet grudgingly, and with his body rebelling. He added a sign of the cross, so as to force his right hand to commit itself as his mouth had done. The gesture was painful, as though he were crucifying himself by a nail.

Grigori's contract brought him no peace. He tried to recite the ancient prayers, but he found relief only in the most florid and affective of them; those which he had recited with Alona in honor of the Virgin. But even their strength soon dissipated. Grigori considered pounding on the wall and waking his neighbor. He was stopped by two considerations, of equal cogency:

If I betray my weakness, he told himself, he will doubt the validity of his absolution.

And:

I am an officer, and I must be strong enough to suffer alone.

He turned on his cot, then turned again.

What if, after all, my absolution was invalid? What if my ordination was only a farce, since I did not truly assent to it? Would my neighbor's sin then be forgiven? Or would his faith supply the validity that this faithless absolution lacked?

Oh, yes, he thought, I'm really in the trap. Maybe the blowtorch is the best thing that could happen to me.

He began to recite the *Kyrie eleison,* the final supplication of a dying Christian. But he could not engage his will in the prayer. He knew the meaning of *eleison.* It meant the blowtorch, the instrument which Grigori himself had used with such alacrity twenty years before. *Eleison* was matches in the beard of the other Grigori, impaled upon the leg of a chair. *Eleison* was Peter, crucified upside down.

The most terrifying prayer in the Christian repertory suddenly came into Grigori's mind: "Choose, O Lord, the way of my salvation." He forced himself to pronounce the words; and then he asked himself whether a prayer offered so unwillingly, with such violence to one's own will, could be of any value.

The passages which Ambrose had been so fond of quoting rose up before Grigori's eyes:

"It is not surrender that I wish, but mercy." This could only mean that the sacrifice of one's body was worth nothing without the sacrifice of one's will.

"Do not bury your talents." What use will I make of my talent for suffering? Grigori asked himself. Will I be able to convert it into grace and store it in your heavenly warehouse, O Lord, where it will be safe from insects? I know beforehand that I won't be able to do it.

"No man can serve two masters." I've spent my whole life serving two masters. How can I be certain that, even now, I've renounced one of them?

In a sense, he had not renounced one. In a sense, he was still a servant of the regime whose uniform he had once worn: the cap, the insignia—and the blowtorch.

It was dawn. The hours passed, and the daily interrogation session did not begin. A delay was to be expected, since the colonel had asked for written orders. Grigori's neighbor knocked on the wall: GOOD MORNING, FATHER.

Grigori answered, without pleasure, in order to provide the man with spiritual food proper to the condition of his soul: PEACE BE WITH YOU.

The man's response harkened back to the religious language of his childhood: AND WITH YOUR SPIRIT.

"Quiet in there," the guard shouted, as he distributed bread and water.

If only it were wine instead of water, Grigori mused, I could have Christ here in the cell with me.

Hours passed. There was no way of counting them.

I wonder how long it will take me to die. If only they'd let a greenhorn work on me. I'm sure I could make him angry enough to finish me off in a couple of hours. But that captain who looks like a Turk—he could make it go on for months. He knows his business. What about the colonel? He'd probably be easier to handle than a greenhorn. But he's careful. He won't get involved.

A tiny ray of hope glimmered.

Perhaps there won't be anything today. No, Grigori reprimanded himself. It's better to get it over with right away.

Nonetheless, he wished with all his heart that his martyrdom might be postponed until the next day.

Immediately, the guard called his number and rolled back the door of his cell. "Let's go."

Grigori got up and was astonished to find that his legs could support his weight. He walked along the familiar corridor, recognizing the odors, the stains on the walls; the unbroken moans from cell 634; the turn where, in his first few days, he had always struck his head against a drainpipe protruding from the ceiling. He reached the iron stairs and started to go down.

"Where do you think you're going? Today, you go upstairs, you fool!"

He turned with an effort. He knew what was downstairs. He did not know what was upstairs. He began to climb, with the guard following him. At the head of the stairs was a long corridor without doors.

Maybe he's simply going to kill me here. A bullet through the base of the neck?

A spark of hope, then an abyss of horror.

Oh, no! Not in a state of sin! Let me make amends! The blowtorch! I want the blowtorch!

Grigori looked fearfully over his shoulder to see if the guard was armed.

"Keep walking!"

He had seen nothing. He continued down the corridor, wishing for a way to escape from the guard.

He did not know where he was. He stumbled against the walls, and he scraped his shins on the treads of a staircase he had never climbed. Suddenly, he saw a window; a real window, opening unto a real sky. The corridor had a floor of wood rather than of cement, and it had been waxed. Grigori slipped. The guard caught him.

Before a door, there was an armed guard, a fresh-faced young man with the jovial face of a peasant, who struggled to maintain his stern, official look. The soldier's submachine gun terrified Grigori.

Is he the one who is going to kill me?

The soldier knocked on the door, and then moved aside.

Grigori saw a desk. A glowing brick stove. On the walls were organization tables, and photographs of the nation's leaders. He noticed immediately that in the place of one familiar face, there was another familiar one. Standing under the photographs, his hands in his pockets, resplendent in his dress uniform (not the fatigue uniform which was worn during interrogations), was the "Turk," plump and dark, with his tinted glasses. Grigori saw that he no longer wore the four stars of a captain, but the two stripes and star of a major.

With his chin, the major motioned Grigori to an armchair covered in oilcloth.

"You mean me?" Grigori asked stupidly.

The major wet his lips. Grigori collapsed into the cold chair, and listened as the major spoke. (First Grouztchik, he recalled, then Verniak, then Nadson, and now this one.)

"My dear comrade," the officer began. "I have no intention of trying to give you a course in Marxist dialectics. But, in the circumstances, it may be useful—since you've been out of circulation for such a long time—for me to bring you up to date on what has happened. As we both know, the laws of historical determinism are fixed, immutable. This sometimes creates apparent contradictions. Individuals sometimes become the victims of these contradictions. They are not done an injustice, in the proper sense of that term, since the only criterion by which we can judge any event is its ultimate utility. Let me give you an example. In cities lighted by gas, the streetlamps are dimmed during the day because their light is useless. The same sort of thing can happen to any citizen of a police state. But the citizen, like the streetlamp, must hold himself in readiness to be used again when darkness falls."

Why, Grigori asked himself, is this man using so many words to say absolutely nothing?

"History, as you know, comrade, progresses sporadically, by stages. We have just entered upon a new stage. I will give you the latest issue of *Truth* so that you can read for yourself the news of our progress and of the new criteria according to which we now live. You will see that there have been a few changes in personnel. Obviously, these do not correspond to any change in doctrine, but to a new direction in the evolution of doctrine. And this new direction has led the authorities to see certain problems in a new light. To be frank with you, I will tell you that so far as the conflict between Church and state is concerned, new ideas have been adopted. No one believes any more in imaginary conspiracies aimed at the very foundations of our government. We know now that the disease of religion is infinitely more pernicious than that; that it infects souls, and not bodies; and that it is at this level that we must fight it.

This theory was true twenty years ago. Today, it is true again. In the interim, other ideas—just as valid, no doubt—took precedence over it. But now history has brought us back to the original idea.

"So far as you are concerned, none of this would have had any immediate effect if the officer in charge of the investigation of your case had not asked for written orders. Upon receipt of his request, the new authorities examined your file and decided that the investigation had been conducted in a manner harmful to the public welfare. As a result, the officer responsible is now in prison, charged with sabotage. I am happy to tell you that I have been chosen to replace him."

The new commanding officer wet his lips again. Grigori did not move.

"Another result of this decision is that all charges against you have been dropped. You will retain your rank, your salary, and all fringe benefits. In other words, you have been restored to the service, and you will take up the mission which, unfortunately, has been interrupted. The absurd idea of transferring you to a professorship of atheism, obviously, has been forgotten. And disciplinary action has been taken against Comrade Nadson for incompetence."

Christ has refused to accept my martyrdom, Grigori concluded. I am damned. I will tell Alona to make some borsch.

His eyes filled with tears.

"I should tell you," the major went on, "that the new authorities clearly recognize the value of your report, and that they have every intention of making use of it. Several arrests took place today at dawn, and already the interrogations look promising. I can also tell you, in strict confidence, that you have been proposed for a medal that will make many of our comrades in the service turn green with envy."

Grigori was silent.

The major smiled. "I can see that you are not in the best possible shape. That is not necessarily bad. I'm going to have you released today. Go immediately to the bishops. Your physical condition can only inspire confidence in them. I have no objection if you tell them that you were tortured. And, since we've just arrested three bishops—on the basis of information contained in your report—I expect that your own nomination as a bishop will be forthcoming shortly. You will be able to take up your mission in the best possible circumstances."

Grigori's hands rested on the arms of the chair. His lips and tongue were dry, and he spoke only with a great effort. "A married priest cannot become a bishop, as you know."

The major cleared his throat sympathetically. "I forgot to mention that a runaway truck struck your wife this morning, as she was leaving your house. She died at the hospital."

Again Grigori thought: Christ has refused to accept my martyrdom. I am damned.

Then:

Never again will I eat such good borsch.

He began to cry like a child. The major tactfully turned his attention to one of the organization tables on the wall.

After a few moments, Grigori spoke between sobs: "How do you know that you can trust me?"

The commander spoke without turning. "Because, comrade, no one can possibly believe in God. You belong to us. We are all you have. Where would you go without us?"

Grigori sighed from the depths of his soul, and he thought his lungs would burst from the pain. "What would happen," he asked, "if I refused the assignment?"

"Come, come," the major answered. "I thought you were stronger than that. You're acting like a child. If you refuse the assignment, we'll put a bullet in your brain and that will be the end of it."

"You won't torture me?" Grigori asked hesitantly.

"I've already wasted enough time on that."

"A bullet?"

"Yes. Right away. In the corridor. I'll report that you attempted to escape. That would be the simplest explanation. You've done the same thing in your time, I'm sure."

"You've already begun to use my report?"

"I've told you so," the major answered. "And you've been proposed for an honor that will very likely be granted."

"How long would the assignment last?"

"That would depend upon the results."

"What results?"

"I don't know about that. For the moment, become a bishop. Then we'll see. Twenty years from now, there must not be a trace of religion left in this country."

"And you say that they need bishops?"

The major smiled. "I can see that a bishopric tempts you." Then he added, proudly: "Yes, we're engaged in creating a few vacancies for them."

"Very well, then," Grigori answered. "I'm at your disposal. Nothing is as simple as it seemed."

"I envy you your mission, you know. There are no risks involved, and there are chances for advancement that one doesn't find behind a desk."

He rang for a secretary. "Take care of this citizen's release." Then he turned to the priest and extended his hand, saying, "Comrade, I wish you the best of luck."

Grigori and the secretary left together.

The major rang for the guard. "Open that window for me, will you? I think we need some air in here."

Then he picked up the receiver and spoke to the chief guard: "Nicolai Fomitch, you will see that all our customers take showers immediately! And clean out their cells!"

Then he sat in his chair, leaned back, and let his head

drop in such a way as to see, from beneath, the photographs of the country's leaders hanging above him. He closed his eyes behind his tinted lenses and dreamed, not without a hint of trepidation, about dialectics.

An acolyte drew near bearing the small tin basin. Around his neck, like a yoke, was draped the embroidered towel. The circle of water reflected dimly. The choir chanted, and their harmonies rose to the cupola and rained down. The faithful, their eyes intent, made the sign of the cross and jostled one another. Behind the barriers stood a group of foreign tourists, half-reverent and half-skeptical, pressing forward for a better view, doubtlessly whispering among themselves of "ecumenism," a word the significance of which eluded them altogether.

The basin was so small that it was difficult to dip six fingers into it. The circle of water moved, flowed to one side, then righted itself. The acolytes bowed in reverence before the young bishop who had already suffered for the faith.

Above the Royal door—one could see them only by craning one's neck—thirteen men sat enthroned around a table. Their dark faces were motionless; their hands, long and white. Their deep, dark-circled, perfect eyes were opened onto another world.

In the sanctuary, hidden by the ikonostasis, there knelt a stout, sly old man in the simple habit of a monk. It was he to whom all was known. It was he who had said: "Yes, that's correct. I'm very much in need of experienced administrators. There will be time enough for martyrdom when you've set up one or two dioceses for me . . . No, no. There is no point in being scrupulous. You are not really betraying your secular masters, since they will find you out sooner or later."

The cleansing water was motionless. It was a plane, a geometric abstraction, a mirror toward which bent two heads, moving toward a common point of encounter, one coming from above and the other from below. Two mitered heads; two beards prematurely gray; two pale, identical faces, without flesh, without whiteness; eyes, black and sunken, as though they had been gouged out from within.